Hard at Work

Books by Brad Saunders

MEN I MIGHT HAVE KNOWN

HARD AT WORK

Published by Kensington Publishing Corporation

Hard at Work

Brad Saunders

KENSINGTON BOOKS
www.kensingtonbooks.com

KENSINGTON BOOKS are published by

Kensington Publishing Corp.
119 West 40th Street
New York, NY 10018

All Kensington titles, imprints, and distributed lines are available at special quantity discounts for bulk purchases for sales promotion, premiums, fund-raising, educational, or institutional use.

Special book excerpts or customized printings can also be created to fit specific needs. For details, write or phone the office of the Kensington Special Sales Manager: Kensington Publishing Corp., 119 West 40th Street, New York, NY 10018. Attn. Special Sales Department. Phone: 1-800-221-2647.

Kensington and the K logo Reg. U.S. Pat. & TM Off.

ISBN-13: 978-0-7582-4627-1
ISBN-10: 0-7582-4627-7

First Kensington Trade Paperback Printing: August 2010
10 9 8 7 6 5 4 3 2 1

Printed in the United States of America

Contents

Introduction

Missed connections occur all the time. Sometimes they spark between single people in search of love. Sometimes they develop between people who are in relationships with others and cannot act upon their feelings. And sometimes they happen in situations where the two would-be lovers cannot declare their feelings—whether because of time constraints or social restrictions.

As in the first installment of *Men I Might Have Known*, this edition is about missed connections. But this time, they will be with men of various occupations. One of the places in real life where people find connections is at work. We spend most of our waking hours on the job, and we form relationships with those around us. In my line of work as a writer, I have come across people in all sorts of interesting fields, and more than a few have sparked my interest romantically, as well as professionally. My theory is, if they are interesting enough to interview, they are interesting enough to go on a date with. Plus, is there anything sexier than seeing someone doing something they're good at?

Unfortunately, for decorum's sake and for the sake of professionalism, we cannot act upon these feelings, and so these connections remain unfulfilled . . . until now. The stories to follow are based on true-life encounters I have had in my various careers, and though nothing ever came of them in real life, as fantasies they live on. That is the beauty of these stories—there are no messy breakups, fights, or what-ifs. However, there is at least a measure of truth to each of them, which is what makes them so scintillating . . . at least to me. I hope you'll find them so as well.

The Mover's Son

In the midst of finals during my freshman year of college, I got a phone call from my parents informing me that they were moving back to my native California in a few weeks, and that they would need my help before I set out for a summer in Europe. I hastily agreed to do whatever they needed and got off the phone as quickly as possible since I was pressed for time, and stressed about an imminent linguistics paper deadline.

I didn't give the move too much thought since I still had all my finals to take, and my parents would only need my help unpacking everything in the new house in California. I would fly straight there after the school year ended, spend a couple weeks helping get the house in order, and then take off for an internship in Paris. I could hardly wait to get to Europe; so even through the drudgery of unpacking, at least I had that trip to look forward to after all the hassle of moving.

When the dust from finals and the subsequent year-end

parties finally settled a couple weeks later, I packed for home and tried to overcome my raging hangover on the flight from the East Coast back to California. I may have been a young, fit eighteen-year-old, but I felt burned out and gross after all my studying and partying, so I was looking forward to a few weeks of good, hard, physical work to clear my mind.

My parents picked me up at the airport late that night and drove me to our new house by the beach. It was a huge, beautiful place, but completely barren except for a couple mattresses on the floor and some fast-food containers in the fridge. My parents explained we were still waiting for the moving trucks to show up, and that they were expected the next day. Then the work would begin.

I wished my folks good night, then fell into a deep, exhausted sleep, anticipating the heavy lifting to come.

Early the next morning, I was awoken by a huge truck pulling into the driveway. The movers had arrived. I watched from my upstairs bedroom window as my parents went out to talk to the driver, then pulled on some shorts and a tank top, and went downstairs myself.

I grabbed a cup of coffee, hoping that would perk me up, and went outside to survey the situation. What a view I got.

The moving truck was owned and operated by a father-son team. From what my mother said, I learned the father's name was Matt. He was a handsome, grizzled guy in his mid-forties, with a mop of graying black hair. He looked tanned and tired, and was opening up the back of the truck for my parents to take a look. What really caught my attention, though, was Matt's son. He was still standing by the truck's cab, getting some equipment out of the front. He looked like he was barely out of high school (and I later found out that he had just turned eighteen and graduated a week earlier), with a young face, an olive complexion, a mop of thick black curls, golden brown eyes, and a sinewy body of long, toned muscles. His back was strong from lifting boxes all day, and his ass was as round as a globe, leading down to some of the most muscular legs I'd ever seen.

I walked up to him and extended my hand, asking his name. When he turned to look at me, he smiled shyly and took my hand, telling me his name was Ty.

"I'm Brad," I told him, smiling back. "Nice to meet you. Let me know if you need any help." Ty blushed and thanked me before turning back to his work. I saw his eyes shift back toward me one last time, though, and I took that as a good sign.

The rest of the day was a blur of bustle, activity, and heat. All I wanted to do was go to the beach and surf all day, but instead I was stuck lugging furniture into the new house and trying to find my boxes mixed in with everything else.

Every time I passed Ty, he looked sexier and sexier, as a healthy, ruddy glow spread all over his body, and the exertion of moving my belongings brought out a sheen of moisture on his skin. A couple drops of sweat even sprung up on his upper lip, and I had a barely resistible urge to kiss them away.

But I controlled myself and channeled my sexual frustration into lugging and hauling and lifting. Finally, it was time for lunch, and I was put in charge of a McDonald's run. I got some cash from my folks and took everyone's orders. I was amazed by the amount of food Ty and his father ordered, but then again, they did manual labor every day of their lives, so they could eat whatever they wanted.

I was about to take off in my mom's convertible when Matt suggested Ty take a little break from the work and go with me to help. My heart leapt up into my throat, but I kept calm as I nonchalantly shrugged, "Sure."

Ty looked anxiously from his father to me, then followed me out to the car. I could tell he was nervous, but I didn't know why. I wasn't just going to jump him! At least, not if I could help it . . .

As I shifted into gear, my arm brushed against his on the armrest. He started to move it, but then he left it where it was, so I left mine there, too, and we stayed like that—sweaty arms touching, but nothing else.

We drove in awkward silence until I turned on the radio and some oldies came on. I started humming along and saw Ty grin a little, so I started singing full voice, and that actually made him laugh before joining in. By the time we got to McDonald's, we were having a good time, and by the time we got back to the house, we were friends.

Soon, I realized Ty was using all his breaks just to come find me and talk to me, even if it was just in furtive little sentences. It seemed like he was just trying to spend time with me. It also seemed like he was specifically searching for boxes labeled "Brad" so he could bring them to my room. I asked him about it, but all he did was shrug and say that the boxes had to get into the house, so he was just bringing them in. He was blushing as he said it, though, and a little smile played on his lips.

The tension was killing me. I wanted to fuck his brains out, especially after he got so hot that he took his shirt off and kept working shirtless. I could see all his muscles contracting and relaxing as he lifted box after box, getting slippery with sweat. His body was perfect, lean and muscular, just like I liked, with a sprinkling of hair around his nipples and belly button. I could tell he wanted me, too, since I kept noticing him looking at me when he thought I didn't see him. Eventually, I took off my shirt, too, so he could see the goods.

I might have felt old and gouty from my recent scholarly cloistering and subsequent alcohol-fueled bender, but I was still just a sporty teenager, and my body looked amazing. I'd been playing intramural sports, getting to the gym, and biking around campus all year, and I was more toned than I'd ever been. No freshman fifteen for me. Instead, I'd put on a few pounds of muscle on my arms, shoulders, and legs, and had the start of a respectable six-pack tautening my stomach. Ty and I could have a really good time . . . if we ever got a moment alone together.

At the end of the first day, we'd made some progress, but the truck was still half full, so Ty and his father were going to come back the next day to finish the job. My parents sent me off to sign Matt's time sheet, and I shook his hand. He got in the truck and honked the horn to call Ty, who was still in the house. Ty ran from the house but slowed when he saw me. He stared at the ground and mumbled a good-bye, and I put a grimy hand on his sweaty, sticky shoulder to squeeze it when I replied and told him I'd see him tomorrow. He looked up at me with an exhilarated grin, then hopped in the truck and the two of them were off.

Luck smiled on us the next day. Around noon, my parents had to rush out on a long errand for the house in another part of the city that would take them the rest of the afternoon, so they left me in charge. Ty's father had to go out, too, since something had broken down in his truck's engine and he needed to fix it so he and Ty could drive it away when we were done with the move. Ty and I were finally alone.

Nothing happened. At least, not for a while. We both became shy again, barely mumbling to each other as we passed one another. Both of us were nervous, not knowing what to do. We worked feverishly, carting box after box into the house, chipping away at the mountains of belongings my parents had brought with them.

As it got hotter and hotter, Ty retreated into the truck to rearrange some things for easier unloading. I went to the kitchen for a cold drink. I got two glasses of water and brought one of them out to the truck for Ty.

I climbed up into the truck and said, "Hey," handing him one of the waters.

He said, "Thanks," and instead of looking away, as he'd been doing, he looked straight in my eyes as he drank it. I smiled and lightly pushed past him, pretending to look for a certain box.

"I'm trying to find a box of my school books," I told him. "Have you seen it?"

"Hmmm, I don't think so," he said, looking concerned.

We worked together, side by side, rearranging boxes and looking for my lost books. We got closer and closer in that cramped, dark space, deep in the truck, surrounded by dusty boxes lit only by the dim lights along the container's roof. It was sweltering in there, with the sun beating down on the truck, and soon we were both covered in sweat and dust.

I was kneeling right next to Ty now, almost leaning

against him, keeping close contact. He wasn't moving away from me at all, and I knew that if I wanted something to happen, I'd have to act now. Fortune smiled again, though, because at just that moment, Ty lost his balance and fell right into me. I caught him as his chest whumped into mine, and we lay on the ground, him on top of me, our faces within inches of each other.

As I looked into his golden eyes, framed by sweaty curls plastered to his forehead, he stared at me with a mixture of lust, eagerness, and fear. I smiled, then suddenly pulled him closer into me and mashed my mouth onto his.

I'm usually a gentle kisser. I like to take my time and work my way from soft, tender kissing to harder, more impassioned making out, but we had no time to waste. Our sexual encounter had been baking in that summer heat for two days now, and it was ready to burn, so we went at each other with a ferocity I'd never experienced before.

Our tongues were lashing each other's, delving into one another's mouths as our lips collided again and again in a frenzied duet. I grabbed his back, feeling those long cords of muscle straining under the damp fabric of his T-shirt. I wrapped my sinewy legs around his waist, pulling him tighter and tighter to me.

I was clearly the more experienced hand at this, and I got his shirt off within seconds, then quickly followed it with my own. Our sweaty chests rubbed against one another, creating a sexual friction that made the boiling truck even hotter. Neither of us had much body hair to speak of, but I had little tufts of it around my nipples and in a happy trail that snaked from my belly button down to my pubes. Ty's chest and belly were completely smooth, though I could feel the sweaty patches of hair in his armpits that were exuding a strong but somehow intoxicating body odor.

We flipped over so that we were both on our side on the floor, kissing each other, and I quickly busied my hands with unbuttoning his shorts and pulling them down. We weren't even speaking, just intensely kissing and rubbing up against one another on the dirty floor of that moving truck.

When Ty's pants were undone, and I had unzipped my own, I shimmied out of them and kicked them away. Then I broke off our kissing to pull his down, too, and threw them a short distance to lie next to my own. He leaned in to kiss me again, but I pulled back so that I could get a glimpse of the gorgeous body that had been twisting against my own. As I stared at him, I stroked his sweaty hair back with one hand and traced the lines of his pectoral muscles with the other.

Ty's body was even better than I'd imagined. I'd already seen his bare torso, but being this close to it, touching it, was even more arousing than merely watching him. His nipples were tiny and dark, capping the curves of his developed chest. He had a hardcore six-pack that contracted and relaxed with each excited breath he took. His legs were so strong from all the squatting and lifting he did working with his dad, with hairy calves the size of ripe melons, and massive quads that looked like they could lift a car.

We were both teenage boys, and we had been waiting for this moment, so naturally we were both fully erect, but even so, his prodigious dick looked delicate between those mammoth, hairy legs. It was framed by a small tuft of the darkest pubic hairs, curling tightly just like the hairs on his head. If I'd had to guess, I would have said that it was about seven inches, but what really impressed me was its girth. In my excitement, I'd already grabbed it, and noticed I could barely wrap my hand around it, especially the throbbing round head. It had gnarly veins snaking all up and down it, and it was surging with blood from Ty's quickened pulse.

I heaved my own hips over so that our cocks were touching, and I could see that my own more slender tool outstripped his by about a half inch. I was so turned on by the sensation of our two rubbery rods rubbing against one another as we frotted and made out furiously for another few minutes.

My cock was burning with the friction of rubbing against Ty's and I did not know how much more time we would have before our parents got back, so I had to move things along. I shifted us so that I was on top of him, and I started to let my mouth wander along his body.

I started with his ears, licking at them, and shoving my tongue into them, making him shudder and grab me tighter. I kissed at his neck, then paused at one of his nipples, giving it a thorough working over with my tongue. Ty's body tasted salty and minerally from sweat that had dried, but as we got worked up again and we both started sweating freshly, the taste became mellower. I wanted to lick his entire body, sopping up every last drop of it.

Ty was whimpering at my nipple work and grinding his hips upward into my body, so I slowly moved farther down his chest to his belly button, tasting the tangy perspiration in that delicious depression before reaching my destination, that inflamed cock.

He was as hard as anyone I'd ever been with, and I

gripped his fleshy rod firmly while burying my nose in the glossy bush of his pubes. His hair smelled so spicy and manly, it was almost too intense, but it only turned me on even more. I shifted my attention to the helmet head of his glans. There was already a substantial buildup of precum leaking from the round hole in it, and I gently licked at it, enjoying the taste of sweetness after the salt of Ty's sweat.

He trembled repeatedly, and I guessed that he had never had his cock sucked before, so I intended to give him the experience of his life. Without hesitating, I swallowed his entire stem, my chin nuzzling into the fleshy curtains of his testicles, and my nose embedded in his short hairs. I gagged slightly but stayed put. It was difficult to keep his impressive girth in my mouth, but I relaxed into it and after a moment I was fine.

I moved my head up and down only slightly, keeping his entire johnson in my mouth, but stimulating as much of the surface area as possible with my tongue, my throat, and the top of my mouth. I sucked and slurped for all I was worth, producing a ton of saliva to lubricate his shaft.

When he started to whimper, I slowly began to undulate up and down, sucking all the way up to the tip, then plunging my mouth down again to deepthroat him. He was losing control and bucking his hips with each of my movements, and I remembered the first time someone had given me a blowjob with a mixture of fondness and jealousy.

Though we didn't have much time, I didn't want Ty to come just yet, especially since I hadn't gotten my own rocks off. I was fully in control of the situation, so I decided to go for it. His legs were splayed on either side of me, so I grabbed them under the knees, and pushed them back and up in the air to get a clear path to his ass crack. It was furrier than I expected, and it had the same musky aroma as his crotch, only stronger. I breathed through my mouth (a trick a fuck buddy of mine at college had taught me) and started to lick his fleshy furrow clean.

Every time my mouth approached his asshole, Ty groaned. He seemed to be really sensitive in the area—in a good way that made me think that he would love getting fucked. I worked over that pungent pink sphincter with all the skill I had, using my lips, my mouth, my stubbly chin, and then when I thought he was good and relaxed, I slid one of my index fingers in.

Ty immediately tensed up, but he didn't say anything, so I gently played around, making my finger vibrate and swirl. Within seconds flat, he was relaxed again and squirming around on the floor, loving every single move I made. I continued licking at his ass and sucked his balls every now and then as I finger-banged him with first one, then two fingers. With bated breath, I dared to slip a third finger in, and he just went with it, riding my hand like a pro as I buried my digits up to the knuckles in the elastic warmth of his ass cavity.

Now that Ty had been attended to, I wanted to meet my own needs, and I was going to give him a treat. I carefully disengaged from him and stood up. He opened his eyes to look up at me and immediately came up to his knees in front of me. I stepped closer so that my stiff meat was right in his face, and I pulled his head toward it. He dutifully opened his mouth to tentatively lick at the tip, and I let him explore for a moment or two. When he was off guard, I crammed my entire shaft into his mouth, making him gag. His eyes widened in surprise, then started watering from the gagging. I kept his mouth on my cock, praying he wouldn't bite me by reflex, but he quickly gained control and stayed still.

I felt his saliva coating my penis, and when it was good and covered, I pulled Ty's mouth off it, lifted him up by his armpits, and turned him around so that he was on his feet, leaning over a pile of moving boxes that came up to just above his waist.

Without losing a moment, I rubbed my wet dick up and down the valley of his ass, mingling his saliva with my own, and using the lube juice of my own spit and the precum that was oozing from my piss slit to get his rosebud nice and slippery.

"Yeah, do it," he said quietly, bracing himself for penetration by bending his knees slightly and reaching back to hold his ass cheeks apart. I pointed my pole straight ahead and eased the aerodynamic head into his asshole. His breathing became quicker as he tensed up, but I rubbed his back and made a *shhh* sound to relax him. When he loosened up again, I pushed in harder and faster, my staff sinking into his puckered sphincter inch by inch.

He took it like a champ, only whimpering slightly. I stood still for a moment, letting him get used to the pressure I was putting on him, and when he had mastered it, I started to grind slowly in and out of him.

I looked down to watch how his hairy hole tightly encircled the circumference of my erection. It was so fucking hot to see it swallow my entire shaft, stretching to accommodate me.

Ty let out an *mmm* sound, and I started to hump him faster. I didn't want to come too soon, but I was getting really excited as I shoved my cock farther and farther into his depths.

I gripped his hips firmly, holding him in place as I began to piston in and out of him. I helped him keep his balance while knocking him into that pile of boxes with more and more force.

He got into the rhythm of it quickly and started to push back on my cock so that each of my strokes became long and powerful as I pulled out nearly to the tip, then dove back in balls deep. Ty started stroking his cock fast and hard to keep up with my impulsion. We were both emitting low, guttural grunts from the exertion, and streams of sweat were pouring off us both.

It was pretty slippery trying to hold on to him, and every time my thighs hit the back of his legs, they made a moist, slapping sound. I leaned over him so that my taut chest lay on his wet, muscled back and I drove up into him with more limited, precise strokes, really using the upward curve of my cock to hit his G-spot.

All my pumping was creating an abrasive friction now as the lubrication of our spit began to evaporate. On the one hand, I could tell we would both be uncomfortable in another few moments; but on the other, it heightened every sensation leading to what I sensed would be an explosive orgasm.

I straightened back up and spat down onto my sheath to give us a little bit more lube, then hit Ty with a few more quick, punchy thrusts. I was really close, so I quickly withdrew from him and started to jack off. Within seconds, I was drizzling cum all over the broad plain of his back, covering it with my white love juice. A few of the last drops slid from my hole to a spot right above the dent of his ass and started to slip down it. I bent down and licked them up before they got too far, enjoying the rare taste of my own semen.

It only made me want more, so I turned Ty, who was still jacking off, around to face me. I stationed my mouth just in front of his reddened cock, which looked like it would blow any second. I licked gently at the very tip of it, which sent him over the edge. He grabbed my head and fed me the tip of his cock, still milking it for all he was worth. He must have been saving that load up for days because it seemed to fill my mouth with syrupy, milky profusion. It just kept coming and coming, but after about a dozen yanks, Ty seemed to finish and pulled out of my mouth, drained.

I swallowed most of his sperm, but left a little bit in my mouth so that when I stood up to kiss him, I could push it into his mouth with my tongue. He stiffened for a moment, then went with it, taking every last drop, and even licking a couple spots on my chin where he had sprayed a few strings of it.

When he had thoroughly cleaned off my face, he grinned and said, "Yummy."

"Yeah, it was," I said, kissing him one last time. "We'd better get dressed, sweet stuff," I said, handing him his clothes.

I used my shirt to wipe the rest of my cum off his back, then balled it up in my fist. We both got dressed quickly, hopped off the truck, and went in the house to clean up. By the time we had soaped up and dried off, Ty's dad was back from his errand.

He surveyed our work and asked, "What have you two

been doing? It doesn't look like you got very much work done."

"That's my fault, sir," I said, taking the blame. "I was having trouble finding a particular box in the truck and I made Ty help."

"Yeah, it was in one of those really hard-to-reach places, but Brad got to it," volunteered Ty.

I almost lost it, but kept a straight face. Ty's father went back into the truck to start working again, and I squeezed Ty's hand before he followed him in. I returned to my room to continue unpacking.

By the end of the day, all my family's stuff was in the house, and it was time for Ty and his father to leave. We shook hands and said good-bye, and it wasn't until the truck had rumbled down the road and turned the corner that I realized I had forgotten to get Ty's number or give him my own. There was no way to get back in touch with him. I was momentarily saddened to think that this had been just a one-time affair. Then again, after the intensity of it, I didn't know how many more meetings with Ty I could take. I just might have to wait until my family moved again to find out. . . .

Riley the Realtor

People always say it's impossible to find a decent apartment in New York, but no one tells you how hard it is to find one in Los Angeles. Even if you're just looking to rent for a few years (or maybe especially if you're just looking to rent), it can take months, even years, to find the right place.

So many of the buildings are leftover prefab 1960s monstrosities, especially in some of the more desirable parts of town like the beach cities of Santa Monica and Venice, or the trendy (and gay) neighborhoods of West Hollywood.

When I first moved to Los Angeles to work in film production (no, not dirty films, get your mind out of the gutter!), I was lucky to find a cheap sublet from a friend of mine. She was off to work on a film in New Zealand of all places, and needed someone to take over her lease while she was gone for several months.

I settled into her little studio and began my own apartment search in earnest. Six months later, I had made no real progress. Every apartment I looked at was either too small, or old, or dilapidated, and they were all astronomically priced. I was reaching my wit's end, desperate to find a place of my own before my friend returned from her film, but still not knowing where to start.

I was griping about my real-estate woes one evening as I had drinks with a group of my friends. One of them, a lawyer named Paul whom I had met through our mutual friends, said that he had a buddy named Riley who was a real-estate agent. Riley normally just handled sales, but occasionally he would help a friend out who was just looking to rent. He was young, ambitious, successful, and very cute. Paul asked if he should call Riley for me, and I immediately said yes.

Paul called Riley right then and there, leaving him a voice mail with my number, then we went back to our drinks. I bought Paul a round to thank him.

The next day, as I was driving to the office, I got a call from a number I did not recognize. I answered the phone and was delighted to hear that it was Riley calling me back.

"I hope this is a good time," he said.

"Definitely, thank you so much for calling me back. I need to find an apartment soon, and I was hoping you could help me," I replied, practically begging.

"Oh, I think I might be able to find something that suits you," he answered. I could hear a little laughter in his voice. It was completely charming, and I saw why Paul had recommended him. Apart from that, Riley's voice was a lilting baritone, and he sounded very fun and lively.

I answered his questions about what I was looking for

in an apartment—size, location, price—and we made a plan to meet that weekend and look at a few places he would find by then. I wanted to hug him through the phone.

That Friday, I got an e-mail from Riley telling me to meet him at one of the big apartment buildings on the Wilshire Corridor in Westwood the next morning, and then he'd drive us around to the various apartments from there. He ended by saying, "Really looking forward to meeting you. Paul said great things!"

I was puzzled but pleased. It sounded like Paul had been telling Riley that I was cute, too . . . and Paul had mentioned that Riley was single. Interesting. Taking all that into consideration, I hit the gym for a hard workout so my muscles would all be primed. I met a few friends out for a drink but went to bed early in preparation for my big day of house hunting.

I woke up early, shaved, and performed all my ablutions with care so I was looking clean and professional, dressed in a sharp shirt and slacks, and gave my hair one last little comb-through so I was looking my best, then I set out for Westwood.

I pulled up to a beautiful apartment building with a driveway right off of Wilshire. It was a great location but looked a little fancy for me. I did not have an opener for the gated parking garage, so I pulled up right in front of the lobby. There was a cute young man standing outside waiting, so I figured it was Riley. I rolled down my window and asked if I should park in the garage since there were no spaces in the driveway. The man looked a little confused but said that the door should open automatically when I pulled up, and that there were guest spaces inside.

I did as he said and parked the car in the garage, then entered the back side of the lobby to meet him. Only, he was gone. What had happened? Was it something I did? I turned to ask the lobby attendant if he had seen Riley when I felt a little tap on my shoulder.

Turning around, I felt a nervous smile creep onto my face. I was looking at a man about my age, in his early twenties, with wavy auburn hair, honey-brown eyes, a golden tan, and a crisp suit that seemed like it would never wrinkle. He was an inch or two taller than me, with broad shoulders and a narrow waste. His suit was perfectly tailored to show off his slim figure, and the pants were just tight enough to cling to his powerful thighs and show off the tight mound of his package, but not in an obscene way. His loafers, I noticed, were very expensive.

He smiled and extended his hand. "Are you Brad?"

"Yes, Riley?" I asked.

"That's me. You ready for a big day?"

"Definitely. I haven't had much luck since I moved here."

"Well," he said, still smiling with those beautiful, perfectly straight white teeth, "I have a feeling that your luck's about to change."

"I hope you're right," I said. "Listen, I really appreciate you taking the time to get all these listings and show me around. I know it's a lot of time."

"It's no problem, that's my job. Besides, Paul said you were really cute, so how could I say no?"

I tittered nervously and blushed, not saying anything else. He led me to the elevator banks to take me up to the first apartment of the day. It was your average Westwood high-rise apartment. Mostly new construction, nice kitchen and appliances, big bedroom with en suite bathroom. But it did not really have any character, the laundry room was three floors away, and the rooftop pool would be under construction for another year. I told Riley my concerns, and he listened gravely, agreed with everything I said, then took me back downstairs to his car.

When Paul had said Riley was successful, he did not indicate just how successful. Riley's car was a gorgeous Jaguar convertible. It was a sunny L.A. day, so we put the top down and commenced our roam around the city.

Over the course of the day, Riley showed me apartments in Venice, Santa Monica, Brentwood, near the Grove, Hollywood, Los Feliz, Silverlake, and downtown. We had started early in the morning, so by the end of the day, we must have been in his car for almost ten hours, though we did stop for lunch around 2:00 P.M. at one of his favorite restaurants in West Hollywood. Without being asked, the host brought over a bottle of Veuve Clicquot champagne on ice and poured us each a glass, then left us to look over the menu.

I raised my eyebrow in question at Riley. "Is that okay?" he asked, indicating the champagne. "I always bring my clients in here, so they make sure everything is the best for me."

"Yes, of course it's all right. Veuve Clicquot is my favorite. I just feel bad that I'm not one of your big-time clients. You shouldn't waste the effort on me."

"I don't think it's wasted effort. Half my clients don't even know what Veuve Clicquot is. It's nice to be with someone who appreciates some of the same things I do."

That did it. The ice was broken, and as we talked about

the champagne, and about ourselves, I found myself liking Riley more and more. Sure, he had that real-estate agent-y vibe to him, but he had not questioned a single complaint of mine that day, and he had not tried to sell me on anything I hadn't liked. If I had to describe his behavior, I'd say he was being a perfect gentleman, and he seemed to be impressed by my house-hunting knowledge . . . not to mention my fine dining background as we talked about restaurants around town.

I could feel the champagne starting to work, making me a little giggly and giving me that delightful warm feeling in the pit of my stomach. I was almost afraid to find an apartment that day because it would mean not spending any more time with Riley. Then again, I could feel his eyes on me as I read down the menu, and his foot brushed mine under the table, but he didn't move it. I smiled to myself as I took another sip of champagne.

After lunch, we looked at about a dozen more apartments. At one point, Riley let his hand rest on my knee in the car, and I let him, discreetly looking out the window as he left it there.

I told Riley the ones I was interested in, and he promised to follow up on them. I'll admit, I included one of them because as we walked up the stairs to the second floor, I got a great view of his ass and imagined what it would taste like if I were eating him out. I nearly got a boner right there, but I controlled myself, and by the time we got to the apartment, I was good to go again. If I moved in there, I'd have that image in my head every day, and that was definitely an incentive.

Finally, we walked out of the last building we saw, a

fixer-upper in West Hollywood, and it was time to call it a day. I asked Riley if there were any more apartments to see, and he looked at me for a brief moment, biting his lip.

"What is it?" I asked him.

"Should we call it a day? We've got plenty of options already. . . ."

"But?" I asked. Clearly there was something he wasn't telling me.

"Well, there *is* one more place I'd like to show you. . . ." He trailed off. "If you're not too tired, that is."

I definitely was tired, but I didn't want my day with Riley to end. "I'm game if you are," I replied.

Relief washed over his face as he smiled and brushed his wavy hair back from his face. "Great, let's go."

We drove for a few more minutes up into the hills above West Hollywood. I didn't know where he was taking me. All the buildings up there are houses, and I certainly couldn't afford them on my film executive's salary. Still, I was curious.

It was getting dark by then, but the top was still down, so it was cold in the car. I leaned in a little closer to Riley so I would be warmer. I felt his shoulder rub against mine as he leaned back toward me, too. We drove in silence, farther and farther up the windy, narrow streets, up into the hills.

Finally, we pulled into a little driveway. I couldn't see the house clearly because it was below the level of the road and it was completely dark. Riley said to give him a second, and he hopped out. A second later, he was inside the house and it was blazing with lights. I got out of the car and walked to the house. It was a beautiful little building, with floor-to-ceiling windows, a flat roof, and incredible views of the city from the back patio. I could see all of Los Angeles lit up below me and it took my breath away.

I walked in the front door and noted the beautiful stone floors in the foyer and sunken living room. The entire house was very contemporary, with clean lines, bare surfaces, dark-colored materials, and very modern furniture. The kitchen had granite counters and all new appliances. The bathrooms were all marble and glass. I wandered into the master bedroom and was taken aback by the bed, with a huge white Lucite headboard, and white-on-white sheets like you'd find in a fancy hotel. It fronted on a 360-degree fireplace like those kinds you see in Swiss chalets. The closet was almost as big as the room itself, and it was lined with shelves carrying shoes and cashmere sweaters, and racks upon racks of neatly lined-up suits.

I looked around the second bedroom, and the small office that opened off the living room. Everything was perfectly in its place. The walls were lined with shelves that held tons of books on every subject from design to wine to travel to literature. Whoever lived here, they definitely had interesting tastes.

I could tell that the house was out of my price range. Why had Riley brought me here? I called out for him, not knowing where he had gotten to. I poked around the kitchen again and even took a look in the fridge. There was not much in there except for a few bottles of Veuve Clicquot. That was interesting.

I started to realize something as I walked back toward the master bedroom. I called out for Riley again, trying to figure out where he was. As I entered the room, my question was answered. The fireplace had been lit. A tray with two champagne flutes and a bottle of Veuve sat next to it. And there, reclining on his side in the bed waiting for me, all tan skin, rippling muscles, and playful grin, was Riley. Completely naked.

I was speechless for a second, just taking in the sight of him. He looked even better out of his suit than he had in it. His skin was flawless. He had just a little patch of auburn chest hair that matched the hair on his head and two little spirals of it around his small, red nipples. His stomach was as flat as a washboard, with a narrow line of hair running down the center of it from his pecs down the groove between his ab muscles and down to his furry belly button. His happy trail continued to a patch of light brown pubes that framed his short, fat cock in a perfect semicircle. He was leaning on one of his powerful arms, the triceps curving beautifully, while the other lay in front of him, his fingers tapping impatiently on the bedspread.

"So, what do you think?" he asked puckishly.

"I guess this house isn't actually for rent," I said, giving away nothing.

"No," he said bashfully, still unsure of how I felt.

"This is where you live, isn't it?"

Still coy, he admitted, "Yes."

"And all those horrible places you dragged me to this afternoon?" I asked him.

"I . . . well, I wanted to spend more time with you."

"I see," I murmured, flattered but still hiding the smile I could feel creeping up at the corner of my lips.

He started to get up, embarrassed, as I walked over to the bed, but I gently pushed him back down, letting my hand linger on his hard chest.

"I definitely like the view," I said, nonchalantly continuing our real-estate conversation as I stroked his chest, "but I'm going to have to explore every nook and cranny before I know whether I want to take it."

"That sounds like a good plan," Riley said, smiling at me again with those big, honey-colored eyes as he pulled my face toward his to kiss me.

I loved being totally dressed lying on top of his completely naked frame, and I ran my fingertips down his bare throat, then fondled his chest and lightly pinched his nipples to pointy hardness before rubbing his taut stomach. Then I brushed my fingers along his furry happy trail and tousled his springy bush of pubic hair. Every so often, I would let my fingers brush past the rubbery stalk of his dick, just to tease him. Each time I did that, he kissed me harder.

He smelled so good, like the expensive Kiehl's products I'd seen lined up in the bathroom, and his skin was so soft and smooth and warm under my touch. He had very little body hair except for some light blond hairs on his forearms and darker, thicker hair on his legs, though that was pretty wispy, too.

I rolled over him and onto my back on the bed, pulling him on top of me so that his legs were straddling my hips. He sat up as he unbuttoned my shirt, and I took the opportunity to rub every square inch of his lithe torso and wrap my hands around his muscular, hairy thighs on either side of me. When he lowered himself back down on top of me to kiss me, I clung to his bare body, enjoying the feel of his naked skin against my own now-bare chest.

We were a pretty evenly matched pair, both of us young, slender, with a layer of worked-out muscle on us. His legs were thicker than mine, but I had the advantage in the upper body with a more fully developed chest, narrower hips, and stronger shoulders. Still, it would have been a pretty fair fight. I preferred the workout we were giving ourselves instead, though.

Riley was right on top of me, his naked skin pressed along the full length of my body, his hands running up and down my torso, and playing with my dark spiky hair. I was running my hands through his wavy mop and down his warm back, pausing at his little bubble butt to give his cheeks a squeeze.

He started kissing my jawline, then moved out to my ears. I have really sensitive ears, and his tongue performed wonders on them. At one point, I thought I might actually come with my dick still in my pants, that's just how talented his tongue was as it ran up and down my earlobe and plunged into my ear hole in all its wet warmness. Meanwhile, he was dry-humping me, him completely nude, and me naked down to the belt. My own monster was beginning to awaken in my underwear as it felt the long hardness of his erection pressing down on my crotch.

Knowing he had me in his control, Riley slithered his way down my torso, licking and pinching at my nipples, getting them nice and hard and sensitive. He kept a hand on them as his face continued farther down my flat abs and paused again at my belly button. I felt his tongue flick into the little dent in my stomach and quashed an urge to fidget because I was so ticklish.

Then, using just his teeth—those pearly whitened wonders—he managed to undo the button at the top of my pants and take down my zipper. By now my cock was really getting hard and surging from the blood being pumped there by my racing pulse. I lay back, closing my eyes, wanting just to feel what he was going to do next.

I felt his face press itself against the light cotton of my briefs, his hot, humid mouth opening over my cock, and his lips tracing its length from the other side of that fabric barrier. He teased me by playing with the elastic waistband of my underwear, dipping a finger, then two, beneath it and brushing up against the tip of my cock, which was pointing due north. I could feel the tube of my urethra and my piss slit getting slick with the precum that I had started to produce, and more than anything, I wanted Riley's mouth all over my wang.

I didn't have long to wait. I felt him start to slip off my briefs, so I lifted my hips to help him slide them down over my butt, and then I felt his hot breath all over my genitals. He seemed to be inhaling my musky, natural scent, and I lay still so that he could get a good whiff. I squirmed a little when his tongue tickled the sensitive skin on my inner thigh, and then I almost jumped in the air as he swallowed one of my huge testicles whole, sucking it way back into the recesses of his mouth. My ballsack was really sensitive and I got a shock in the pit of my stomach with each swish of his tongue over my scrotum.

Releasing me from that agonizing bliss, he slowly and deliberately traced a course up the curving length of cock with his mouth, licking the entire underside with his wide, wet tongue, and causing it to twitch involuntarily and produce even more clear precum. I wanted just to clamp my hand on his face and make him deepthroat me, but I relaxed into his calculated pace and eagerly awaited what was going to come.

Brushing his tongue back and forth over the sensitive little triangle of skin just beneath the tip of my cock, Riley very nearly brought me to orgasm right then and there, sending volts of electric energy from that minuscule spot to the outer reaches of my entire body. Thanks to his attentions, I was now sporting a raging woody, and it was unfurled to its full eight thick inches. I could feel him sizing it up, wondering how he was going to get it all in his mouth, but I had faith in my realtor and knew he could appraise it just right.

Starting with the very tip, he got me all worked up and trying hard not to come from all the stimulation of his strong tongue passing again and again over my nerve centers. Then he swallowed the first couple inches of my staff, getting just past the wide-rimmed cockhead. With another suck, he was down a few inches farther, and a few sucks more, he had managed to get within an inch of my pubic bush. He was almost there but couldn't quite seem to make it all the way down, so I helped him out. Massaging his jaw while he sucked me a few times, I waited until he was a little more relaxed and then, when he least suspected it, I bucked my hips upward and forced the last inch of my sausage down his throat. His eyes widened with surprise, his jaw looked like it might crack open, and he barely managed to suppress a huge gag, but he handled it admirably, and once he'd gotten over that hurdle he deep-throated me for several minutes, lighting up every arousal spot I had as his tongue passed over each of the heavy veins that ran down the sides and top of my shaft.

I felt my body notching those first few steps toward climax, so I gently laid a hand along one of Riley's beautifully formed cheekbones and pulled him back up so that we were face-to-face. I thanked him for his fine service, kissing him full on the lips and delighting in the taste of my own cock on his mouth.

I took hold of his bony hips and began to pull his body up mine until his cock and balls were dangling tantalizingly close to my mouth. He had developed a massive hard-on while servicing me, and his cock had actually turned out to be a bit of a surprise. I thought he was a beer can kind of man, but he was a grower, so he actually had some length to him, as well as some meaty girth, and I knew I was going to have to work at sucking him off.

A little dribble of precum leaked from his slit onto my chin as I gently stroked him, making sure he was completely hard before I latched my mouth onto his organ. Raising and lowering my head from the comfort of the bed, I set to work milking his cock with my mouth and playing with his floppy balls like some low-hanging fruit I had a craving for. They were pillowy and soft, their wrinkled skin completely free of unwanted hair, while the tough skin of his shaft was likewise hair-free. That just made my job easier as I slid my mouth back and forth over its entire length and tasted his fresh, clean skin.

It wasn't long before my neck got tired, though, so I laid it back down on the bed, and guiding his hips with my hands, indicated that he should fuck my face. He was gentle and slow at first, gingerly plunging his cock straight down into my waiting mouth, but I pulled down on him as he thrust and he got the point that he could give me a harder rogering if he wanted to. That was all he needed, and soon enough he was punching his cock as far down my throat as it would go, and it took all of my concentration to keep my mouth open wide and my throat relaxed so that I wouldn't gag.

Riley was starting to perspire, and I loved the feel of his hot, damp skin as the sweat sprang up on it. I rested my hands on his lower back, feeling the heat rise off him as he flushed with the exertion of basically doing push-ups into my mouth.

I needed a little break, so I slowed him down, and used my mouth to suck at his testes instead, especially the left one, which was the lower hanger. At the first touch of my tongue, they withdrew into his body. So this was his weak spot, I thought to myself, he had really sensitive balls. I let them drape over my nose as I scooched farther back underneath him and licked at his taint. His skin there was musky and coated with fine hairs that led up into his moist ass crack. He didn't smell pungent—his skin was still clean with the scent of expensive soaps and products—but there was something else there. Something a little spicy and a little funky that was all Riley, and that was what I loved.

When I had worked my way to the bottom of his crack, I was actually no longer beneath Riley's kneeling body, so I slid out from under him and pushed him down, face-first, onto the bed before eating him out. I licked up and down his entire hairy furrow, glossing it with my saliva. Prying his firm ass cheeks apart, I got my first view of the tan gulch that hid his pink chasm, which was encircled by a few fine, dark hairs. It was such a beautiful ass, I wanted to kiss it and eat it and plunge my tongue as far into it as I could, so that's just what I set about doing. I knew I had made the right choice when I heard Riley begin to moan, almost imperceptibly at first, but gaining amplitude as I tongue-fucked him with all my might. As my tongue probed farther and farther into him, I tasted more and more of an acrid note, and I knew his tight little hole was going to be the fuck of a lifetime. Apparently Riley thought so, too, and after a few minutes, he was ready for it.

He flipped over and sat up to kiss me so that he could taste his own musky scent on my lips, then said, "Not here. There's one more room I have to show you."

He took my hand and led me toward the closet, both of our rock-hard cocks pointing the way ahead. He turned on the bright closet light and I looked around, confused. There were just hanging racks and tons of built-in drawers, but I didn't see anywhere to fuck. Then he pulled aside a curtain at the back and revealed something very special in a corner I had not noticed before.

Hanging from the ceiling was a leather love swing. It had a saddle for someone to sit on, a head-and-neck brace, and then two sort of stirrup things that loosely attached to the seat and to the ceiling so that someone could hop into the thing and spread their legs for the fuck. Riley handed me a condom and a bottle of lube to prepare while he got into the contraption. This was the first time I'd ever contemplated using such a device, but I was excited . . . especially once I saw how limber Riley was.

I unrolled the condom onto my dong, stretching the latex to its limits. Rubbing a few pumps of the lube onto it, I got my pole nice and greasy, then pointed it perpendicular to my body to aim it right into Riley's wide-open fuck bud. He was firmly ensconced in his swing, his legs splayed to either side, and his ass presented and waiting for me. I bent my knees to achieve the proper trajectory, then I eased my way inside him. His pink little pucker was nice and relaxed from my lip service, and with the lube running down my prick, it was an easy matter to slide all the way into him in one quick motion. His ass cheeks quivered with the effort of stretching to take in my dowel, but Riley gritted his teeth and reached up to rub my chest as I started vibrating slowly back and forth.

I was not used to the swing, so with my first few thrusts, I popped out of Riley since the contraption overcompensated for my motions and elongated my strokes. Each time I plugged into him, it moved away from me, so that when I pulled back, I miscalculated the distance and had to penetrate him all over again. Holding the chains by which the love swing attached to the ceiling, I fixed Riley in place and began to fuck him with quicker, shorter strokes. Eventually I let go of the chains, enjoying the sound of them rattling and clinking with each pump of my hips, and keeping my strokes brief so that I could remain within the moist confines of Riley's hospitable internal fuck chamber.

Eventually, I figured out how to let the swing do all of the work. I barely had to move as it swung back and forth like a pendulum while I stood still and let Riley's ass fuck me like that. I basically had very little to do except remain standing up straight, which was difficult enough since Riley's ass muscles were giving my cock a mind-blowing workout as they squeezed and contracted around my girthy shaft. The seat swung farther and farther, my low-hangers slapping against the clenched muscles of Riley's smooth little ass. I reached a still lubed-up hand down to his solid cock and began to fondle his balls and jerk him off as the swing did its work upon us both.

After a couple minutes of lazy yet incredible, swing-creaking sex, Riley wanted to switch positions. He managed to extract himself from the swing rather fluidly, then made me lie down on it on my back, the brace cradling my head, my ass on the seat portion, and my legs swinging freely down to the floor. As I settled into position, I felt the warm residue of the puddle of sweat on the seat that Riley had worked up while I was fucking him, and I nestled into his humid heat.

I gripped the two harnesses that anchored the swing behind where my head was while Riley climbed on top of me to face me cowboy-style, then impaled himself slowly on my waiting spear, taking its length inside him inch by massive inch. He anchored himself by placing his legs on the floor, and he started bouncing up and down on me like that, causing us to swing back and forth slightly. Restricting the swing's movement was quite an arm workout for me, so I loosened my grip slightly and just let us pendulum more freely, enjoying the ride.

In this position, Riley's ass felt even tighter than before. Though the range of motion was smaller than when I had been fucking him on his back, he made up for it by using all his internal muscles to massage my cock toward a quaking orgasm. His lubed-up tool was ramrod-straight and pointed directly up. Each time he bounced up and down on me, it slapped down onto my belly with a wet thud sound and then ricocheted back up to slap his belly. We both had a cock-shaped lube pattern on us within seconds, and I loved the feel of his flesh slapping down onto me as he ground his ass down on my pelvis even harder.

The swing was surprisingly comfortable. Usually when I was fucking someone in that position, the longer we made love, the more I felt it in my lower back as their weight came down on me again and again, but the swing had so much lumbar support, and moved so freely, I didn't feel Riley's weight at all. It was like fucking a cloud. A really hot, muscular, sweaty, sexy cloud. I loved the feeling of weightlessness as we swung to and fro, back and forth, like fucking in midair.

I reached forward and took hold of Riley's flopping prick and began to thoroughly massage it with both my hands, one concentrating on rubbing the knob, and the other working its way up and down his long, thick shaft. My labors were turning his skin a bright pink to match the splotches of rosy color created by our aerobic exertions, and he had started to produce a thick flow of precum. I knew that, just like me, he was getting close to climax.

I redoubled my efforts, tugging more forcefully on his prong and bringing him steadily closer to the inevitable. Riley responded to my ministrations by gyrating and swirling his hips, pushing back on my cock 'til it was completely enveloped inside him. I was going to lose it at any moment, but Riley went first.

Without much warning, he gave a primal grunt and began to quiver. My first clue that anything was happening was a sticky, wet feeling in the hand that was twirling around his cockhead. My second was the burst of cum that shot past my left ear onto the floor. The next hit me square on the chin. Riley, meanwhile, just kept riding me as hard as he could, bracing himself against my chest and clawing into my muscles as his orgasm overtook him, drops of cum landing between his delicate hands and covering my entire torso.

Each time Riley shot a load onto me, the walls of his ass cavity flexed involuntarily, squeezing my tool and pressing me further and further over the edge. Finally, I could control it no longer. My back arched, I shoved my cock as deep up into Riley as I could and sent rushes of cum surging into the condom. I jackhammered up into him several times, trying to finish myself off completely by punching my cock into him as hard as I could and making Riley moan even louder.

Finally, I went rigid, every last drop of ejaculate drained from my aching balls, and Riley collapsed onto my cum-covered chest, plastering my face with grateful kisses. He lay on top of me in a sweaty, swinging heap as we both recovered our breath; then he reluctantly rolled off of me and led me into his immaculate bathroom.

After we both had cleaned up, we padded, still naked, into Riley's kitchen for a drink of water to help cool off. He also cracked one of his bottles of Veuve. The icy golden liquid was like drinking sunshine, the carbonation making it even more thirst quenching. I quickly gulped down a flute of it and got a refill. It was starting to make my cheeks rosy again, but I didn't care. I knew we would be here all night and finish the bottle.

Raising his glass in a toast to me, Riley said, "Here's to finding you the perfect apartment."

"I'll drink to that," I replied, clinking glasses with him.

Finishing his sip, Riley spoke again, this time a rascally

grin pulling up the corners of his beautiful lips, "We've got another full day tomorrow. We could be together for hours and hours. I hope that's okay with you."

"I think I'll be able to put up with you somehow," I told him, grinning in turn.

"That's good, because boy do I have a great property to show you tomorrow. . . ."

"I'll make sure to stretch first this time," I laughed, pulling him in for a champagne-laced kiss.

Pierre the Pâtissier

Life had brought me back to Los Angeles after years away on the East Coast. I had cultivated a career in book publishing only to grow bored, spend six months traveling the back roads of Europe, and return to my native California without a clue as to what I should do with my life.

Though I eventually found work in the film industry—no, not *that* film industry—on the production side of some big studio flicks, my heart was never truly in the work. Unfortunately, that was all I did: work. Though I was making good money, meeting interesting people, and found the work to be challenging, I had no free time to pursue any of my interests.

I didn't mean to take up guitar or learn Russian or anything like that, but time and again I found myself thinking: What good is making money if you don't have time to enjoy it? So after a couple of years, at an opportune moment, I quit.

That was it, I just up and quit. Granted, I had more of a

plan than that, but my plan did not extend beyond a few months. If I really stretched things, I figured I had the savings to live on for a little less than a year, but I didn't want to go back to the daily grind anytime soon, so I quickly started casting about for an alternative career.

As luck would have it, I met a food writer while I was out one night, and he indulgently gave me some helpful hints about how to start freelancing. Before that evening, if you had asked me whether I would have ever thought I'd be employed as a restaurant reviewer, I probably would have laughed in your face. I had always been interested in food, and loved eating out, but until I really started to think about it, I never thought I was qualified.

Turns out that if you are a good writer, curious about food and restaurants, and are driven, you can be a food writer. I was all those things, and on top of it, I started cataloging all the fine restaurants I'd eaten in around the city and figured out that I had an excellent base of reference for becoming a restaurant critic.

Once I started thinking this way, I found out I could write about just about anything, especially once I got a few sample clips published. The more I wrote, the more writing work I got. Editors seemed to appreciate the way I punctually met deadlines, my fastidious research, the fresh angles I took, and the genuine passion I had for the work.

Before long, I was pretty much fully employed, though I made my own hours, worked from home, and got to spend my days wandering the city in search of the best places to eat. Not only that, but I also got to travel and write about my experiences. It also gave me a good excuse to eat at really nice places while on the road. For research purposes, of course. Life was good.

Most important, however, was keeping up-to-date on the food scene in Los Angeles, since that was my bread-basket, so to speak. Whenever I heard about a new restaurant, bar, or café, I hastened to try it, hoping to get a review up before the competition.

That was why one day when I was strolling through my neighborhood doing my errands, I was interested to notice a new pâtisserie right near my dry cleaner. I had been traveling a lot, so I had not even noticed that the place had been under renovation. The sign said: PIERRE'S PÂTISSERIE.

That was a little too cute for my taste, but I decided to pop in anyway, and I had to concede that the baking smells that were wafting from the door were incredible. The places smelled like heaven. Buttery, *pain au chocolat* heaven.

I dreamily walked in the door prepared to order up a pastry from the shelves and shelves of golden croissants, colorful petits fours, and assorted bonbons, but no one was in sight. "This is a fine way to run a business!" I thought.

I hungrily wandered the bakery, looking at all the different goodies; then I noticed that there was a little door-man's bell on the counter. So, not knowing what else to do, I rang it, fully expecting some grandmotherly type woman to come flouncing in from the backroom.

Imagine my surprise when the person who came from the kitchen was actually a scrappy young man in his late twenties with dark, spiky hair, smoldering brown eyes, an earring, and tattoos winding their way up his sinewy forearms. He gave me a little smirk, which was funny because *he* was the one with some flour smudged on his face.

Then he asked, "May I 'elp you?"

Hearing his accent, I realized he was French. I picked my jaw up off the ground and answered him in his mother tongue, saying, "Yes, I was wondering what you've just baked, I'd like to take home the freshest product."

He smiled at me, saying still in French, "Ah, you speak French?"

"A little bit," I modestly replied. "I have spent a lot of time in Paris."

"That is where I did most of my *stage* when I trained to be a chef," he told me. Then he introduced himself. "I am Pierre."

"Ah!" I exclaimed. "So this is your pâtisserie?"

"That is correct. I am a chef, but I was always most interested in being a baker like my grandfather. I came to California to work, but wanted to start my own business."

"Well, it looks wonderful," I told him. "Where in France are you from?"

"A town called Aix," he told me. "Do you know it?"

I had indeed spent a little time in Aix. It is in the southeast of the country in Provence and is known for its fields of lavender that thrive in the sunny Mediterranean climate. Hearing he was from Aix also made me smile, because the city is known for a particular pastry.

"You're from Aix?" I repeated. "Then I would love to try some of your *calissons*."

Hearing me say that, Pierre positively lit up. His huge smile completely transformed his smirking, mischievous face into that of an excited little boy.

"You know of *calissons!*" he exclaimed, completely surprised.

These special treats are tiny sugar cookies trimmed with pine nuts, and have been a specialty of the pâtissiers of Aix-en-Provence since the Middle Ages.

Suddenly, Pierre was my new best friend. He invited me behind the counter and started to ply me with the treats of his trade.

There were *chaussons aux pommes* with flaky buttery shells surrounding fresh-picked apples swimming in cinnamon. The fruit tarts were made with the most colorful berries I had ever seen. There were fluffy meringues, nutty *dacquoises*, dark chocolate ganaches, creamy financiers, and utterly delicate napoleons. My favorite, as Pierre soon figured out, were the cream-filled éclairs that he had made with a variety of glazes. He made me try the chocolate, the mocha, the caramel, the maple, and his own homemade buttercream.

I was going to go into a sugar coma, but I couldn't get enough of Pierre or his pastries. He would dip his finger into an éclair's creamy center and make me taste it. When I didn't suck all the cream off his finger, he would finish the job himself, giving me an impish little grin as he cleaned his finger with his tongue.

Each pastry was more delicious than the last, and I made sure to sing Pierre's praises. Everything was so delicate and decadent, yet simply made from the freshest ingredients. I made a mental note of what I was tasting so that I could write about it later.

The rest of my concentration, however, was taken up by checking out Pierre whenever he wasn't looking at me. He was definitely French, but not in that annoying, mousy way. He was like a celebrity chef, with real machismo, though with each passing moment and each additional goodie, I could tell that he was gay and that he was definitely into me.

As for me, all I could think about was working off my sugar rush by fucking his brains out. He was my height with a svelte body that was knotted by the muscles he had gained plying his trade. It takes hard work and effort to run a bakery: long hours, hauling ingredients, rigorous mixing, stoking the ovens. His arms were pure muscle, and I could make out the outline of a round little ass through his flour-stained jeans.

I asked him more about himself and learned that he had been in the U.S. a few years. He had been dating another chef, but when their relationship soured, Pierre decided he needed a big change and that it was time to start his own bakery, just like his grandfather had.

I asked him specific questions about his techniques, ingredients, and his culinary background so that he could see I was no common dilettante. My plan must have worked, because after the last éclair, he raised his eyebrows and gave me a searching look.

I looked back at him, questioningly, then grinned. Something I did must have convinced him to do what he did next.

Taking my hand, almost gently at first and then more insistently, he led me into the back of the bakery, telling me, "Come, there is something I want you to try."

I was ready for anything.

Leading me into the back, past his cavernous ovens and a large marble preparation table to the gigantic stove that occupied an entire wall, he pointed out a huge copper pot that was sitting over a tiny open flame. Reverently lifting the top, he bent down to breathe in the fresh cloud of steam. I followed his lead and got a nose full of spicy, fragrant, chocolatey bliss. I couldn't fathom what would make such a combination and I asked Pierre what he was making.

He told me that he was experimenting with creating different chocolate bonbons and that this was something completely new. He was creating the base ingredients for a new truffle that incorporated three different kinds of Asian chilis, natural bee honey from Scandinavia, and Turkish citrus fruits.

Before I could ask him any questions, he had ladled out a spoonful of it, and was holding it up to my lips expectantly. I compliantly opened up my mouth to try it, and he stepped closer so that our mouths were almost touching, and he blew on the steaming liquid to cool it slightly for me. I was touched by the thoughtful gesture, and leaned forward to take the spoon into my mouth.

The chocolate had cooled slightly, and at first that's all I tasted; but as I swallowed the thick liquid, it made my throat tingle and burn, while releasing the most heavenly citrus vapor up through my nose. There were so many flavors going on, I found myself craving more just so I could try to parse them out more exactly.

Pierre was still standing inches away from me, and I wrapped his spoon-holding hand in my own so that I could lick the utensil clean, trying to taste every single element in the candy. He looked thrilled and nervous, asking me what I thought.

I didn't even answer him, I just pulled him into a sweet, long, messy, wet, chocolatey kiss. I had just gorged myself on this beautiful man's baked goodies, and now I hungered for his sex. My appetite was insatiable and I was going to be fulfilled one way or another.

As we kissed, my lips scratching against his supple, pink mouth, we began to tear at each other's clothes furiously. I quickly unbuttoned his chef's whites while he tore off my shirt. I kicked off my shoes and started to undo my pants while Pierre took off his jeans. We were naked in seconds flat, and then we were back to kissing one another ravenously.

The harder I kissed him and the deeper I shoved my tongue into his mouth, the harder he kissed me back. We were clawing at each other so intensely, embracing so tight, it was like we were wrestling right there in the middle of his kitchen, and I delighted in the feeling of his muscles flexing and contracting in counterpoint to my own.

Pierre's chest was more hirsute than my own, with a huge patch of fur covering the entirety of it, tapering over the space of his abs and then widening again to form a diamond patch around his belly button. I could barely see the light pink nipples at the tip of his flat pecs for the mat of hair that covered them, but I still managed to tweak them a few times, making Pierre kiss me even harder.

I reached around him and grabbed hold of his tiny ass, pulling the cheeks apart and really kneading into the muscle like an unformed lump of Pierre's bread dough. I nuzzled into his chest hair and savored the smells of sweat, deodorant, and a slew of baking spices like cinnamon and nutmeg that had left faint traces on his skin.

I sucked on his fingers, tasting the vestiges of chocolate still on them while Pierre reached down to coax my swelling cock to life. His own meaty éclair was already up and ready for action, and I couldn't wait to taste its cream filling. He was, unsurprisingly, uncircumcised, and was sporting a nice, thick baguette, about the same size as my own eight inches. The shaft thickened from its base and was the widest at the middle, then tapered to a finely pointed head that was just barely revealed by the turtle-neck of his foreskin. The whole thing curled in a down-ward arc shape. I'd seen one or two dicks like that in my time, so it was still a novelty.

We slammed back into one another, making out again as we felt each other up and down, leaving bright red marks where our hands rubbed each other's skin. We dry-humped each other standing up, our two cocks chafing each other like soft sandpaper. My own cut sausage was getting tickled by Pierre's unruly mound of black pubic hair. He was so European and went au naturel, with no manscaping at all, and his shaft and balls were forested with a thick layer of downy hair.

As we frotted, my cock pushed up and down against Pierre's, causing the foreskin to stretch and retreat with each upward hump we made on one another. His rolling pin was dribbling clear precum all over the place, wetting both himself and me, and lubricating our dry-humping.

Without my realizing it, Pierre maneuvered us back through the kitchen to his large preparation table, right in the middle of everything. He swept his arm across it, spilling utensils and kitchen implements everywhere. Then he grabbed me in those muscular arms of his and set me on my back on the table, pinioning my legs against his hairy chest.

This was his work space, so there was flour, spices, and various other ingredients like sugar and butter everywhere. Within a moment, we were coated in all kinds of baking necessities, my back stained white with flour. Pierre reached for a bottle of cooking oil and poured it freely over his bright pink cock, and sent another squirt right at my ass.

He rubbed my crack with his hand a couple times to get it coated in the oil, then holding me firmly in place with his strong hands, he stuffed his meat thermometer as far into me as he could go.

I reached up and squeezed his arm, hard, because I was not ready for full penetration, and my insides burned with the intrusion, but as he started to vibrate slowly, loosening me up and massaging the walls of my ass, I soon became more comfortable and let go of him so that he knew it was all right to start fucking me.

He worked my ass with the same finesse he used to style his pastries, switching rhythms and directions frequently, keeping me guessing, and hitting every one of my internal erogenous spots. He would ram me for a few strokes, then gently swirl his hips, making me moan with ecstasy. He would anchor himself by leaning over me and placing his hands on my chest, pinning me to the table, and thrust down into my cavity. Then without warning, he would lean back and jab up into my prostate.

Every new movement was a surprise, and my mouth hung open as I let the waves of electric pleasure wash over me. Pierre ran his hand along the surface of the table, dusting it with confectioner's sugar, and then stuck his fingers in my mouth, wiggling them around so that my tongue sucked every last granule clean.

He turned me on my side, with one leg wrapped around

him and the other in the air. With each thrust, his hairy, sweaty balls whacked against my ass, and they stuck together for a moment until Pierre withdrew again. His sprout of pubes tickled my testes and made them ache with ecstasy.

Pierre poured another cupful of cooking oil onto his hands and greased up my junk as he continued to hump me. With the precision of a master baker, he manipulated my rod into a throbbing erection while teasing my balls by lightly brushing them with his fingertip.

For my part, I grabbed on to his rug of chest hair and pulled hard, making him gasp with delicious pain and redouble his efforts to bring me to fruition. He was talented with his hands, using all the coordination that years of carefully dressing cakes had trained in him, and he was quickly sending me to a finish.

Pierre continued to tenderize my ass with his mallet of a cock, sparking every single nerve inside me and sending jolts of electricity to every extremity. Meanwhile, he was rolling the circular tip of my johnson in his hands, leaving my breath ragged and irregular as the nerve endings became overworked.

Finally, I could hold back no longer. My berries knotted up into my body, and I let loose a colossal gush of semen, spilling sperm all over Pierre's hands as it issued from deep inside me. Torrent after torrent of the stuff arced through the air onto the prep table, even hitting my own throat and shoulder as Pierre persisted in milking out every last drop.

I moved my ass around on Pierre's dick a few last times, savoring the last sensations of completion. He coaxed a final drop of jizz from my spent cock and gently dabbed at it with his finger, bringing the goo to his lips and licking it off with his tongue. He smiled and pronounced it to be *délicieux*.

Pulling out of me, Pierre started to jerk himself off. He had gotten some flour on his hands, and it had created patchy lumps on his sweaty torso and dusted his cock. He didn't pay any attention, though, as he whipped the foreskin back and forth over his cockhead. He concentrated on the tip of his dick, getting it really lubricated with cooking oil and swirling his finger all round it inside the foreskin.

With a low groan, he twitched his hips a few times, and his knees buckled, and he poured a cascade of his cream down onto me. When I had seen he was about to blow, I spun myself around so my mouth was inches from his cock, and as he shot his load, I opened my mouth to catch some of the custard. It was delicate and hot, sliding down my throat in a mass of slippery goo, and as he finished dribbling drops onto the edge of the marble table, I smacked my lips appreciatively, enjoying the last remnants of flavor.

When Pierre finished, he hunched over, taking a moment to come back to life. Then he leaned toward me to plant a final kiss on my mouth, which was still smeared with a mixture of our cum.

He licked a drop of it off my chin and kissed me again. We passed the little white ball of salty fluid back and forth between our mouths, sharing the snowball until it became too diluted with our saliva to taste, then he swallowed it and kissed me again one last time.

"That was better than anything else I tasted today," I told him.

"You have a very discerning palate," he joked back.

We dressed quickly—a customer could come in at any moment, after all—and Pierre sent me on my way with a bag of croissants and a package of chocolate bonbons before cleaning up his kitchen.

As I left, Pierre told me, "It's nice to meet someone who appreciates what I do. I hope that you will come back."

"I plan to be a regular. You can count on it," I replied. "I'm going to tell everyone I know to drop by."

"I'm not sure I can handle all that business," he said, grinning. "But I can try."

Samuel the Barrel Master

As a writer, I cover everything from current events to art history to food and wine. Basically I am a curious person, and that helps you when you're a writer since you always want to get to the bottom of everything, so to speak.

While I lived in Los Angeles, I wrote a lot about the food scene, and because it was California, wine played a major part of what I talked about. That was just fine by me, since I am an avid oenophile, and I often plan entire trips around wine-tasting. Living in California was like heaven since I could visit so many different wine regions in my own state. While I lived there, I hit all the big ones, like Napa, Sonoma, and Santa Barbara, and even some of the lesser known regions, like Lodi, and Temecula, which is in the high desert near Palm Springs.

The most memorable trip by far, however, was a road trip I took, à la *Sideways* to the Santa Ynez Valley north of Santa Barbara. It's home to some major appellations like the Santa Rita Hills, as well as iconic wine towns like Los Olivos and the Danish-themed Solvang.

I only had a few days, but I made the most of them since the two wines the area is known for, Chardonnay and Pinot Noir, are two of my favorite varietals. I think I managed to hit about six wineries a day, but toward the end of the trip, I slowed down, pacing myself more by plotting wineries that were farther away from the main towns.

That was how I ended up, at the conclusion of my last day, driving for about an hour down the winding roads through the Santa Rita Hills trying to find a particular winery whose wines were supposed to be amazing. I had made an appointment for the end of the day since it was so far removed from anywhere else I had been. I felt like a drunken explorer, wending my way through the little mountains past vineyards and fields dotted here and there with cows and various farm sheds.

After a little while, the road became unpaved, the signage stopped, and I was beginning to get worried that I was on the wrong track, but then I noticed a crude wooden sign for the winery I was seeking that pointed down an even rougher dirt track.

Downshifting, I pulled onto the ranch road and drove another five minutes past some sheds and a trickling creek before pulling up to a rusty iron gate that was flung open to reveal a gravel driveway.

With more than a little trepidation, I slowly pulled onto the drive and continued another couple minutes until I pulled around a bend and saw a huge shed in front of me. I'd arrived at the winery.

Unlike the places in Napa and Sonoma, the wineries

down here were more casual, functional affairs. If the building kept the temperature cool, it was good for the wines, and good enough for the winemakers.

I gingerly stepped from my car and walked around the shed to where I could see the huge front doors. No one seemed to be around, not even a ranch dog. I knocked on one of the doors but got no answer, so I meekly stepped inside and started to look around.

I could hear some clanging from one corner of the shed, so I followed the noise, calling out, "Hello!"

The clanging immediately stopped, and as I continued walking, I saw a figure appear from between the fermentation tanks in front of me.

The person who greeted me was a burly young guy in his early twenties, with sparkling green eyes, reddish hair, and the start of a beard. He was about my height, which is to say, not tall, but he had at least forty pounds of muscle on me, which he'd amassed from harvesting grapes, hauling crates, and cleaning the huge tanks. When I met him, he was jollily stomping around in a pair of waterproof boots—the costume of his trade—and he came forward to meet me with a hearty handshake.

"You must be Brad," he said, smiling broadly.

"I am, thank you for having me," I said, trying to be polite, though I was immediately charmed by him.

"I'm Samuel, the barrel master. I've been expecting you."

"Sorry to have kept you waiting!" I stammered. "The drive up here was longer than I thought."

"I know it, I've got to make it every morning!" Samuel said, laughing. "Everyone else has gone home for the day, so it's just you and me. I hope you don't mind."

"Not at all," I told him, struggling to hide my grin.

"I'm about done here anyway, so let's get tasting," he suggested.

I followed him to a little makeshift tasting bar that had been set up in the corner. It was basically a couple planks of wood thrown over two barrels. He raised an eyebrow at me, and asked, "Why don't we go out and enjoy the sunset?"

"Sounds good," I replied as he picked up two wine-glasses and handed them to me, then scooped up several different bottles in his arms and tromped outside.

He led me around the shed to where there were a couple of beach chairs set up in a clearing that overlooked the hills all the way to the ocean. The sun was almost dipping into the sea as we set everything down, and Samuel poured each of us a taste of the first wine.

The sunset was just spectacular, illuminating the few clouds in the sky with shades of orange, pink, and lavender. Samuel and I sat there, enjoying it in silence for a few moments before starting to discuss the wines.

I was pleased to see that he was drinking them with me. Unlike some of the more formal tastings I'd been on, where one was expected to spit out the wine to avoid getting tipsy, we were both downing our tastes, then comparing opinions.

We didn't agree on much. He tasted one thing, I tasted another. He liked this one, I liked that one. We were both getting a little "happy," and our disagreements only contributed to the congenial mood, giving us something to keep talking about.

Now, I thought Samuel was very handsome, with his ruddy cheeks, his beefy physique, and his friendly manner, but I did not have even the faintest suspicion that he might be into guys. That is, until I noticed he kept refilling my glass before his own, letting his hand linger on mine as he held my cup steady.

I watched him out of the corner of my eye, and I could see that he was checking me out when he thought I wasn't looking. I didn't blame him. My cheeks were ruddy, too, from a day of wine tasting. My skin was tanned from the L.A. sun, and from spending a few days roaming the wine country and enjoying the glorious weather. The fresh air had done me a world of good, and I was already in great shape from hiking and hitting the gym. Though I was more slender than he was, I still had the muscle to take him on. My straight dark brown hair contrasted sharply against my bright hazel eyes, and it was long enough almost to touch my shoulders in kind of a Euro way, but not cheesy or girly since I never tied it in a ponytail. I was a sophisticated city dweller, and I wanted to cowboy up.

When we had tried the last wine, I gazed pensively at the last rays of sunlight emanating from the horizon, and I felt like I never wanted this moment to end, so I figured out a way to prolong it. I asked Samuel for a tour of the winery.

"Of course!" he exclaimed, flustered. "I can't believe I didn't show you around before we had the wine."

I laid a delicate, uncalloused hand on his massive shoulder, comforting him. "We had a sunset to catch, remember?"

"Oh yeah," he agreed, grinning. He took my hand from his shoulder and pulled me up. "Come on," he said, still grinning.

Samuel gathered up the bottles and I grabbed our glasses, and we both went inside, depositing them at the bar. Samuel gave me a mischievous smile, then opened a door I had not noticed before and stepped inside a dark room. Was he leading me into his love lair?

I stepped forward, but just as I did, he reemerged with a dusty bottle. It was about seven years old and was one of the estate's reserve wines.

"I don't usually do this," he told me, "but you really seem to appreciate our wines, and since we don't agree on anything, I want to know what you think of it."

I couldn't believe my luck. The bottle he was holding was worth several hundred dollars at least, and I was going to get to taste it!

I kept thanking him as he carefully opened it and poured us each a new full glass. Then he led me to one corner of the winery and showed me where the grapes came in. He told me about how they treated the grapes and the methods they used to ferment them, age the juice in barrels, and then blend the barrels into their different wines. I was very interested in everything he was saying since the wine was delicious, but I found myself distracted by watching him talk animatedly about what went on in the winery.

I wanted to kiss him so badly, especially when he grabbed my shoulder and guided me to the next point of our tour. I held back, though, waiting for the right moment. Waiting for some sure sign that my feelings were requited. I gulped down my last drop of wine, barely noticing the rich flavor that had made me so happy earlier.

Samuel looked at me quizzically but gulped his down,

too, then put both our glasses down on a counter next to one of the aging barrels.

"Come on," he said, taking my hand and leading me to the main barrel room. When we reached it, I was over-whelmed by the comforting, toasty smell of the oak, with just a little hint of yeast giving it some tang.

"This is my room," Samuel told me proudly.

"It's wonderful," I breathed, taking in the sight of all the barrels and shivering a little in the cold. Wineries must stay cold to control the rate of fermentation and the aging process of wines, so they can get a little chilly.

Samuel noticed and came to stand next to me, throwing a heavy arm over my shoulder and pulling me close into his warmth. Before I knew what I was doing, I turned my face toward his, gently grabbed his head, and guided it to-ward my own for the kiss we had both been waiting for.

His lips were chapped, and his beard poked my face, but I didn't mind either discomfort at all. It felt so good, so right, to be kissing a real man after all the pansies I came across in Los Angeles. I loved tasting the wine we had just drunk on Samuel's lips, feeling his rough tongue scrape against mine as it probed deeper and deeper into my mouth. His thickset arms were wrapping around me, squeezing me tight so that I found it difficult to breathe all the way in, but I wouldn't have had him loosen his hold for all the world.

His hairy, thick forearms pulled me into a bear hug as we made out, and I felt pressed against the wall of muscle that was his torso. A few more years and he'd be a world-class bear, but for right now, he was just a stocky, pumped young guy. I ran my hands along his broad back and felt the hard-worked muscles of his shoulders, rounded as they were from the manual labor he performed at the winery. His legs, too, I could feel, were solid as wine barrels, stretching the fabric of his work overalls. As soon as I reached down to cop a feel of his burly, juicy ass, I knew he could fuck me 'til I wouldn't be able to walk straight.

Samuel's hands, meanwhile, were busy as well, feeling my entire body up and down. He especially seemed to like my well-formed pecs and the six-pack that had taken me years of crunches to achieve. Before I knew what he was doing, he had lifted me up under the legs so that I could wrap them around his waist and he could carry me over to the nearest racking barrel.

It was a big, traditional Burgundy barrel, fully rounded in the middle, so when Samuel put me down on it, he didn't even have to bend his knees. He started to pull back, but I held him close to me by keeping my legs tightly wrapped around him, and smiled as he leaned back in to kiss me. My face was growing warm and red from all the saliva swapping, but it was still freezing in the barrel room. I wanted to get naked with Samuel so badly, but I couldn't imagine having sex in such a cold, dank place, no matter how hot we got.

By this time, I could feel that both our packages were getting hard, mine beneath my jeans, and Samuel's making a bulge beneath the denim of his overalls. I loosened my legs around him and let them drop to either side of his massive trunk while Samuel reached down and carefully undid my zipper. He didn't have to root around for long to find my prick. It popped right out like a jack-in-the-box, and he coaxed it to maximum hardness with one of his meaty paws.

Placing a hand on either side of my narrow hips to brace

himself, Samuel bent down and began to play with the knob of my cock using just his tongue. First, he sopped up the film of clear precum that had drooled out of my urethra, smacking his lips at the salty, sticky taste. Then, he started to dip his head up and down on my champagne flute, taking more and more of it down his throat. Finally, he hoovered the whole thing, and made his cheeks and tongue undulate around it rhythmically, producing the sexiest slurping noises and giving me chills.

The scrubby hairs on his lips and chin tickled my shaft when he took it out of his mouth to play around with his tongue. I had a hard time maintaining my balance each time his sandpaper face jolted me, but it felt so good, so manly, that I just grabbed on to his bushy hair and forced his face farther down to suck on my balls.

The contrast between the soft, downy flesh of my nutsack and his rough-bearded face only heightened the stimulation as he sucked both my testes at once. I inhaled sharply as he mildly pulled at them with his teeth, sending volts of electricity down to my very toes.

When my cock was perfectly hard and totally wet with his spit, Samuel pulled me off the barrel and turned me around so that I was leaning over its curve. He yanked my pants and underwear down so my ass was completely exposed to him, and I went completely limp, leaning over the barrel and ready to let him have his way with me.

The first thing I felt was the weight of his titanic hands, one seizing each of my ass cheeks and pulling them apart to expose my sensual valley. The next thing I felt was the coarse whiskers on his face as he bent near and inhaled a huge whiff of me. Then I felt my abdomen loosen as a molten liquid warmth enveloped the entirety of my bull's-eye. His tongue worked magic on me, and before long, I was both quaking with uncontrollable tingles of ecstasy and totally loosened up and ready to be ravaged.

Samuel's tongue glossed over the length of my ass crack, licking each square inch of skin and sending me into an even higher state of excitement when he concentrated his efforts on my little wing nut. I reached behind me, grabbed hold of his skull, and mashed his face even harder into me until I felt his tongue delve deep into my love tunnel. That was quickly followed by one of his sturdy fingers, which slowly crept into my fudge chute, then wended its way deep into me.

He started to finger-fuck me while continuing to lick the sensitive nerve endings in my butt furrow, but I knew I would have to brace myself when I heard him stand up behind me. I hadn't yet felt Samuel's hard-on, but I reached back to take hold of it and guide it into my waiting ass. It was hefty and thick, just like its owner, with a head that was as big and round as a snow globe . . . at least it felt that way to me.

He had already managed to get it wet and slippery with a mixture of spit and the precum that I felt practically pouring from the hole at the tip of his dick. Holding his penis in one hand and pulling aside one of my cheeks in the other, I slowly maneuvered his corkscrew into my shy pink pucker.

I breathed in deeply, trying to loosen up enough to take in his remarkable girth, and it was only after a few seconds that I was able to decontract for him to push his way inside me. As every inch of his slab of meat entered me, I felt

Samuel lean over onto me with his heavy bulk, pressing me even harder down onto the barrel. When he had totally penetrated me, he took a moment to kiss my ear and the back of my neck, letting me get used to his volume; then he smoothly pulled almost all the way out, leaving just the tip of his cock head inside me before gliding it all back into my ass cavity. He did that a few times; then he started to pump in and out of me with more purpose.

The bramble of his pubes was tickling my ass cheeks, and I could feel his balls whacking against my taint, making a sweaty slapping sound each time they came into contact with my skin. Samuel's hands were prying apart my ass cheeks, opening them as far as they would go and stretching the skin of my sphincter as he plunged in and out of me with his fat hard-on. He stood back up and took a firmer grip on my pelvis, really plugging me with all he had. I took it for a few moments, but then I stood up, too, and arched my back in order to slow him down and make him punch deep up into me in order to hit my G-spot. I turned my head to kiss his scratchy face, sending my tongue on a caving mission into his mouth while he, in turn, went spelunking in my nether regions.

After a minute or two in that more intimate, profound position, Samuel asked me if we could change it up. I breathily agreed to do whatever he wanted, and so he pulled his knob out of me and set me back up on the barrel, facing him. Then bending his knees slightly, he launched himself back inside me with the precision of a guided missile, barely pausing when I issued forth a sound that was half moan and half whimper.

We were both totally warmed up, so Samuel started at a

fast pace, jamming me several times a second as his breath came faster and more shallow. I loved being able to see the changing expressions on his face. His cheeks were puffed out and totally flushed from the exertion, and a line of sweat had broken out on his fair forehead. We both still had our tops on since it was cold in the barrel room, but I reached up to feel out the hard, rounded muscles of his husky frame, and I shifted my ass back and forth so that each time his sturdy, hairy legs slammed into me, we met with a powerful impact.

Our motions combined to create long, vigorous strokes that stoked the fires within both of us. I pulled Samuel's face down to my own, his hefty weight resting upon me, so that we could kiss as he fucked my brains out. I could barely concentrate on anything except the fact that my ass and my back were aching—my ass from the pounding of a lifetime, and my back from the strange arch shape the barrel made me conform to. I didn't care, though. I just wanted this to go on forever, though I knew that within a minute I would be spewing enough cum to fill one of the room's stainless-steel fermentation tanks.

Each thrust sent me further and further toward the precipice. I had barely even touched my own dick since Samuel's oral entertainments, but I could already feel the precum coating my piss pipe and the sperm flowing up from my prostate and through my balls to where it would erupt from my groin.

I could no longer resist giving in to my impulses, so I demanded that Samuel fuck me as hard as he could, and I gave myself a few final squeezes, getting ready to pop my cork. I told Samuel I was going to cum any second, and he

panicked . . . with two results. The first is that he pounded
me even harder, faster, his whole body becoming stiff as a
board. The second was, after screaming that if I came on
the barrel I'd ruin the wine, he bent down with a flexibility
I found remarkable for someone as powerfully built as he
was, so that his mouth was suctioned over the very tip of
my cock.

That was it. He sent me right over the edge when his
mouth latched on to me like that, and I began to ejaculate
right into his orifice. Wave after wave of undeniable gratification swept over me as each burst of semen flew out of
my body.

Samuel struggled to gulp it all down. I always produced
big loads, but his massive cock had kneaded out every last
bit of semen I had to offer, like a fully inflated winepress,
and I was sending it all down his throat. He managed to
suck down most of it, but he was quickly overwhelmed
and let a few drops spill back onto my pelvis. He was considerate, though, and as soon as he knew I was done, he
released my dick from his mouth, and licked up the remaining splatters from my body.

The least I could do was return the favor, so I climbed
down from the barrel. His prick was completely engorged
and red, with veins sticking out in every which way. He
had to be close to completion. With the same attention
he'd given me, I fastened on to his cock with the single-
mindedness of a leech and sucked for all I was worth.

Using my hands, I coaxed and caressed moans of pleasure from him, and when the flow of his precum became
particularly heavy, I knew he had only seconds left to resist
me, so I employed my hands to jerk his slobbery cock off

while I continued to suck and lick at the sensitive skin on the bottom of his shaft right below the head. That did the trick, and he began to shudder, while his balls shriveled way up into his groin.

Keeping my mouth over the entire head of his cock so that not even a jot of juice would escape me, I continued to tug at his shaft until I felt surge after surge of body-hot goo hitting the back of my mouth and running down my throat. He kept gushing for almost a half-minute more, then, treating me to one final trickle of his mineral-tasting slime, he shifted back and pulled out of my mouth. I wiped at my chin to be sure I had polished off all his gunk, then stood up to kiss him, tasting our mingled substances on both our mouths.

Standing back at the rudimentary bar a few minutes later, Samuel poured us both another glass from the vintage bottle he had pulled out earlier. We swirled our wine, sniffed at it professionally, then tasted a hearty swig of it.

"Delicious berry notes and a strong alcohol content, but still a fine, young acidity. Just beautiful," I sighed, taking another sip.

"For once I agree with you, but it's nothing compared to how you taste," said Samuel.

"Well, that was just one sample. You'll have to try a few more before making your final judgment," I told him, knowledgeably.

"I look forward to it. You know, we could use more wine writers like you around here. Ones who are really willing to get their hands dirty . . ."

"Well, it helps to have a barrel master who can show you the ropes and really let you delve into every aspect of

the winemaking process," I replied, taking another sip.
"That's how you learn."

"I plan to teach you everything I know," he told me.

Raising my glass to toast him, I replied, "I look forward
to it."

Twin Trickery

I'm going to preface this by saying that I am *not* the type of guy who picks up other guys at the gym normally. Nor, more importantly, have I ever had a fetish for twins. Oh, sure, I know the gay pornosphere is totally obsessed with them—let alone triplets who are willing to get naked together. Well, not me. The tinge of incest is just too much for me to handle. Or so I thought.

Let me start at the beginning. When I lived in Los Angeles in my mid-twenties, I joined a gym that I frequently referred to as "the gay epicenter of the universe." Yes, it was one of those kinds of gyms. Muscular, overly tanned actor boys working out all day in the testosterone-saturated weight room. Wiry, granola-crunching yoga boys stretching, shirtless, in the yoga studio for hours on end, demonstrating just how far back behind their heads they could get their legs. Harried publicist gays running to spin class, then primping for an hour afterward in the locker room, making sure every little label-conscious accessory was in place. Basically every stereotype imaginable came through that gym.

I never intended to join it, but it was the closest gym to me, the facility was brand new and kept extremely clean, the rates were low, and you can't blame me for wanting a little bit of eye candy as I worked out, can you? Unlike some of the other WeHo gyms, not too much dirty stuff happened in the sauna or showers, so I was happy to prance in and out of there for my workouts and leave the dirty stuff to others.

Due to my writing schedule, I came at all hours of the day and tried to make it when I didn't think it would be too busy. It's hard enough to motivate in the first place, but when you have to wait for equipment, going to the gym becomes a downright burden. Usually I would just mind my own business as I used this weight machine or that, and then did a bit of cardio to work off my nervous energy. Occasionally, I'd loiter a little in the locker rooms for a few delicious looks at some of the guys I lusted after, but my experience overall was pretty PG.

Unlike many of the other gay guys at the gym, I did not really make friends there. I didn't wear earphones to discourage conversation or anything like that, and I was usually pretty cheerful, but no one talked to me much. That was fine by me, since I really was there just to work out, but sometimes I was jealous of the posses of gays I saw around me having so much fun and gossiping as they worked out. Sigh, back to the weights.

After a few months, I was doing very well and getting pretty buffed up, with veins running down my arms from my hard-packed shoulders over my bulky biceps and down my sinewy forearms. My abs were washboard flat, and my legs were 100 percent sculpted muscle, too. A friend even commented that my ass was hard enough to break his hand on. All in all, the gym was doing my body good. Still, I kept mostly to myself. . . .

Until one day when a new guy I'd never seen before came up and asked if he could work in with me on a fly machine. He was taller than me, about six-foot-two if I had to guess, with curly brown-blond hair that coiled off his head. He had bright blue-green eyes, bushy eyebrows, and a lean, muscular body that made me just want to rip his shirt off. Did I mention that he had the cutest smile I'd ever seen?

I politely said that he could certainly work in with me. He thanked me and hopped on the machine. I had noticed that he had a funny accent. Liverpool, England, I guessed, but what I said was, "You sound like Ringo Starr."

He laughed, and said, "That's because I'm from Manchester, mate."

"Ah, not Liverpool," I said, disappointed. "But at least that's still Lancashire."

"That's right!" he exclaimed. "You're the first person I've met in L.A. who knew that."

"I'm an anglophile," I explained. "When I think of Lancashire, I always remember Tennyson's 'The Charge of the Light Brigade' and how it's meant to sound. That's how I knew where you were from."

"What do you mean?" he asked, his weight lifting forgotten.

"Well, in 'The Charge of the Light Brigade,'" I started, "Tennyson, who was from Lancashire, rhymes the words *thundered* and *hundred*. In standard English, they don't rhyme, but in Tennyson's—and your—accent, they do. That's how I knew."

"You're a bit of a brain, then, are you?" he asked, punching me lightly in the shoulder.

"Total dork here," I admitted, blushing.

"A hot dork," he said, causing a rosy blush to bloom brightly on my cheeks. "And you like Tennyson. I think I'm in love," he said, chuckling, but holding my gaze.

"You must be a poet, too, then," I said, trying to keep things light, though by this time, I wasn't sure I was not in love myself.

"No, just a musician. I've got a band with my brother," he explained.

"That's awesome. What do you play?" I asked.

"Guitar, and I do the vocals with him," he replied.

"When are you guys playing?" I asked.

"We've got our first gig next week at the Viper Room," he said, not a little proudly.

"I wouldn't miss it. I'm Brad, by the way," I said, introducing myself.

"I'm Alastair," he answered, running a hand through his wiry hair. "If you're not busy after the gym, why don't we do something tonight?"

In response to my quizzical glance, he elaborated, "It's not every day you meet a California boy who quotes Tennyson. I don't think I can wait until next week to see you again."

Debating whether to play hard to get or to just give in to my own impulses, my hormones won out. "Okay," I said, as coolly as I could manage. "I'll meet you outside in forty-five minutes."

"It's a deal, mate," Alastair said, smiling. As I turned to walk away, I felt his hand briefly pat the space on my back between my shoulder blades, and I smiled to myself.

Just as I started down the hallway to the cardio area, though, I saw Alastair walking toward me. Only he was wearing different clothes. I was so dumbfounded that I just sat there, mouth agape, as he walked past me, giving me a quick once-over as he walked by.

Turning to follow, I traced him back to the weight room and saw him head toward the fly machine where we'd just been talking. And that's when I realized: when Alastair said he was in a band with his brother, he meant his *twin* brother. This was just getting more and more interesting.

I walked back over to the machine and heard the tail end of their conversation. Alastair was saying something like, "cute guy . . . Tennyson . . . dinner," but I didn't wait to hear the rest before clearing my throat so they would notice me.

Alastair stood up abruptly and said, "Brad! Sorry, hi, this is my brother, Ewan."

Extending my hand, I said, "Nice to meet you. Alastair, you didn't say you were a twin."

Ewan piped in, "Yeah, mate, we usually try to weed out the pervs who just want to get with us because we're twins."

"Understandable," I replied, shifting gears quickly. "They would only want the two of you to fulfill a fantasy. I'm just looking for good conversation and nice date, which your brother seems to fit pretty perfectly."

"And now that you know we're twins?" asked Ewan, ever protective.

"I think it's sort of silly to label people as twins when

one of them is charming and personable and friendly, and the other is suspicious, guarded, and defensive. Don't you think? Besides, why would I assume you were gay, too?"

Alastair laughed, and Ewan—after taking a moment to determine whether I meant what I said and apparently deciding that I was an honest bloke—laughed, too, wishing his brother and me a good time on our date. Then he chucked Alastair on the shoulder and called him a wanker for finding such a cute boy to go out with first.

I walked away from the pair with a spring in my step and hurried to go get ready for my date.

That evening was the first of many dates Alastair and I went on. The more time I spent with him, the more time I wanted to spend with him. I found him endlessly fascinating, what with his working-class English background, the fact that he and his brother had scrimped and saved to come to L.A. and try to make a go of their band, and just the fact that he was so nice and friendly, not to mention utterly, completely hot. He seemed just as smitten with me, and even Ewan warmed up to me pretty quickly once he determined that I was not some sort of twin-obsessed sex fiend . . . though I do have to admit that sometimes I caught them shaving side by side in the mirror, and I was extremely turned on by the double image of their perfect musician bodies, bare to the waist.

I was content just to be with Alastair, though, because like I said, in no way did I have a twin fetish. Plus, the sex was amazing. He was a conscientious, considerate lover; but he could also be primal and forceful. He always took care of my needs, but he made sure to take care of his own

as well. It was one of the most satisfying sexual relationships of my life. The one hitch was that he did not like to
bottom at all, so I usually took that role, though he often
offered to change it up. Every time we did, I felt kind of
bad because he clearly was uncomfortable, but I had
needs, too, so I took him up on it a few times a month and
left it at that.

It was also just plain fun dating him. As we got more
and more serious, I would start coming to every show that
he and Ewan played, and eventually I was a full-fledged
roadie. I would help them lug their equipment around
town and set up for shows when I had the free time. I sold
tickets, T-shirts, and CDs, and even set up their Web site to
help raise their image. When they went on mini-tours
around California and the Southwest, I would try to join
them wherever I could for moral support. Being a musician was such a huge part of Alastair's personality, I couldn't
help but find him sexiest when he was up onstage doing
what he loved. Sure, the sex was hot, our connection was
deep and strong, but there was nothing that could turn me
on as much or as quickly as watching him sing his heart
out for a crowd of adoring fans.

The other fun perk about my relationship with Alastair
was how jealous all my friends were of me. They kept asking about what it was like dating a twin, and if the two
boys had ever offered to double-team me. Once they both
got used to me, even the brothers started joking about it.
Ewan used to pretend he was going to make out with me,
telling me in all seriousness that they "shared everything"
while Alastair mildly looked on. At times, I felt a jumble of
unease and pride when I heard Alastair talking about the

amazing sex he had with me, and that Ewan was really missing out. I felt like an object, but at least I was an object of desire.

I laughed off their suggestions—both my friends' and the brothers'—saying that I was in the relationship with just Alastair, and that I had come to appreciate all the tiny nuances that differentiated the twins. Or so I thought, until one night when the two played a big gig in town a couple months after I started dating Alastair.

The truth was, the twins were remarkably identical. Even their mother had trouble telling them apart. They didn't have any distinguishing birthmarks or freckles, not even a tattoo, and their faces looked exactly alike. They were also workout partners, doing the exact same routine as each other every single day, so their bodies were mirror images of each other. Granted, their personalities were slightly different, with Alastair being the friendlier, more outgoing brother, but once Ewan got to know me, he treated me the same as his brother did, so it got harder and harder for me to tell them apart, and I would often mix them up. Still, I was dating Alastair and that was that. I didn't even entertain thoughts of hooking up with Ewan. I let down my guard despite their jokes about playing a trick on me, and I just enjoyed my time with Alastair.

So back to the night of the gig. It wasn't anything fancy, just an early set down at the Troubadour on Santa Monica Boulevard on a Tuesday night. The twins had another show scheduled there in a few months, but they got called in at the last minute to substitute for a group that had missed their flight to Los Angeles. I was out on assignment for a writing job that night covering another event, so I had to miss it, but when Alastair called to tell me about the gig, I told him I'd meet him back at his and Ewan's apartment later that evening.

When I got to the boys' place that night, I let myself in and called out to see if anyone was home. No one answered, but I heard the shower running, so one of them must be in there. I figured it was probably Alastair who had come home to meet me while Ewan had stayed at the Troubadour to hear the other bands. The twins shared a two-bedroom apartment with a single bathroom that they shared and a separate living room. I dropped my stuff in Alastair's room and grabbed a beer from the fridge, then sat down in the living room to wait for him to come out.

Soon enough, the shower turned off, and a few moments later, the door opened, billowing out a roomful of steam. As Alastair stepped out of the bathroom, I said hi, and gazed admiringly at his figure. He had a big, fluffy towel wrapped around his narrow waist, but above it, I could see the hard outline of his eight-pack, the tough muscles of his shoulders, the beautiful curves of his worked-out biceps and triceps, and his strong hands, not to mention those muscular calves and big, smooth feet. His normally bushy brown-blond hair was slicked back with water, and he looked all fresh and rosy from the shower, his blue-green eyes shining brightly.

He replied to my greeting, seeming unsurprised to see me, and said his usual, "Hey, love!"

I had gotten up and strode over to plant a big kiss on his mouth. I hadn't noticed that he had turned slightly left instead of right, as if he was going to Ewan's room instead of his own, so preoccupied was I by the thought of his naked body beneath that downy towel. He seemed momentarily stiff in my arms but quickly relaxed into the kiss, as though not sure what to do. But within seconds, he was kissing me just as splendidly as he normally did.

I tasted something funny on his breath, though. "Were you smoking?" I asked him, suddenly suspicious. Alastair never smoked. Ewan enjoyed the occasional cigarette, but I'd never seen Alastair take a puff.

He fumbled for an excuse, but said quickly enough, "Yeah, yeah, mate, I took a drag off Ewan's. Sorry 'bout that, I know how you hate it, babe."

I was still unsure, but said, "That's okay," and took him by the hand to lead him to his room.

"I've been looking forward to this all day," I told him as I seated him on the edge of the bed. He looked like he was cornered, but I was too busy taking off my clothes to notice. Within seconds, I had stripped naked, revealing my fit V-frame torso, my stacked legs, and my juicy cock, all within a foot of where he sat.

His expression quickly altered from cornered to incredulous. He was grinning like an idiot who couldn't believe his luck, and he quickly reached up to touch my body. I had been working out with the boys a lot lately, and it showed. My body had begun to resemble theirs, knotted with all kinds of new muscles, and ready for action. I had just trimmed my thick mat of dark pubes into a tidy little triangle right above my pendulous cock, making it look even bigger than the five flaccid inches it already was.

He kept touching me like a starving man at a feast, as though he could not get enough of me. I bent over at the waist so my face was level with his, and I started to kiss him again, sending my tongue straight into his willing mouth. He kissed me with a new urgency and excitement. I couldn't remember the last time Alastair had kissed me with such force, but I was enjoying it.

Dropping to my knees between his powerful legs, I unwrapped his towel while still kissing him. As soon as I had unknotted it from his waist, I threw the ends of it to either side of his legs like I was opening a present.

Now, I loved Alastair's English cock, and was proud to have studied it in great detail. It was about four inches long flaccid, and almost nine inches when it was erect, with a tight foreskin that narrowed to a tiny eyelet that had about the same thickness as a heavy-duty rubber band. It was a little darker than his normally golden skin, and it hung slightly to the right, pushed that way by his left testicle, which was about a quarter inch bigger than the right one. Both of them hung pretty low, but the left one was really voluminous. The cock in front of me looked pretty much the same, but it didn't curve as much as I could have sworn Alastair's did, and the testicles looked to be about the same size. Not only that, but Alastair groomed his pubes a certain way, not really shaving the bush, but trimming it down to a manageable length. The twin whose pubes I was now observing were completely shaved in parts and trimmed down almost to the skin right around the base of the cock.

I looked up at my man's face, arching my eyebrow, and asked, "Did you do something new?"

"Oh, uh, yeah," he answered quickly, "Ewan showed me how to do something different. I . . . I thought I'd try it out and see if you liked it."

"I do, I do," I said, truthfully enthusiastic. "But, well, this sounds crazy, but tell me the truth now," I demanded, looking him right in the eye. "Are you Alastair?"

He blushed bright crimson but quickly recovered, going on the offensive. "What kind of question is that, love?"

"Just answer me."

"Yes, of course I'm Alastair, what do you think?" he said, looking me straight in the eye.

"You're not Ewan, just having a little fun with me?" I asked, very suspicious still.

"No, we been through that, mate. It's me!"

I wanted him to prove it, but I couldn't really think of anything that would do it. Then he added, "Besides, like I said, we share everything," and he smiled a naughty little grin, but that didn't make me feel any better.

"That's not funny, I don't want to jeopardize my relationship with him . . . er, you . . ."

Caressing my face under my chin and pulling me to sit up level with him, he told me sincerely, "You won't. I know that." And he laid those soft lips of his over mine, setting my mind at ease. After all, he kissed like Alastair, and maybe I was just seeing things with his cock. I mean, he had trimmed his pubes in a new way. That could make everything down there look different. I stopped my mind from wandering and began to concentrate on the task at hand. In my hands, actually.

Like it was second nature, I had reached down and started to rub Alastair's tool, flipping the foreskin back and forth over the tender head of his dick. Likewise, he had also reached down to where my own elephant trunk was swinging between my legs. It soon resembled more of a giraffe than an elephant as it began to rise to a steep angle. Alastair's cock was mimicking mine and quickly extended almost to its full length under my careful manipulations.

He smelled so fresh and clean—apart from the smoky breath—I wanted to kiss every inch of his frame, and I began to lick my way down his athletic chest, across the grooves of his cum gutters, dipping into his shallow navel, and ending at the moist tip of his Big Ben. I lolled my tongue around the entry to his foreskin, mingling my saliva with the tiny reservoir of precum that had accumulated there, then shoving it inside that skin membrane so that I could twirl it between the foreskin and the sensitive head. That made Alastair flinch with flashes of titillation, and I attacked his peaked cock head with even more zest before starting to work my mouth farther down onto his shaft.

I tickled his balls with my fingertips, causing them to compress close to his body, then pulling them back down to hang out again. His hand flew to the top of my head, and forced my face farther and farther onto his stiff rod. It was as hard as I'd ever felt it, and I lashed my tongue every which way over its silky surface, tracing the outlines of the veins that ran along it.

"Use your hand," he breathed. It was an unusual direction for him. For the most part, he liked it better when I blew him with just my mouth. Still, I put my skepticism aside and did as he asked.

He began to moan almost at once and laid back on the bed, his hands covering his eyes, and I sucked away, enfolding his cock in my capable hands and stimulating every erogenous zone I knew of. I paused my neck-cramping undulations to suck first one testicle, then the other. Despite his new trim, I could swear that something else was different down there. He smelled like Alastair usually did, but the balls were not the same size I was used to, and they didn't seem to hang as low. I was growing more suspicious, but I wasn't sure what to do.

If this was indeed Ewan, why had he let me go through with this? Where was Alastair when he knew I was coming home? And did he know what his brother had been planning? I didn't have answers to any of these questions, but first I had to find out whether this was my twin or not.

I gently left off my oral arguments and slithered up Alastair's (or Ewan's, who knew?) soap-scented body, taking a moment to rake my teeth over his pink nipples and the halos of fur that dusted them. It was practically the only other body hair he had except for his pits and his pubes. Kissing Alastair on the mouth, I continued my ascent until my erection was right in his face, pointing at his nose.

I whispered, "Open wide, baby," and dangled my tackle along his lips. He obligingly opened up and began suckling the wide pink head of my cock, really licking hard at the hole and sending shivers down my body so that I had a hard time maintaining my balance on shaky arms. Then he did half sit-ups so that he could work his mouth farther and farther along my cock, eventually taking in almost the whole eight inches of its rock-hard length. After a few moments, he released my dick, and it sprang up against my stomach with a wet smacking sound; then he stuck his tongue out to help pull my peach-fuzzy stones all the way into his melting pot of a mouth. Alastair knew how sensitive my testicles were and probably wouldn't have attempted this move. Indeed, my stomach immediately tightened with a dull ache from the overture, but I didn't want to give anything away, so I let him continue, relaxing again as he moved onto my ticklish taint, and even sending his tongue a short way up my ass crack.

Alastair didn't really enjoy tossing salad, but if this wasn't him, how was he to know? I crept forward slightly on the bed so that my ass was now over this man's face, and sure enough, he didn't even hesitate before beginning to eat me out. Now, I loved Alastair's work on my nether regions, but he had never tongue-fucked my ass like this. This twin's tongue was like a high-speed, multigear, ass-eating machine, switching intensity, direction, and pressure in all the right increments. Before I knew it, I was rocking back and forth on my knees, making sure his talented tongue covered every little spot. What turned me on even more were the sounds of delight and gratification that were coming out of his mouth, like he was enjoying a fine meal, and I was only too happy to indulge him.

Clearly something was going on here. By now I was certain it was Ewan, not Alastair, who was underneath me. Well, if he was going to play a trick on me, I was going to beat him at his own game. When I'd had enough ass action, I hoisted my leg up over him so that I was kneeling next to him. I reached behind me to the nightstand drawer, and pulled out a condom and the tube of lube that Alastair kept there.

"All right, baby, you ready for a fucking?" I asked him, fire in my eyes.

"Yeah, darling, I want you so bad," he said, extending a hand to accept the condom.

I feigned confusion. "What are you doing? Don't you want me to tear you up? Like I always do? Like you like it?" I asked him, making sure to sound suspicious so that he would be sure to go along with whatever I said.

"Oh, sure, I . . . I wasn't sure if you wanted to switch things up is all," he explained.

"No, I think we better stick to our routine tonight. It's going so well so far," I said with a smirk.

I had him turn over on his stomach and pull his ass cheeks apart for me. I squirted a generous amount of the lube over his Hershey's kiss—a circle of tight, dark skin smack dab in the center of his crack. Rubbing some more lube on my latex-enshrouded dick, I hovered over him and directed my fishing pole right into his pond. I wanted to keep him relaxed—little did he know what I had planned— so I pushed into him gently, giving him time to ease into the pressure that my instrument was putting on his ass cavity. When he was good and loose, I started to thrust slowly and gently in and out of him.

I kept my first strokes long and neat, pulling out almost to the tip, then leisurely reentering his pit until I was balls deep. He made a high-pitched *mmmm* sound, but I just shushed him, telling him it was all right. I wasn't actually sure it was, though. He was really tight, and like his brother, he probably didn't like to get fucked, preferring to top. But he also was in too deep, so to speak, to admit he wasn't Alastair, so I knew he would take whatever I gave him.

"You good, baby?" I asked him, leaning down and nibbling on his ear.

Shifting his ass around on my cock, he answered with a strained, wordless, "Mm-hm." His eyes were shut tight, and the veins on his neck and forehead were standing out.

I felt bad for a moment, but then I remembered that he

had been trying to pull one over on me, and that got me feeling ornery and even resentful. I was going to teach him a lesson.

Without warning him, I began to fuck him harder, picking up my pace to double time. He tensed up, and I could tell I was giving him some pain, but I just kept going because he didn't say anything. I was in a sort of upward facing dog position, my legs pinning his to the bed, but my torso up in the air supported by straight arms. I was relying on my strong lower back to do the thrusting, and I was in good form. I reached over with one of my arms and pulled back his head, seeing his face contorted with both pain and intense pleasure as I slugged him with my cock. I bent down to lick his face and plant a deep tongue kiss on his mouth, but he was breathing hard and couldn't return the affection.

I let his head drop to the mattress and resumed the walloping I was giving him, wielding my massive member like a pickax that was mining for gold within the cave of his ass. He started to keen and whine, emitting loud, high-pitched cries. I lowered my body down onto his back and held his arms with mine in a vise-like grip, delving as deep as possible into his fuck furrow and putting the squeeze on his pulpy prostate.

"That's more like it," I told him, picking up my pace even more so that I was cudgeling his hole two or three times a second. "That's how I know you like it, baby."

"Arghh, ughhh!!" was all he could manage to cry out in response.

I wasn't through with him yet, though. He was being a real trouper and taking everything I had to give, so I figured I might as well try out another position. I heaved over onto my side, pulling Ewan with me so that I was still positioned behind him and inside him, holding his top leg up in the air by the knee. He was covered in sweat from absorbing the force of my fucking, but his dick was still rock hard, and his balls were curled up into his groin. Maybe he was a bottom, after all. Though this position did not allow me the same range of motion I had had before, I could poke him at a few new angles, and I hit him at every degree you'd find on a protractor.

Ewan was gasping and wheezing now, but he was getting looser by the second and had started to stroke his cock. The bastard was enjoying this! I needed to keep up the intensity, so I popped up onto my knees right in front his ass while he stayed on his side. I held his top leg against my sweaty chest and kept sending my spear into him at a ferocious pace while my pubic area bashed into his sticky nutsack. He stopped jerking himself off to place a hand on my hard torso, squeezing my chest and just feeling the hardworking muscles of my abdomen as I continued to clobber him.

I had been concentrating so hard on the punishing asswhooping—literally—I was giving him that I didn't even hear the front door open, so I was startled when the door to Alastair's room opened, and there stood . . . well, at that point I was almost certain the newcomer was, in fact, my boyfriend Alastair, but I was still taken off guard.

"Oi! I told you he'd know!" he shouted at his twin, laughing.

I had stopped pummeling Ewan's manhole as soon as I'd seen Alastair. Ewan, a hot, sweaty, exhausted mess, was still confused, though. "What do you mean?"

"He knows that's not me he's fucking, don't you, love?"
he asked me, coming over to plant a quick peck on my
lips. "I could never take the mickey he was just giving you,
could I, Brad?"

I was too stunned to answer with words, so I slapped
him. Then he was the one who was stunned. "What'd you
do that for?" he asked, dumbfounded.

"Why the hell do you think? I come home expecting to
make love to my boyfriend, and I find out he and his evil
twin have hatched a plan to fool me? Nice boys, real
nice." I had pulled out of Ewan and began to climb off the
bed, whipping the condom from my dick and starting to
search around for my clothes.

"You guys always talk about how creepy it is when guys
are into twins, then you go and pull this shit. It's unbeliev-
able."

Before I got too far, Ewan had jumped off the bed and
grabbed my arm, pleading, "Brad, I'm sorry. Brad, listen
to me." I stared at him in stony silence, so he went on. "It
is creepy when guys just think of us as fuck toys, but
you're different. Alastair is in love with you and is always
saying how great the sex is. I just wanted to know what it
was like."

I softened a bit at that. It was a sweet sentiment, after
all, but still pretty fucked up. I said so, and Alastair explained, "I know it is, but neither of us has ever been in a
relationship. We've always just been single or had flings,
so it's been hard for us to adjust to one of us having a
boyfriend and the other not. He just wanted to see all the
things I've been telling him about you for himself. You
can't blame him for that. We made a deal that if he ever

got you alone, he could take you for a test ride. And I said I was okay with it because I knew it wouldn't mean anything."

"It means something to me. How can I trust the two of you?" I asked, totally serious.

"It doesn't mean anything," insisted Alastair, starting to smile. "You knew all along it was Ewan you were fucking, didn't you? I saw how you were rogering him. You were taking it out on him, weren't you?"

I blushed, caught. "Maybe . . ." I conceded.

"You right git!" cried Ewan, punching me on the shoulder. "You nearly broke me, you bastard!"

"Serves you right, mate," said Alastair. Then he turned back to me and brushed my lips in a sweet, swift kiss. "Now, Brad, I know you're mad and all, but . . . well, we've never done this with anyone else, and from the looks of your willy, you're not altogether opposed to the idea of finishing up with both of us." He was right, my joystick was up and ready for round two. Alastair continued, "So I know you aren't into the whole twin thing, but if it's all right with you, can I join in?"

I looked back and forth from his to Ewan's expectant faces and weighed my options. As long as the two of them didn't touch each other, I wouldn't be grossed out, and that just meant more attention for me. My balls were aching to shoot their load after the intense fuck session I'd already had with Ewan, but I didn't want the boys to think they were off the hook yet. I nonchalantly shrugged, and replied, "Well, since we're all here . . ."

That was all it took. Ewan was back on the bed, Alastair had his clothes off within seconds, and we were all getting into position. I decided that I'd topped enough for the evening, so I was going to let Alastair have a go at my ass while I sucked Ewan off. Thanks to Ewan's earlier work, my ass was all loosened up and ready to go, so I assumed all fours in the middle of the bed, and gritted my teeth as Alastair jerked his cock erect, slapped on a condom, and steered it into my love canal.

I let him pump me for a minute or two, waiting for the pain his nine inches was inflicting on my insides to subside and be replaced by pleasure. As soon as my prostate began to tingle and quiver from his thrusting, I turned my head to face Ewan, who was standing directly in front of me, and opened my mouth to take in his heavy prick. With just a few sucks I was able to get him totally hard again and spewing a stream of yummy precum.

Alastair was going easy on me. I think he felt sorry for what he'd done and wanted to accommodate my needs before his own. I reared back on my knees to kiss him and let him know it was all right to fuck my brains out as hard as he wanted, and once he got the green light, he peeled rubber, taking my curves as hard and fast as he could. I was so turned on by what was going on—surprising myself with how okay I was by having my two twins fucking either end of me—that I stayed completely hard even though I wasn't jerking myself off. I looked in the mirror that ran along one wall of the bedroom, and was entranced by the image I saw there of my two gorgeous Brits stuffing both my holes.

It was difficult withstanding the assault Alastair's behemoth was inflicting on my butt, but it helped to concentrate on what I was doing to Ewan's pipe with my mouth and hand . . . since I knew he liked that now. Apparently Ewan was as turned on as I was by our twin-symmetry fuckfest because he was staring in the mirror, too, rubbing his nipples and stomach, sticking a finger up his own ass, and beginning to ram his meat deep down my throat. Within a minute or two, he was ready to come, probably partially thanks to the anal mauling I had given him earlier.

He plopped his cock out of my mouth and jerked himself the last few strokes to completion, hunching over as he yanked. Each time his foreskin pulled back to reveal his cockhead, he released another fountain of cum. The first flew far above my head and hit Alastair's stomach. He kept fucking me, but scolded, "Dude!" The next spattered in warm puddles on my back, getting me nice and sticky. Ewan finished with a few shots right at my face level. I opened my mouth to take in the spray, curious to see if he tasted like his brother. That mystery was quickly resolved: no. His semen was clearer and thinner, but also slightly sweeter. I wondered what he'd had to eat that day. I decided to be a good sport, and I approached Ewan's softening cock with my mouth, sucking gently at the tip and tasting the last drops of cum directly from the source. He laid a hand on my cum-spattered back to steady himself, then crumpled back on the bed.

Though still going at me full force, Alastair had been transfixed for the whole process. I think it kind of blew his mind to watch his twin come all over his boyfriend, making him ache to finish up himself. He was the newcomer to our naked workout that evening, but he was the next one to climax. After Ewan had finished, I began to jerk myself off, and that's what I was doing when Alastair abruptly pulled out of me, ripped off his rubber, and beat himself off. His strokes were more prolonged and manually forceful than his brother's. He really dug into his cock each time he tugged at it, but it only took him a few yanks to begin painting the canvas of my back with his sperm. I felt a rainstorm of hot white juice strike my skin, coating me with my man's juicy essence. He unleashed rope after rope of the stuff onto me, hitting my neck and ears, and even over my shoulder onto the bedspread. It was a full minute before he was finally done—I could tell because he had stopped groaning and begun to sigh softly. I skittled around, still on all fours, and just as I had with Ewan, sucked the last drops of nectar from his piss slit. Creamier, richer, but definitely more sour. I smacked my lips.

So then it was my turn. I stayed on my knees and began to whack off, but Alastair stopped me, crouching down so that he could blow me in a show of gratitude. Ewan was still on his back on the bed, but as soon as he saw what was happening, he sat up to join in the fun. The boys took turns milking my wang, one of them concentrating on the head and shaft while the other sucked at my balls. Then they would switch and take over the other chore. At one point, the two of them ran their lips back and forth down either side of my cock at the same time. It was a heavenly sensation that I wished could go on all night, but before I was really ready for it, I felt my orgasm rising up from the pit of my stomach.

All at once, my penis began to twitch involuntarily, my balls knotted tight up into me, and my creamy serum was erupting all over the twins' surprised faces. Alastair maintained his grip on me and kept jerking me as I sent load after load of thick goo onto their cheeks and chins, giving them a cum facial. They eagerly lapped at the drops they could catch in their mouths, savoring my extract appreciatively, and I got a thrill watching their smiling faces yearning to clean up the mess I was making all over them.

When I had finished, I collapsed on the bed, ready for a shower and a good night's sleep. I didn't want to think anymore about what had happened that night. At least, not until the next day when I could start fantasizing about it. Wiping their faces off on the sheets, the twins lay down on either side of me, each of them spooning either side of me.

I was the first to speak. "That was more fun than I'd imagined, but I think that has to be the only time we do this, boys."

"Agreed," said Ewan. But he added, "But it was really brilliant, Brad. Thank you. I'm not going to be able to sit down for a week."

"Serves you right," I replied, planting a friendly kiss on his cheek.

"So, Brad . . ." started Alastair. He had that tone he always got when he wanted to winkle something out of me.

"Yes?"

"Well, Ewan and I were wondering . . . which one of us was better?"

So that's what this was all about! "What do you mean?" I asked, playing dumb.

"We just wanted to know, you know, who you liked better. In bed, that is," ventured Ewan.

"Oh, boys, that would be like comparing an apple with . . . well, another apple," I said, refusing to give up anything.

"Come on, darling, we won't hold anything against you. We just wanted to know," said Alastair.

"Well, in that case, I'd have to say it was Ewan," I said, pretending to be thoughtful about it.

Ewan gleefully pumped his hand in the air in triumph, but before he could get too celebratory, I feigned a puzzled tone and said, "Or Alastair. Maybe it was Alastair I thought was better." Now it was Alastair's turn to gloat, but he didn't get the chance because I continued, "No, that's not it. Ewan? Hmmm, or Alastair. Huh. You know, I just can never tell the difference between you two. . . ."

And before they could say anything else, I hopped off the bed and scampered to the shower for a few minutes of peace. Let them figure it out for themselves.

Smooth Sailing

I have traveled a lot in my life, but one of the best trips I have ever taken was a sail down the Aegean coast of Turkey. It was the year after I graduated college, and I was twenty-two. Though I didn't have much money myself, a bunch of my friends had gotten jobs at big banking firms in New York, so they were swimming with cash. However, because of their long hours and few vacation days, they didn't really have much time to spend it. That summer, though, a few of them got some time off and decided to charter a yacht in Turkey through one of their father's connections.

At the last minute, one of the guys dropped out due to a work emergency, and I was asked to take his place. He still paid for his share of the yacht since it was too late to pull out of that, so all I had to cover was my plane ticket. The trip was only a week away, and the airfare was rather steep, but I figured I might not have another chance for a trip like this, so I said yes, bought my ticket, and stocked up on bathing suits and sunblock.

As was my custom, I also purchased as many guide-books about the area where we'd be sailing as possible. We would start and end in the coastal town of Bodrum in the south of the country. It is an international destination thanks to some amazing coastline and beaches, and many of Turkey's glitterati spent their summers there, sort of like the St. Tropez of Asia Minor. Personally, I was looking for-ward to exploring the Crusader fortress at the mouth of the harbor, and the Underwater Museum inside it where you can see the jetsam of an ancient shipwreck.

I was also looking forward to seeing two of the Seven Wonders of the Ancient World. The first was near Bodrum itself: the Mausoleum of Halicarnassus. It is the tomb of a man named Mausolus who was a satrap (or governor) of the Persian Empire around 350 B.C.E. Gross fact alert: He was actually married to his own sister (as was customary back then), and the two were buried together in the mas-sive structure, which was over 100 feet high.

The second wonder I wanted to see lay farther north up the coast. The Temple of Artemis once stood in the ancient city of Ephesus, though now only its foundation and a few sculptures remain. It was even older than the Mausoleum by about a hundred years, but it was destroyed by a fire right around the time the Mausoleum was being built.

On the flight from New York to Istanbul, I dorked out, imagining all the amazing sights I would see, but eventu-ally dozing off for a few hours. Thanks to my penury working in a publishing house, I was stuck in steerage, but my banker friends up in business class came back periodically to sneak me drinks and snacks. One of them even lent me his laptop so I could watch movies he had downloaded. All in all, it was a fun flight, though uneventful. I thought the rest of the trip would be, too, since I was the only gay man on it, but at least I'd have some eye candy of my fit friends frolicking in their bathing suits.

Finally, we arrived in chaotic Istanbul, hurried through customs, and caught a small plane to Bodrum. About ninety minutes later, we found ourselves in the dusty little airport, lugging our bags around the small terminal and trying to find the driver who was supposed to meet us.

No one was holding a sign for us, so we all stuck our bags in a corner and settled there to wait for a few minutes. I excused myself to use the restroom, and walked down the terminal. As I did, I could see another young man about my age rushing up in my direction. He was a gorgeous Middle Eastern man with tan olive skin, a full head of curly black hair, and the most surprising almond-shaped silver-green eyes. He looked like one of those Greek statues, a *koroi,* come to life, though there was nothing boyish about him. He was all muscle, and the button-down shirt and shorts he wore seemed ready to burst at the seams, especially where the sleeves constricted his massive biceps. His thighs also stretched the fabric of his shorts, and I could just make out the curling outline of his cock through the thin cotton fabric.

I tried not to stare, but he caught me glancing at him. I'll admit that, after the long journey and the heat of the airport, I was not looking my best, but he still gave me that telling half-smile I get when guys want to hit on me. He did not seem to have time to stop, though, and kept walking by as I went into the restroom.

I sighed as I emptied my bladder. How would I find that Turkish guy again so I could have a fling? I gave it up for hopeless as I washed my hands, and exited the bathroom to find my friends again. When I got back to the corner where they were all waiting, they whooped when they saw me and said the driver was pulling the car up. We grabbed our bags and made our way outside the terminal to where a Jeep was waiting for us . . . and who should be at the wheel but the handsome Turkish man I had made eyes at.

He hopped out of the Jeep to help everyone with their bags. I was last, and as I handed him my small duffel, my friend Darren introduced me to him.

"Brad, this is Aslan. He's going to help out on the yacht, too. His uncle is the skipper."

"Nice to meet you," I said, extending my hand.

I saw a hint of recognition flit briefly across Aslan's features, and he smiled at me and shook my hand but said nothing.

"He doesn't speak much English," explained Darren as the three of us went to the front of the Jeep.

"Ah, too bad," I said, giving Aslan one last furtive look.

He went around the other side of the car to get in the driver's seat. Our friends had all crammed in the back, so Darren and I were stuck up front. I was smaller, so he made me sit in the middle, but that was just fine by me since it meant that I was mashed up against Aslan's solid frame. My arm touched his, and my thigh was pressed against his, even as he shifted gears to get us going. I could see the sweat break out on his olive-toned brow and I smirked.

When we got to the harbor, Aslan helped us unload our bags, then led us out to the docks to where the yacht was waiting. It was a beautiful seventy-foot sailboat with a white hull and two masts.

One of the other guys whistled that he was impressed, while another said, "Wow, it's a schooner. Beautiful."

Without thinking, I said, "Actually, it's a ketch."

It was one of those things that slipped out and that made me feel like I was being snotty without meaning to. I wished I could take it back immediately, but it was too late, so I went on, explaining, "See how the second mast at the stern is shorter than the main mast? That's what makes it a ketch. On a schooner, it would be bigger. Or at least the same length."

"Such a size queen," chortled Darren, to the rest of their amusement.

Okay, it totally sounded snotty, but I could tell my friends were impressed, despite their jibes about not knowing "they had a mariner in their midst," and that I "must have picked that up hanging out with the sailors down by the docks."

I turned crimson as I saw Aslan laughing along with them in that way that people who don't really get a joke do to try to fit in. But he gave me a little wink as he hopped onboard the boat and started taking our luggage.

We spent that first night in Bodrum, hitting the bars and dancing in the discos. I had come to relax and see the sights, but my friends were all there to party hard. I had a good time drinking with them—though thankfully they were the ones paying for the expensive bottle service—and we met some interesting *Istanbulu* down from the big city on vacation and living it up. I was more interested in the daytime activities I hoped to get to over the coming ten days, though.

We all got back to the boat around dawn and slept in. By the time I awoke to the smells of Turkish coffee, it was noon, but I was still the only one of the Americans awake. In my hangover haze, I wandered into the kitchen in just my briefs to find some coffee. It was a second before I noticed Aslan was there measuring out coffee beans by the sink. I was about to rush away when he turned and saw me. I was mortified, there with my pale body out for anyone to see, my hair a mess, some dry drool on my cheek. I looked like hell.

Well, not like *hell*. After all, I was still only a year out of college, and my frame was wiry and lean. I had some great arm muscles going on thanks to hours spent lugging boxes of books around at work, and my morning wood was just starting to dissipate, so my package must have looked substantial beneath the fabric of my underwear.

I murmured a good morning to Aslan, took a cup of coffee from him, and slunk back to my room. I quickly groomed myself and dressed, trying not to wake Darren, who was my bunkmate for the trip, then snuck off the boat without anyone seeing me.

Though I was tired, the jetlag had kicked in, and I had a burst of energy, so I thought I would take advantage of the gorgeous weather and some blessed alone time to explore Bodrum a little and to stop by the fortress. The yacht was not scheduled to leave until the following morning, so I would have all day to see the sights.

I stayed out for the entire afternoon, stopping first at the Underwater Museum, then having a light lunch before hitting the Mausoleum of Halicarnassus. By the time I got back to the boat, it was well into evening, and the other boys were already getting ready for a night out.

They had all slept most of the day, and Darren said they were all starving, so they were going out to dinner and then back to the club we'd started at the night before. I said I'd meet them there and quickly undressed to take a shower once they had gone.

When I got out, dripping wet, I walked back to my room to find Aslan making the beds. He looked up and seemed surprised to see me. He muttered something in Turkish as though making excuses and apologizing, but I waved him off, trying to indicate it was no big deal, though I was also trying to cover myself up with the minuscule towel they had provided me. He squeezed past me in the narrow corridor, his shirt getting wet from the droplets pooling on my skin, and his nose almost brushing against mine as he looked bashfully into my eyes. Then he was gone.

This was the second time in a day Aslan was getting an eyeful of me, and this time, it was he who rushed off. Though not before I could see the start of an erection beneath the tight fabric of his shorts.

When he had gone, I got dressed, whistling merrily to myself. I didn't see Aslan as I left the boat, and by the time I made it back to the dock that night, it was almost dawn. Some of the guys had found girls to hit on, so they were still out. I just hoped they made it back to the yacht in time for our launch in the morning.

As with the day before, I awoke around noon. This time, however, I made sure to clean up a little bit before heading to the galley. I went in my underwear again, hoping to catch Aslan by himself so he could see what I could really look like, but the only person at the table was Darren. As soon as he saw me, he yelled at me to put on some clothes. I was mortified and ran back to my room to get dressed.

That day passed the same way as many of the following ones. We spent the morning sunbathing as the yacht cruised to our next destination. Around mid-afternoon we found a beautiful cove to moor in, and I took a swim while Aslan and his uncle took aboard any provisions we needed and got lunch ready. Sometimes we would use the Jet Skis that came with the yacht, though everyone liked them so much that it was often a long time between turns. Then we would eat a cold lunch, though sometimes we ate the fish that Aslan had caught that day, had a few beers, and sunbathed on the deck as the yacht sailed farther north. By evening, we would anchor in a harbor and either cook something over a campfire to eat with our ice-cold beers and ouzo or head into the nearest town and have dinner at a taverna until all hours.

Aslan's uncle, learning that I had some experience sailing, soon put me to work on some of the lighter tasks, like helping fold sails or hauling them up one of the masts. Often I was assigned to help Aslan with whatever he was doing. As time wore on, he became more familiar with all of us, chucking us on the shoulder or smiling to say hello. I was disappointed to see he was as nice with everyone as he was with me, but I was still the only one allowed to help out on the boat since I knew what I was doing, so it was often just him and me working on something.

A day or two in, he would spend most of the time with his shirt off. With all the hard work he did, he was usually a little sweaty, though he came for swims with the rest of us to cool off. All the hard work on the boat had made him into a brawny young man, with the shoulders and torso of a linebacker. I loved the way his chest hair curled tightly around his eggplant-colored nipples. His muscles rippled as he pulled up the anchor. His legs clenched and his ass flexed as he clambered up the mast to retrieve a flown halyard. He was like a roughneck stevedore . . . except for his glittering white smile and shy almond eyes.

By the third or fourth day, we were working together as a team even though we could not speak the same language. I enjoyed my times of silent, side-by-side work with him more than relaxing with my friends. There was just something comfortable and sweet about Aslan, not to mention how sexy it was to be performing manual labor alongside my own personal Hercules.

One day, Aslan's uncle let me hoist up the colorful spinnaker so that we could really cut through the water on our way to the next harbor. When we arrived, I left it up, but untied the lines on deck and knotted them into a makeshift swing so that one person at a time could sit on it and be flung up into the air by the wind. It was like the best roller coaster ride ever. All of us took turns, even Aslan. He was able to stay on the whipping swing the longest, and when he came splashing into the water, we all applauded. He swam up next to me as we watched the next person take his turn, and I could feel his legs and arms brushing against my own as we treaded water. I wanted to look at him so badly, but a moment later, he was gone, swimming back to the yacht.

I watched as he climbed up the little ladder onto the back deck of the boat, admiring how his wet shorts clung to his body, and loving the view of his flexing back and arms as he shook the water out of his mane of curls, and then his stomach contracting into a perfect eight-pack as he blew out a mouthful of air.

A few days later, I consulted Aslan's uncle about when might be best for me to head to Ephesus. He told me that the next day we'd be stopping at Kusadasi, a harbor not far from there, and that he'd have Aslan rent a scooter to drive me so I wouldn't get lost. He looked puzzled as I thanked him overenthusiastically for his help.

The next day, I got up early to prepare for my sight-seeing mission and found Aslan in the galley as usual preparing coffee. With a mysterious grin, he handed me a small steaming cup of the strong stuff, and when I had finished that and a roll with jam, he beckoned me to follow him out onto the dock.

A few minutes later, we came up to a ragged hut that rented scooters. Aslan haggled with the old woman who was manning it, and I forked over about twenty dollars for the day rental. I gestured to indicate I would like a helmet, but the old lady just shrugged and Aslan chuckled. Guess we were going commando, so to speak.

I had never driven a scooter before, so I let Aslan take the handlebars. It was about the size of a Vespa, and that's to say, not large, so we were going to have to get cozy on the seat. Aslan swung one of his tree-trunk legs over the bike and took his seat on the front. I hopped on from the back with a little more force than necessary, and my chest slapped into Aslan's back, making us both lurch forward. I said sorry, but he just turned to look back at me and give a little laugh. Then he started the engine and we shot off onto the dusty road.

I wasn't quite prepared and hadn't grabbed onto anything to steady myself, so without thinking, I frantically wrapped my arms around Aslan's torso. I could feel his abs tighten as I gripped him, but after a second he relaxed, and I found myself relaxing my grip a little, too. Not too much, though. Every round ball of muscle on his eight-pack felt so sexy, I wasn't about to let go.

I shifted my weight forward so that my chest and stomach were flat against his back again, and I could smell how clean his hair and skin were. My crotch was right against his tailbone, right above where his ass crack would start, and I had to concentrate in order not to get hard.

When our ride quickly drew to an end only a few minutes later, I was sad to let go of him. I didn't want things to be awkward, though, so I quickly hopped off the scooter and walked quickly over to where the single remaining column of the Temple of Artemis stood. It was still early in the day, so we had the place to ourselves, but Aslan waited patiently for me by the scooter. After a few moments, I'd had enough, and I came back to show him where else I would like to go on my map. I wanted to see the Roman Agora with its old buildings, and after studying the map for a second, Aslan hopped back on the bike and off we went.

A few minutes later, we pulled up to the tourism parking lot in the old Agora and I began to explore the ancient city while Aslan had a coffee at the café. We seemed to be the only people there, and I enjoyed having the ruins to myself.

I wandered through the ancient gymnasium and peeked through the harbor gates out to sea. Next, I took a stroll across the area where the stage would have been in the great amphitheater. It was such an impressive and humongous space—thought to be the largest outdoor theater of the ancient world—I could only imagine what performing for an entire crowd there must have been like. My favorite building by far was the Roman Library of Celsus, with its gorgeous façade that reminded me of the Mint at Petra in Jordan.

When I had finished in the Lower Agora, it was starting to get crowded with other tourists, so I hiked up the Street of Curetes, stopping for a moment to scope out the remains of the brothel and of Hadrian's Temple. I got to the top of the hill to the Upper Agora and headed to the Temple of Domitian to take in the view of the hills, but I discovered someone had already beaten me there. Just as I walked down into the building foundation, the other person came out from behind one of the remaining columns, and I saw that it was Aslan.

Like me, he was slightly perspired from the hike up the hill, and he wiped a hand across his brow self-consciously when he saw me. I did the same and fixed my shirt, hoping there were no sweat stains on my chest.

We came to a stop standing next to each other, and stood looking around us for a moment in silence. Aslan broke it to say something in Turkish while sweeping his arm to encompass the site. I took it that he meant to say that it was impressive or breathtaking or something like that, so I nodded and smiled, taking a deep breath. It was starting to get stiflingly hot outside, but I stayed standing next to him like that, our hands lightly touching at moments.

Finally, I decided to take a chance and turned to face him. As the sea breeze whipped our hair, I took another tiny step toward him so we were face-to-face, and I started to lean in. He looked slightly terrified but also thrilled. Just as our lips were about to touch, and I could even smell the faint remains of strong Turkish coffee on his breath, we heard a commotion coming from the path. Instantly, the moment was broken, and we split apart as a group of pale British tourists descended on the site. I walked off toward one corner and Aslan walked toward another, pretending to look interested in the old quarried stones of the temple.

A few minutes later, I called out to him and gestured that I was heading back down the hill. He caught up with me on the path, and after a few minutes of walking silently together, we found our way to the car park and returned the scooter to the rental shop.

By the time we got back to the boat, everyone else was already having lunch. Aslan headed toward the captain's cabin while I joined my friends at the table, pouring myself a glass of water and a shot of ouzo.

"How was it? See anything interesting?" asked Darren above the hubbub.

"Could have been better . . . stupid tourists," I answered, downing the ouzo.

Darren looked at me questioningly, but I kept mum, sighing at the lost chance for romance among the ruins.

A few days later, our Turkish cruise was finally drawing to an end. We were to spend our last night in the harbor of Göltürkbükü, on the northern side of the Bodrum Peninsula. Then we'd drive overland to the airport for our flight out the next day. Göltürkbükü was just becoming *the* place to see and be seen on the Turkish Riviera. It was a very popular vacation spot with the artists and cognoscenti of Istanbul who wanted to avoid the international crowds in Bodrum.

We spent the morning fishing for sole just outside the harbor. When we had caught enough for lunch (though Aslan really did most of the work), we sailed past the two islands at the entrance and moored near the busy little vacation town of Türkbükü on one side of the harbor. After lunch, we swam over to the jetties of the waterfront hotels and restaurants, and spent the day sunbathing and drinking in the open air, swimming from dock to dock and making new friends whom we'd meet up with that night.

That evening, Aslan and his uncle sailed the yacht to the other side of the harbor near the quieter village of Gölköy. I liked it much better on this side of things. As the sun set, we had perfect views of the dramatic hillsides forested with tangerine and olive groves, dotted here and there with bright slashes of fuchsia bougainvilleas. The air smelled like a wonderful mix of ocean, orange blossom, and cooking spices. I was going to be sad to leave Turkey.

The guys decided to hit the nearby town of Selçuk and see if they could rustle up some action for the night. I was tired from our day of sunning and drinking, and I couldn't bear to watch them hitting (unsuccessfully) on more girls, so I stayed back on the boat. They left after a late dinner, and though I'd been tired before the meal, I felt a second wind come over me. On the last night in Turkey, I wanted to go for a moonlight swim and really savor the experience, so I changed into my bathing suit and went topside. Only two other yachts were moored near us, with no wind to ripple the water.

I heard a noise from the bow of the boat and saw Aslan

squatting on deck as he coiled some of the sail lines for the night. He didn't see me, so I stayed hidden behind the cabin, watching him. When he had finished his work, he stood up, stretched his arms, and then started unbuttoning his shirt.

He threw it onto the deck, then undid his shorts and let them slide down his legs, too. It was only then I noticed that he was not wearing underwear. I wondered if he had been going commando this whole time, and bit my lip in frustration. I prayed he would turn around so I could get a glimpse of what I was sure was a fat, uncut cock, but he stayed in that position, facing out toward the water.

I felt a little dirty watching him like that when he had no idea I was there, but I could not take my eyes off the hardened triangles of his calves or the geometrically round globes of his pale ass, separated by a furrow darkened with pubic hair. His back was knotted with muscles, and I started to pant as I watched him stretch like an ancient Greek athlete. Then without a moment's hesitation, he dove into the water.

I slowly let out my breath. Maybe I should just go back downstairs and go to sleep. I started to walk down the steps, but as I felt frustration well up inside me again, I came to a decision. I walked back up on the deck, stripped off my shorts, and dove in after Aslan.

He had been swimming toward shore, but the noise of my splash must have stopped him. When I surfaced, I was only a few feet from him and I could see uncertainty on his face until he recognized me and it was replaced with anticipation.

Without a word—for I would not have understood him anyway—he swam right up to me, aligning our bodies underwater as we treaded. I wanted him to feel my body, and his eyes practically bulged out of his head when he realized I was naked, too. Then before I could even react, his mouth was on mine and he was kissing me with all the pent-up sexual energy of our ten-day journey.

If you haven't tried to tread water as you made out with a gorgeous Olympian god, let me tell you, it's not easy. Sure, you can kiss, but it's hard staying level with the person, and practically impossible to get a hand on their body for more than a moment or two at a time. Aslan seemed more proficient at it than I was, though, and he was able to encircle me with one of his strapping arms while treading water with his powerful legs.

I didn't realize it, but he had swum us back to the boat and we both quickly clambered up the metal ladder at the back. I made to cover myself up and run for my clothes at the bow, but Aslan stopped me by placing a large hand on my chest, while he pulled my hand away from my genitals with the other. Holding my arms out, he gave me a frank and thorough once-over, smiling broadly the whole time. My dick had regained some of its volume after the refreshing cool of the water, and I relaxed and breathed deeply so my balls would descend to their full distension.

Though preoccupied, I couldn't help checking him out in turn, and what I saw was even better than I'd imagined. His torso looked as athletic as ever, but I was finally able to see what he looked like beneath the cotton shorts he always had on. They had given him an attractive farmer's tan—not like the cheesy Speedo-shaped ones I found most gay guys had, but one that looked like what a real man would have. It turned his skin into an olivey pale color just below his pelvic bones, where his waistband usually covered him up, and ran down to mid-thigh. A couple inches beneath where his waistband sat, he had a thick block of pitch black pubic hair that, though untrimmed, was not unruly. It formed a neat little triangle from his pelvic bones to the stem of his cock, and then dissipated again on either side of his package, forming a lightly furry halo over the skin of his scrotum. As I had suspected, Aslan was uncircumcised, and his dark foreskin was one of those that formed a thin, tight membrane that completely covered the bright pink head of his dick. I couldn't wait to pull it back and explore him with my tongue.

When he had looked his fill, Aslan nodded his appreciation, then pulled me back into an embrace and kissed me deeply. Pulling away a few moments later, he brought a finger to his lips in the international signal to be quiet, and he motioned for me to stay where I was. He crept below deck, leaving me for a couple minutes by myself, wondering where he'd gotten to. When he emerged again, he gestured to inform me that his uncle was asleep and snoring, so we wouldn't wake him up. Then he took my hand and led me to the large cushioned daybed that sat at the stern of the ship. In his other hand, Aslan held a bottle of clear ouzo and two glasses.

I reclined along the daybed, extending to my full length, letting the warm night breezes wick the water off my skin while Aslan first lit the propane torch at the stern and then poured us each a healthy dose of ouzo to enjoy by the mellow light of our lone beacon.

I sat up as he handed me a glass and entwined his arm around mine, looked me deep in the eye, and said, *"Serefe,"* which I'd learned was a Turkish toast. I repeated after him, and then we drank together, never breaking eye contact.

Aslan took my glass and refilled it, then refilled his own. We toasted again and threw back our drinks. He made to take my glass again, but I'd had enough and I wanted a taste of him instead, so I brushed his hand away, taking his glass instead and setting them both down on the deck. I took a moment to drink in those soulful almond eyes again, shining gold in the firelight, and then pulled him in to kiss me as we both lay down on top of the cushion.

Though my skin was mostly dry by now, Aslan's was still quite wet, and I could feel the little goose bumps popping up on his bulging arms. His breath was warm and tasted like spicy licorice from the ouzo we'd drunk. Its heat was beginning to radiate from my stomach to my extremities, making me feel all warm and bubbly so that I smiled as I kissed Aslan's warm lips again and again.

I ran my hands through his wet hair, luxuriating in its thickness. My other hand glided over his back—that back I'd been staring at and fantasizing about for over a week now. I trembled as I caressed him, barely able to believe that I was actually enjoying the object of my desires, and afraid that I would wake up from this beautiful and terrible dream at any moment.

His rough sailor's hands scraped against my body like sandpaper as they ran up and down the length of my athletic torso, giving me a squeeze here or there before coming to rest wrapped around my back. We stayed coupled like that for the longest time, just kissing, sometimes passionately, sometimes tenderly, enjoying our quiet moment together.

The torchlight flickered in the evening breeze, setting our shadows playing against the boat's white hull and amplifying the prodigious curves of Aslan's muscular frame. I flipped us over so that I was on top of him, then began to kiss my way down his broad chest. I nuzzled the patch of curling black hairs that covered it and nibbled on the aubergine nipples that delineated the end of his firm pectorals. Cupping his chest muscles in my hands, I squeezed and rubbed at them, really working into the muscle and making Aslan tingle with anticipation.

His skin tasted of the sea, though beneath the briny layer of salt on it, I could also taste a smell that I recognized as Aslan himself. It smelled like sun-kissed skin, Middle Eastern spices, dark-roasted coffee, ouzo, and some sort of soap. I breathed in deeply, wanting to remember this smell so I could always associate it with this special moment.

Sliding farther down Aslan's sizeable frame, I rubbed my face against his muscle-rutted stomach and patted his abs with my hand. He had one of the best bodies I'd ever seen, let alone touched, and I wanted to get to know every square inch of it. After kissing his belly button and the grooves of his cum gutters, I finally eyed my prize.

His uncut cock was already at attention, the bright pink head slipping out of its brown cowl to show me the tiniest drop of precum glistening at its very tip. It rested in his dense nest of pubic hair like an oversized cigar. I gave his dick a few short swipes with my tongue, making it twitch reflexively as Aslan looked down his long body to where I was teasing him. I rubbed just the tip of my nose gently against the furry cushion of his balls, causing them to pull upward, then distend again as he relaxed.

Separating his legs slightly, I began to kiss his hairy inner thigh, tickling him and making him groan as I lit up the nerve endings that were concentrated there. I kissed his taint, feeling the muscles in it contract and relax with each touch of my mouth, while my own lips were tickled in turn by the prickly hairs that grew there. Licking up the center seam of his testicles, I noticed his left one dangled asymmetrically almost a full inch below the right, and I grinned at the fact that at least something about this Mediterranean demigod was not perfect.

I sucked on his longer gonad 'til it was all wet, then moved on to the shorter one, all the while rolling my hands around his solid ass and cupping a mighty cheek in each hand. Each time I hit a nerve or did something Aslan liked, his ass would flex, and I felt the meaty muscle grow even harder and rounder in my hands while my mouth kept at its work.

As his groaning grew softer into more of a whimper, I figured it was time to stop teasing him and give him a taste of what he was in for, so I stuck my tongue as far out of my mouth as it would go and I used it to lick up the entire, rock-hard length of his prick. Aslan shifted his weight and I felt one of his hands come to rest on my messy brown hair. His cock had been pretty long flaccid, making me think he was a shower rather than a grower, but under my very eyes, it had continued to lengthen and expand until it was nearly nine inches. This was going to be fun.

I loved sucking uncut guys because there was a lot more skin to play with, and their glans were always more sensitive than those of circumcised penises. Pulling Aslan's foreskin back, I sucked delicately at his cock tip, enjoying the sticky solution of his precum as though I were eating a lollipop. I pulled the foreskin back over the head and stuck my tongue inside the skin membrane, running it round and round his helmet, and making him shiver as I stimulated both the outside of his cockhead and the inside of his foreskin. Opening my mouth wide, I swallowed as much of his dick as I could before its pointy tip hit the back of my throat, making me gurgle while trying to suppress a gag. The hairs on Aslan's shaft felt wiry and coarse in my mouth, but I loved the feeling of servicing a real man, and I sucked for all I was worth as I began to move my mouth up and down the entire length of his cock.

My hand soon joined in the effort, jerking him off as it trailed my mouth up and down on his dick. Wads of my spit drooled down on his package and coated his entire dick, balls, and my own hand. I was driving him crazy with my skills; he kept almost convulsing with each suck, and his hands squeezed and pinched his nips, as well as reaching down to tweak mine as I worked away. After a couple minutes, he was ready for primetime.

My own meat mast, meanwhile, had been hoisted and was ready to set sail, so I clambered back up Aslan's body to kiss him, the taste of his tool on both our mouths now, and lay down on top of him. I jerked myself off with my spitty hand for a moment or two, then sat back on my knees so that Aslan's enormous rod lay just under my waiting ass.

Reaching behind me, I pointed that massive flesh cannon directly up so that its length was buried in my ass cleft. I rocked back and forth a few times, getting used to the feeling of Aslan's prick pushing against me and loosening up to accommodate his girth. Then when I was ready,

I reached behind me again, aimed his pecker skyward as I sat farther up, then leaned back and onto it.

I let out a sharp gasp of pain as his penis penetrated my sphincter. I had known this was going to be a challenge at first, but even I was surprised at how difficult it was to steer his battle cruiser into my narrow grotto. Gritting my teeth and using my own weight to help me, I slowly sat farther and farther back until his was totally buried inside me up to the hilt.

I sat very still, letting my ass muscles stretch to take him entirely in and to get used to the foreign object I had shoved in, then I began to shift my hips back and forth slowly. Tugging on my meat to get me back to the pleasure zone, I got myself completely hard again within seconds, and let myself rock forward and back with a bit more range of motion on Aslan's shaft as I grew comfortable.

When the pain of entry turned into the pleasure of total invasion, I really started to get active. I lifted and lowered my hips off Aslan's pelvis with longer and longer strokes. He anchored me by placing a hand on either of my muscular thighs, letting me do all the work and take total control. I used my lower back to buck backward and forward on Aslan even as I pounded up and down on him, working every direction I could manage at once. His prong was hitting all the good spots inside of me, but I wanted more.

I shifted my legs so that I was crouching on top of him with my feet flat on the daybed; then I went to town humping him, raising my ass until Aslan's cock almost popped out of me, then slamming back down on top of him. My ass was starting to hurt, and I was going to be so sore the next day on my long flight back to the States, but

I didn't care. It was pure ecstasy as I rode him like a pogo stick. My rock-hard cock was pointing straight up, and with each of my motions, it would first slap down onto Aslan's stomach, following the rest of my body, then spring back up and slap my own taut tummy when I raised myself. My balls made a little smacking sound each time I impacted downward, and my cock was turning red and tingling from all the slapping it was getting.

Leaning even farther back and placing my arms on the cushion, I lifted my ass even higher so that I was in a sort of crab position, and I slackened my pace so that I could lengthen the strokes and really exert some pull on Aslan's cock with the muscles of my ass walls. He liked that, placing a hand on either of my ass cheeks to help support me and letting his eyes roll into the back of his head with a guttural sigh.

As his rod probed my crater again and again, I felt a stream of precum oozing out of my insides and down my dick 'til it leaked out in a steady flow from my piss slit. It formed an unbroken strand of liquid from the tip of my dick down to the spot on Aslan's stomach where it fell, and noticing it, Aslan swiped it with a finger, then tasted my milky fluid, grinning as he licked it all up.

That seemed to reinvigorate him, because he held me still, crouching above him in my crab position; then he started bucking his hips up and down, plunging his jackhammer into me twice as fast as I'd managed to ride him. I could feel his nutsack bouncing up and hitting my crack even as his tool lit up all my pleasure sensors. I could barely think, let alone speak, and the only thing that came out of my open mouth was an incomprehensible moan. Aslan's breathing grew more and more shallow, and I couldn't take much more of this pounding, but he just kept going. His manly hands squeezed me harder and harder, running up and down my chest and belly as he rammed me. I felt like I was going to break at any moment, so I reached down and touched his chest to let him know to slow down; then when he had stopped ravishing me altogether, I carefully disengaged myself from him.

I had been right, he was about to come. I could tell by the involuntary pulsing his cock was performing as I pulled off of him, but he still had some more work to do before I was going to let him finish. Smiling down at him, I grabbed hold of his hips and flipped him over onto his stomach. He turned his head to say something over his shoulder. His voice sounded nervous, but he did not move.

Kissing my way back down his strapping back, I came to his round globe of an ass and quickly massaged the muscles to help him loosen up. Straddling him, one leg on either side of his hips, I spat a huge wad of slippery saliva onto my hand and rubbed it onto my cock; then pointing my flesh gun into his hairy valley, I slowly pressed my way inside him. His asshole was so tight, if my dick had been any less hard, it would not have made it past the back door. As it was, I had to keep very still and set a precise trajectory in order to penetrate him at all.

He half-groaned and half-cried as I slid inch after inch of my long stick into him, going slowly and carefully so that I would not hurt him. He helped me by reaching back and pulling apart the fleshy muscles of his ass cheeks so that I had a better view of the tight tan pucker that I was attempting to violate.

When I got most of the way in, I stopped and let Aslan take a few deep breaths, petting his back soothingly to help relax him. When I felt the mouth of his sphincter loosen, and his internal ass walls slacken, I pulled out a little, then pressed back in. He gasped shallowly but stayed relaxed, and I kept lengthening my strokes until I was pulling most of the way out and entering all the way back in.

Within moments, Aslan got the rhythm and managed to stay loose, so I had free rein and I could fuck him with more momentum. Based on his nervous chattering earlier and how tight his hole was—it was becoming more and more pink with the friction of each of my thrusts—I guessed that this was the first time anyone had fucked him, and I felt both honored and so turned on that it was me.

Each time he let a squeal of pain escape, it thrilled me to the core and only made me pick up my pace. By the end, I was banging him as hard as I wanted, my strokes lengthening to the extent of my eight-inch cock. I particularly loved seeing how the pink lip of my helmet head would make the edges of his asshole stretch to their greatest circumference, straining the skin and making Aslan cry out.

In order to have my way with him, I pulled myself up into a kind of push-up position, with my back as flat as a plank, and I plunged down into him at that trajectory, knowing that I would hit his prostate with my pounding. I steadied myself by placing my hands on Aslan's broad, manly shoulders, pushing him down into the daybed cushion with each thrust. At one point, I grabbed his curly hair and pulled his head back so that I could kiss his open mouth, then let his face fall back onto the pillow where he had buried it in order to avoid making too much noise and waking up his uncle. He was completely within my power, and I enjoyed every second of domination over my Turkish muscleman.

But as with my wonderful Turkish seaside idyll, this fuck session had to come to an end. Only it came more quickly than I anticipated, and I barely had time to pull out of Aslan's ass before I was shooting load after load of steaming cum onto his ass. My orgasm was so sudden and violent, I could see stars and had trouble staying conscious. My knees buckled, my body convulsed, and I had to remember to breathe. By the time I was done shooting, I had virtually unloaded an entire pool of my jizz into Aslan's ass crack, making one of the juiciest cream pies I'd ever seen.

He was still moaning, but looked back to see what was going on, and wiggled his ass to slosh around my baby batter and get it all over himself. He got up on all fours and was about to turn over, but I stopped him. I wanted a taste of myself mingled with Aslan's ass, so I stuck my tongue right into the middle of that hot mess and got as big a dollop of my cream as I could, swallowing it down like a salty oyster. It was the same temperature as my own overheated body and felt good as it slid down my gullet.

After I'd drunk my fill, I crouched lower and licked the last drops off Aslan's taint, and the few little trails of it that had crept down his scrotum. Lowering myself even farther, I flipped over and squeezed my head between Aslan's muscle-knotted legs and began to suck off his still-hard meat muscle.

As before, I used my hand in tandem with my mouth, simulating a real fuck as I sucked him closer and closer to completion. I must really have worked his ass chute well with my prong, because he was already completely stimulated, and I didn't have long to wait before he started to shoot.

Roughly grabbing hold of my mane of hair, Aslan forced my face all the way down on this dick as it started to twitch within my mouth. Wave after wave of tepid semen splashed down my throat, making me gag for air and my eyes water. I stayed hermetically sealed to his cock, though, and took as much as I could until he had finished ejaculating.

When he was done, I mumbled his dick around in my mouth a few last times, then scrambled up beneath him on my back, pulling him down to me for a kiss. He ran his tongue deep into my mouth, getting the last flavors of his jizz, and then also licked my chin where a few drops had gone astray.

Aslan dropped down beside me on the daybed, both of us silent, flushed, and in awe of what had just happened. We lay like that for a few minutes, letting the now-cool gusts of air dry the sweat off our bodies. Aslan sat up again and poured us both another ouzo. This time, he toasted, "To American friend."

"I'll drink to that," I said, mirroring his beautiful smile with my own.

We threw back our shots, then Aslan climbed off the cushions and took my hand to pull me down after him. Walking quietly back up to the bow of the yacht, we stood along the rail, then climbed over it and jumped back in the water together, still holding hands.

My Naked Neighbor

I'd been out in California for a few years working in film when I finally decided that I needed a change of pace. So I quit my job and decided to try my hand at writing. Unfortunately, that would mean cutting back and living more frugally; but with all my extra free time and creative energy, I hoped that, though I would be going out less and spending less money, I would enjoy my new lifestyle more.

At first, it was a little hard not being able to go out to dinner or order takeout any time I wanted, and it was difficult explaining to my friends why I couldn't go out every night of the week anymore or go in on a house rental in Palm Springs. But they all understood, and even covered my share a lot of times, so I didn't really feel the financial pinch right away.

Plus, I was so happy working on scripts and books, and starting to write freelance articles, I didn't even care about my changed circumstances. After a few rent checks came due, however, it became clear that I would have to move to a smaller apartment. I didn't mind too much, though. I love moving. It's like starting over and becoming a new person—making a new space entirely your own. I found it very exciting, and I felt years younger than I had in a long time.

I started to look around Los Angeles, paying attention to apartment listings and visiting open houses whenever I could. It was early summer, so a lot of new apartments were coming online as people moved out and students moved back home. Finally, I found a cute little studio in the heart of West Hollywood. It was in an older building that was still pretty well maintained, with a pool and a parking place. And it was rent-controlled. It was perfect.

I submitted my application and eagerly waited to hear back from the building's management. After a week of pins and needles, they got back to me to tell me that the place was mine and that I could move in the next month. I began preparing immediately, writing checks, giving notice, packing all my things, and arranging for some movers to help me out with my furniture.

The big day arrived, and I was all set to go. My movers arrived promptly at 10:00 A.M. and started carting my boxes out to their truck. I had been afraid that I had packed the boxes too heavily since I was trying to save money and buy fewer supplies, but they were no problem for the burly Eastern European men that the moving company employed. One of them could barely have been out of his teens, but his arms were sinewy pythons cabled with veins, while his older compatriot was a burly barrel of a man with a thick neck and bulging back muscles. I enjoyed watching them work.

We drove the couple miles to my new apartment, which

I was amused to see the movers appraise approvingly, and they managed to unload all my stuff within an hour. There I was, alone and ready to start my new life in my new apartment.

It was already blazing hot in my apartment on that July day, and I was dripping with sweat, so I stripped down to a little pair of shorts and a baseball cap to rearrange the furniture. I was looking forward to taking a dip in the building's crystal-blue pool later that afternoon, but first I had to unpack my boxes . . . only I realized that I had blundered by packing my scissors in one of them! How was I going to cut all the tape that I'd used to pack? This was going to take forever.

Luckily, I had heard music coming from next door. I think it was Belle and Sebastian. Make-out music, I called it. Or study music. Mellow. I figured my neighbor was in, and maybe he or she would have some scissors I could borrow. Plus, it would be a good chance to introduce myself.

I didn't bother to put on a T-shirt or shoes since it was broiling in my apartment, and not that much better outside. Besides, after I'd quit my job, I'd been hitting the gym pretty hard, and it was showing. My stomach rippled with a six-pack, my arms were coiled with muscle, and my legs looked fantastic. I tucked my sweaty hair under my cap and wiped away a few trickles from my forehead so that I would at least make a decent impression in case it turned out that my neighbor was a cute guy. A boy can always hope, right?

I walked across the hall to where my neighbor's door was open and the screen was letting in a brisk cross-breeze. I peered in and could see someone with his back to me typing at a desk in the corner. When I knocked on the door frame, the man turned around, revealing himself to be a strapping young college-age guy in only his briefs. He looked like he'd just sprung to life from the pages of an Abercrombie & Fitch ad, what with his spiky blond hair, piercing violet-blue eyes, and a moist sheen of sweat covering his well-muscled young body.

He raised his eyebrows in an unspoken question. I cleared my throat, beginning, "Uh, hi. I'm, um, your new neighbor. Brad?" My voice went up at the end because I was so nervous after seeing him. It sounded like I'd forgotten my own name and was asking him what it was.

Seeing me, dressed not much more modestly than he was, my new neighbor grinned, then turned to hit something on his computer to shut off the music. He got up, not bothering to put on any more clothes, and came over to the doorway to open the screen.

As he sauntered toward me, my eyes could not help drifting down his body. He was about my height—that's to say under six feet—and looked like he was a track and field guy with narrow hips, wiry shoulders and arms, and some big but elegantly formed legs. He was wearing boxer briefs that clung to his upper thighs, and I could make out the bulge of his balls and the slight curve of his cock to the left as he came over.

He was still smiling as he opened the screen door and extended a hand. "I'm Nick," he said, simply.

"Nice to meet you," I said, shaking his hand. "I'm sorry if I'm bothering you," I continued, indicating his work at the computer.

Following my gesture, he said, "No, no, not at all. I need a break anyway. It's my first project for next year."

"Project?" I asked.

"Yeah, I'm in the screenwriting program at USC and we have to have a feature-length script ready for the start of the new school year."

"Wow, that's amazing," I effused. "So, you're what, twenty? And already on your way."

"I hope so!" he said, laughing. "Yeah, I'm twenty. Why, how old are you?"

"I'm twenty-six. I'm a writer myself, though I'm just getting started," I explained, suddenly feeling like we were both very naked.

"Well, you don't look twenty-six. Welcome to the building," he said, giving me the once-over. People always thought I looked several years younger than I was, and one of my boyfriends had even said that he loved the fact that my ass looked like that of a fifteen-year-old quarterback. I tried to flex my torso muscles inconspicuously.

That reminded me of what I'd come for. "Oh, yeah, thanks! Um, I was actually wondering if you had a pair of scissors I could borrow?"

"Oh, sure, I think so. Come in for a second while I find them."

I bashfully followed him inside, closing the door behind me and looking around his apartment. Wandering about, I stopped to stare at an aquarium with all sorts of exotic fish he had set up in a corner. In another, he had a guitar and some music books strewn about, while on his bed, he had a motley assortment of textbooks and clothes. Yep, he was a student all right, but boy, did he seem interesting. "I really like what you've done with your place," I said.

"Thanks!" he called from the kitchen.

I walked over to his computer and leaned over to look

at the script he was working on. I had only managed to pe-
ruse a few lines when I noticed that a pair of scissors were
sitting in a coffee mug Nick used to hold his pens. I
grabbed them, straightened up, and started to call out,
"Hey, I found them!" but then I realized that Nick was
standing right next to me, breathing hard and with a huge
hard-on pooching out the cotton of his underwear.

"Yeah, you did," he said quietly, not moving.

I turned to face him. We were inches apart. I could feel
his quick breath on my face as he waited to see how I
would react. I didn't move an inch, letting him know that
I liked him standing so close.

In a moment, he had taken my hand that was holding
the scissors in his own and was gently guiding the tip of
them down his torso. First along the line that separated his
broad, flat pecs, then along the shallow ditch that ran the
length of his abdomen, into his divot of a belly button, and
finally down to the waistband of his boxer briefs.

Then gently, his hand still cupping my own, he used
them to cut his boxer briefs off his body, inch by tense
inch, being careful to avoid his sensitive areas. When the
blades had reached the lower hem of the shorts, he put the
scissors aside on the desk. He took my hands and made me
slide the shorts from his groin. My hands grazed his hard
penis and soft balls as they made their way over his private
parts.

In a moment, he was completely naked, and I stood
there with him, gazing into his eyes. I looked down to take
in the sight of the rest of his body, loving the fact that he
had no body hair except for under his arms and around
his crotch, where it was only a shade darker than the
blond hair on his head. It made a little upside-down trian-

gle that ended in a point at the stem of his dick, which was a sleek seven-incher, and slightly darker than his fair skin. I was amused to see that it was ram-rod straight, though it pointed a few degrees to the left, like my own.

I reached down to fondle it, tickling the lollipop head with my fingertips and watching Nick's rippling stomach twitch as he breathed in and out. I reached down farther and took hold of his nads, juggling them around a little to massage them. That made Nick breathe even harder and brought his mast up to full sail.

I looked back into his eyes and slowly moved in to kiss him. At the same time, I could feel his hands start to undo the button on my shorts and to slide them over the ripe peaches of my ass and down my legs.

In one swift motion, he pulled down my shorts, then cupped my ass in his hands and lifted me a few inches to sit on the desk, my legs splayed on either side of his waist. Then he leaned over to kiss me full on the mouth, biting down slightly on my lower lip as he cradled my face with both his hands. Then his hands were running up and down my body again. A little clumsily, I thought, but then again he was only twenty. I was just going to have to show him how it was done.

Reaching around to grab his full, round ass, I pulled him closer in to me so that our cocks were wrestling against each other. Though Nick had a head start on me, my own was getting harder by the second and was beginning to feel like a steel beam as it frotted against his own beanstalk.

Nick's hot mouth began to work its way down my neck and along my collarbone to one of my nipples, where it suctioned on like a lamprey. He kept licking it 'til it was almost raw, but I didn't stop him 'til the skin got really sore. I guided him farther down by planting a hand in his spiky crop of hair and pushing his head toward my waiting skin flute. I really hoped he could play it with some talent.

Like the rest of Nick's strategy, his cocksucking was anything but subtle. Then again, who needed subtlety when you had a hot guy milking your man meat with his mouth? Without preamble, he opened wide and deep-throated the whole thing at once, swallowing my entire sheath in his moist mouth.

I don't know whether I was more turned on by the rough sucking he was performing or the messy slurping sounds that he emitted as he bobbed his head up and down. Both were driving me crazy, making me shift my hips from side to side as he revved me up. After he had crammed my whole cock in his mouth one more time, I felt the little muscles around my balls start to tense, which meant I was halfway ready to come, so I placed a hand under his chin and guided his mouth off my package with a big plop.

I kissed Nick just to taste my own cock on his lips; then I hopped off the desk and walked around him, pushing him down so that he was bent over the desk, his legs spread, with me standing right behind him. I started by kissing his ear, then licking down his neck and planting a few more pecks between the bony precipices of his shoulder blades. I continued my trek down his long, lithe back, nibbling at the tender skin above his hip bones and making him squirm.

Then I got to the pale, firm cushion of his ass. We were both completely sweaty thanks to the heat, and since I'd

closed the door to his apartment, it had turned into a fur-
nace. We were both getting gamy, but I thought the pungent, tangy scent from his butt crack smelled heavenly as I
sent my tongue snaking down the top of it where he had a
few little blond hairs growing. Kneeling down farther, I
parted the cheeks of his butt so I would have full access to
his honey pot, and I spat a few wads of saliva to get it nice
and wet.

Before I started to eat him out, I dug my nose deep
down under his full moon and licked at his low-hangers,
which were fully distended in the heat, and I knew I'd
done right when I heard him start to moan. I reached
under his balls and pulled his semi-erect cock back and
gave the head a few swirls with my tongue, like I was licking a dollop of whipped cream off a sundae.

I sucked him a couple more times, then relinquished his
prong so I could get to work loosening his ass up for the
pounding I was about to give him. I started by licking up
and down the entire length of his crevice, my chin getting
tickled by the prickly little hairs that grew along either side
of his sphincter.

When he had stopped tensing up his muscles with each
pass of my tongue, I began to lap at his hole with my
tongue, teasing it and taunting it. He opened it up to me
and I could shove my tongue farther and farther into its
dank recesses with each pass, and soon I had invaded it
completely, getting it all slobbery and slack for my dick.

"Do you have a condom?" I asked, my voice muffled by
the muscles of his ass.

Without speaking, he opened a drawer in his desk and
grabbed one, along with a tube of lubricating jelly. I stood

up and unfurled the rubber over my meat, then smeared a healthy helping of the gel over both my rod and his flesh inner tube.

Then, holding both his hips straight, I slowly navigated my ship into his slip, pressing the pointed bow ever deeper into the tight berth of his ass canal. I forced it in, inch by throbbing inch, and watched in perverse fascination as his virginal rose bud stretched to handle my girth. My cock looked so huge and bloated as it pressed its way into him, and I started gently undulating in and out of him with no small sense of pride.

At first, Nick seemed to be taking it like a trouper. He made a few small squeaks and whinnies, and he liked what I was doing. I could tell because when I reached around to play with his dick, my hand came away covered in a tacky layer of his glistening precum.

I picked up my tempo, pulling in and out at a quickening pace. Nick was still bent over, so I leaned forward, reaching under his arms and grabbing hold of his shoulder, clinging to him as I plowed him. I pulled him upright, still holding on to him so tightly that there was no space between his back and my front, and I rammed myself up into him with the force of a jackhammer, having to step up onto my tiptoes to complete each thrust.

It was getting to be more than Nick could take. His head began to loll as he cried out again and again in pain, but when I asked if I should stop, he told me to keep going. He kept moaning and even screamed a couple times. I loved that I could make him do that, but I was afraid that our neighbors would hear since there were quite a few people still around the building that morning. I silenced him momentarily by gruffly slapping a hand over his mouth and holding his throat with my other, stifling his cries. Again, I could feel my ejaculation blooming way down deep in the pit of my stomach, so I slowed and then eventually stopped, relieved that Nick's cries had abated as well.

I wanted to give Nick a turn seeding my cornrow, so I disengaged from him and turned him around to kiss me as I pulled off the condom. His face was splotchy and flushed from the discomfort of having my cock rip him open, but he kissed me hungrily and threw me down on the desk.

He groped around for another condom and quickly unwrapped it before sliding it down his rod. He greased it up and then dipped his knees a little so that it was pointing directly level at my waiting cookie jar. I swung my legs up into the air and rested them against his tight shoulders, my big toes meeting just behind his head.

As he drove his sharp spear into me, I muffled a cry of the briefest anguish before giving myself over to the waves of unbridled ecstasy that his invasion of my ass cavity produced. His long prong poked every stimulating spot on its way to brushing my prostate, and Nick's amateurish but thorough thrusts were fomenting a mind-blowing orgasm deep within me.

Nick might not have had much practice or finesse, but he was a power top in training if I'd ever come across one. He had found his rhythm, and he was sticking to it, assaulting my foxhole again and again, pounding me in an ever-mounting pitch of mindless, frenetic energy.

Sweat streamed from both of us, making us both slippery. Every few moments, Nick would have to readjust our position to get back into his rhythm, and each time he did so, he hit another erogenous zone inside me. I was haphazardly massaging my cock, and I was not going to be able to hold back much longer, but I didn't have to wait.

Nick had started emitting a low keening noise, somewhere between a moan and a whistle. His eyelids hung low as he furiously fucked me, and his jaw was slack. He was going to blow at any moment, and I urged him on, telling him to keep humping me until he shot. Suddenly, his eyes widened for a moment, and his thrusting took on a wild, chaotic trajectory. His whole body grew rigid, and I watched as the muscles of his arms and his torso all contracted, and his face turned red because he was holding his breath. He clung to my legs for dear life, pinioning them against his hard chest and shoulders, the veins popping out with the effort. Then all at once inside me, I sensed his meat jerking hard several times in a row as Nick gave a few final, stiff, short thrusts.

That was all it took to send me over the edge. As Nick's pubic region slammed into my balls, I let my surge of sperm work its way up, creating an itchy, warm feeling as the semen flew down my piss tube and out the dilated hole of my cock all over my chest, stomach, and hands. I unleashed current after current of the hot white stuff onto myself and the desk. Some of it even landed on Nick's stomach as he slowly regained his senses.

As the river slowed to a trickle, I shivered a few last times and felt Nick slowly pulling out of me. I opened my eyes and looked up at him. He was still out of breath but smiling a broad, beautiful smile. He leaned down to embrace me and shove his tongue carelessly back into my mouth.

We kissed messily for a moment, our whole bodies

touching, smearing us both with my jizz. Nick stood up and helped me off the desk, handing me a paper towel from the kitchen so that I could wipe off, then taking one for himself.

"That was a pretty good welcome to the building," I quipped, "and I didn't even ask to borrow any sugar."

Nick laughed and asked if I wanted to go for a swim. Pulling on my shorts, I said sure, and we set off to take a dip in the pool, where a few other of our neighbors were already hanging out.

Nick introduced me to all of them and we shared a knowing look when he joked to them that he had thoroughly checked me out and that I was cool. One of our other neighbors, another hot young guy named Jeremy who was sunning in a pretty revealing Speedo at the moment, pointed out his apartment and told me not to hesitate if I ever needed to borrow anything. He smiled at me before turning over to tan his back.

As I dove into the cool blue water, I thought to myself that I was going to like living in my new apartment.

Trivia Night Threesome

I was depressed. It was October. I was in Berlin. I was alone. A couple friends had met me in the city a few days earlier for a quick European getaway, but they had to get back to their jobs while I continued on to France.

Don't get me wrong. We had spent a fabulous few days in that most conflicted of Western European cities. I was twenty-three and I had never been to Germany before, so I had really been looking forward to seeing all the places I had studied in school, and learning about the city's dramatic past. My friends were more of the . . . party persuasion. They had done the research on the nightlife and gay scene while I had had my nose buried in guidebooks.

I let them pick the hotel, which was ideally situated near many of the historical sights I was interested in, and during the day, I was in charge. First thing, I booked us on a walking tour of the city, and we learned all about the history of Berlin as we walked around Museum Island in the River Spree and strolled down the famous Unter den Linden boulevard to the Brandenburg Gate. We marveled at the Reichstag, took in the Holocaust Memorial, passed parts of the Berlin Wall and Checkpoint Charlie, and ended in the picturesque Gendarmenmarkt between the imposing Deutscher Dom cathedral and the Schauspielhaus, or symphony hall.

We also trekked over to the Alexanderplatz, with its Soviet space needle tower, and then across town to the bustling Potsdamer Platz, with its huge open urban spaces and contemporary malls. My friends humored me as I went hunting for famous paintings in the Gemäldegalerie, and though they dragged their feet, I knew they loved the ancient structures preserved at the Pergamon Museum, especially the colorful Babylonian Gate of Ishtar.

In the evenings, we searched out dinner at both classical German restaurants and in the new wave of ethnic eateries springing up in the old Jewish quarter around the Oranienburg.

We were staying just east of the city center in the up-and-coming hipster haven of Prenzlauer Berg. It was located in what used to be East Berlin, so the architecture was pretty depressing, but the ambiance was sort of like Williamsburg in New York or Silverlake in Los Angeles, thanks to the droves of young artists and professionals drawn to the neighborhood by the low housing prices. Little cafés and boutiques were popping up everywhere, not to mention sushi joints, art galleries, and every other hallmark of a revitalizing neighborhood. It was a very exciting time to be there, and when I felt my friends had put up with enough of the tourist thing, I was happy to just amble along the Prenzlauer Allee looking at all the people and shops.

At night, my friends were in charge. They had found our little hotel through some German friends who knew everything that was going on, and so we heard about all the newest bars and clubs to hit. We did everything—gay, straight, mixed. It was just fun to be out in a European city where no one cared and everyone was ready to have a good time. Night after night, we danced until the wee hours, stumbling home with new friends we'd made along the way, and stopping for a last falafel to stave off a hangover before collapsing back at our hotel.

It was one of the most fun trips I had ever taken with friends, but by the time they were ready to go back home four days later, I thought I was going to die of exhaustion. I had one more night in the city by myself before I had to catch a train to Paris, so I saw them off to the train to the airport, went back to the hotel, and snoozed for a few more hours.

When I woke up, it was just after noon, so I washed up and went out for a little last bit of sightseeing and bought a ticket to the opera. I was in one of the Western world's musical capitals, after all, and I thought I just had to see a performance while I was in town.

I took another quick nap at the hotel, then got ready for the evening. At home, I would have dressed up for a night out at the opera, but I was backpacking it that trip, so I didn't have anything too nice to wear. I put on a pair of clean jeans that just happened to look really cute on me, a fitted black polo shirt, and a light cotton jacket that hit me in all the right places. I grabbed a sandwich on the way to the opera house and ate it as I walked. When I got there, I found I had mistaken the performance time, so I had about an hour to kill before the curtain rose.

Luckily, the bar was open, so I had a lovely glass of champagne while I waited and struck up a conversation with a young woman who happened to be waiting for her date to show. It turned out she was native Berliner, but when she had grown up, the city had still been split between east and west, and she had grown up on the west side. We had a fascinating conversation about her experience as a child in that society, and when her boyfriend showed up, we all exchanged information so that we could keep in touch.

The opera was actually sort of disappointing. Since I only had the one night, I had not had much choice of program, so I was forced to see *Rigoletto*. Only it had been translated into German, and, well, it just lost something. The performances were okay, but the house was half empty, and you could just feel the weight of it sagging on the actors.

I was relieved when the curtain came back down two hours later and it was time to leave. I had thought to go back to my hotel for a good night's sleep since I hadn't gotten many of those with my friends and I was sure I wouldn't the following night on the train, but I didn't feel at all sleepy. I thought about what I could do, and an idea occurred to me.

While my friends had been with me, I had wanted to visit an area in the former West Berlin called Schöneberg. Before all the cool kids had migrated east to Prenzlauer Berg, it had been a big bohemian area with lots of gay bars. Even though there were still quite a few bars, mostly centered around a little street called Motzstrasse, my friends had wanted to stay on the east side of the city, so we hadn't even explored the area.

Consulting my map like the true tourist I was, I found the U-Bahn stop I would need to get to Schöneberg, and I hopped on the train at the nearest station to make my way there. About forty-five minutes later—wow, Berlin was bigger than I thought—I arrived and found myself walking down Motzstrasse. I was not terribly impressed by what I saw. It was a cute little street, sure, but nothing much seemed to be happening on it. The first couple of bars I stopped in at were pretty much deserted. I should have known better than to expect a fun evening out on a weeknight, but I had come this far, so I was determined to find something to do.

Finally, I found a bar with some people in it. A lot of people, actually. It was a small space with two rooms. The front housed the bar just inside the door and large front windows, as well as some small booths where people were drinking in groups, and then little nooks and crannies where people were clustering to chat and socialize. In the dimly lit back, there were a few tables where more people were drinking and carousing. The music was loud, the mood was lively, and everyone seemed to be having fun. I'd found my bar.

I shouldered my way through the crowd to the packed counter and waited until one of the barmen acknowledged me. Not speaking any German, I ordered by pointing at the large green bottle of Beck's beer my neighbor at the bar was drinking. The barman understood and brought me my drink.

When I had paid, I wandered away from the bar and took up residence in a free corner wedged between the front door and the booths. Looking around, I could see a lot of cute guys, though quite a few older men as well. This was going to be interesting. I tried to strategize about how to talk to people. Everyone seemed to be off in their own world, just talking to their tablemates or ordering drinks, but not really making friends with those around them. Combined with the fact that I didn't speak German, I wasn't sure what I was going to do. Maybe I could just try to make eyes at some hot young thing and we wouldn't have to speak the same language in order to accomplish what I intended. I looked around to see if there was anyone on whom I should set my sights this early in the evening, and took another pull at my beer.

Out of the corner of my eye, I noticed two guys around my age sitting at a two-top table toward one end of the bar. They were looking back and forth from me to each other, and speaking animatedly. I pretended not to notice, though I checked in on them every few moments to see what was going on.

One of them was short and burly with buzzed red hair and a lot of stubble. From what I could see of his thick forearms, they were furry and veined from manual labor. His tight jeans accentuated the powerful muscles of his thighs and constrained his bubble ass into a round sphere. The other man at the table looked like he was a good eight inches taller than his friend. His hair was blond and long. I might have said it looked a little girly even because it was so pretty, but it was wavy and just the tiniest bit unkempt, making it look like he'd just gotten out of bed after a protracted sexual adventure. I thought they both looked really sexy, and wasn't sure why they had their eye on me.

While I was still scanning the room for a likely victim,

one of the bartenders stood up on the bar with a microphone and started making announcements in German to the cheers and jeers of the crowd. Some of the other bartenders and busboys came through the crowd handing out pieces of paper and pencils.

I was given one by a busboy who winked at me, but he was already on to the next table before I could ask what it was for. The paper had numbered lines from 1 to 30, but that was all I could tell.

The bartender was back on the microphone making more announcements. I had no idea what was going on, but just as I was looking around to find someone to explain it to me, the redhead from the table near the bar got up and walked straight over to me.

I could feel a surprised expression register on my face, but I plastered a grin on instead as he stepped up. Up close, I could see that his arms were furry with the same red hair that was on his head and face. He had a beautiful smile of straight white teeth and playful, deep brown eyes. Freckles scattered on either side of his nose and forehead, like he'd spent too much time in the sun as a child. He smiled back at me and said something in German. I shrugged and indicated that I could not understand him.

"English?" he asked.

"Yes, I speak English," I said, relieved that he did, too.

"Fantastic. Would you like to be in a threesome with us?" he said, gesturing toward his friend.

I was confused. "Er . . . a threesome with you? Do you mean . . . ?"

He gave a deep belly laugh and punched my shoulder playfully. It still hurt, though, since he was so strong. As I rubbed the sore spot, he explained, "No, not that kind of threesome. Um, I think the word is 'team.' It is trivia night and each team needs three people. Would you like to join us?"

Now, I love a good bar trivia night. I am a master of the arcane, and I usually end up in the top three and get a prize. Even if I don't win overall, at least part of the bar tab gets taken care of, or I get a free pitcher or round or something, so I always have a good time, but this was different.

"But I don't speak German," I said timidly. "I don't know how much help I'll be."

"Ah, but that is okay! The trivia is in English. You will be our secret weapon!"

"Well, in that case," I said, smiling, "I would love to. Thank you!"

Without hesitating, he took my hand, gave it a friendly squeeze, and led me back to the table where he'd been sitting with his blond friend, who stood up as we arrived. He was indeed a lot taller than his friend (and me), with a thin, lanky body, and the most beautiful gray-blue eyes. His skin was completely fair and clear, with a roses and cream complexion that would look perfect in a Dove commercial. He extended a hand to me and said something in German, to which I just replied, "I'm Brad, nice to meet you."

"Ah, American! Wonderful!" he said, shaking my hand. "I am Max."

"And I am Marius," chimed in the redhead.

They quickly found another chair for me, and we got ready to start the competition. There were about twenty teams in all and a bunch of spectators. The quizzing was simple. There were three rounds of ten questions each. You had ten seconds to write down your answer for each question, and no using PDAs to Google the answers.

As the bartender started firing off questions, I could tell that we'd do well. Max and Marius spoke English very well and got the gist of the questions, and even some of the answers, but I soon took over the task of writing our answers down just because I was processing the information faster than they were. Plus, I knew a lot more of the answers. By the end of round one, they were impressed. By round two, when we'd gotten another perfect score on the section, they were entirely pleased, patting themselves, and me, on the back for having made such a fine, random choice of quiz partner. They had really lucked out.

I'll be honest and say that none of the questions was really that difficult, most of them coming from general trivia categories like arts, history, and sports, so anyone who'd played Trivial Pursuit a few times stood a good chance of doing well.

Round three was touch-and-go. There was one question that I did not know the answer to, so we all had to guess and keep our fingers crossed. Turns out we were right. When the scores had been tallied, we were tied with one other team.

The bartender told each team to pick a representative to answer a tiebreaker question in front of everyone. Only I didn't understand what he was saying since he was back to German. Max and Marius immediately volunteered me, pushing me up and sending me off toward the bar. I was so confused, but I went along obligingly.

The other team sent up their representative, and it was just the two of us facing off. The final question was: What two actresses played Jane and Blanche in *What Ever Happened to Baby Jane?*

The other man raised his hand first and answered Bette Davis and Olivia de Havilland. The bartender looked down at his answer card and declared that he was wrong, then turned the mic over to me. If I got the answer right, we would win the game and a free bar tab of fifty euros.

I pondered for a second, then said, "Bette Davis and Joan Crawford." Taking a moment to build suspense, the bartender looked at me, then around the whole room, then back at me, then said, "YES! That is right, you've won!"

The whole bar erupted in hoots and cheers, and everyone was patting me on the back. Max and Marius came up to accept the gift certificate, and both of them gave me a kiss on the cheek and a big bear hug. I was the man of the hour.

After a few minutes of flirting with every cute guy who came by to give me congratulations, I finally made it back to the table with the boys so we could gab over what had just happened. We were all flush with victory, and kept congratulating ourselves. Every so often, one or the other of them would squeeze my leg under the table.

As we talked, I learned that Max and Marius were boyfriends and had been together for a few years. They were both originally from Berlin and had grown up on either side of the Iron Curtain, Marius on the east and Max on the west. They had met as teenagers at university and then had gotten together after school when they reconnected at a party thrown by a mutual friend. It was as romantic a story as I'd ever heard, and it made me wish I had a boyfriend, too.

We finished up another round. It was getting late, and I had my train trip the next day, so I got ready to leave, thanking the boys for a lovely evening and trying to find a piece of paper so I could give them my contact information.

As I was writing down my e-mail address, Marius put his hand over mine and stopped me. "I thought you were going to be in our threesome . . . ," he said, smiling devilishly and taking a second to glance at Max, who nodded almost imperceptibly while also smiling at me.

I could feel the mood shift at the table, but I wasn't quite sure what was happening. "I . . . I was in your threesome. We won."

"No, I don't mean that kind of threesome this time. I mean the kind you thought I was asking you about when we met." He shot me a look of expectation, smirking as he awaited my response.

I weighed my options. I had two hot German guys whom I'd just spent a great evening with asking if I wanted to go home and have a threesome with them. That had never happened to me before, and I wasn't quite sure what to do. On the one hand, I had my trip to Paris the next day and I needed to get home and pack. On the other . . . well, I envisioned a night of sweaty, dirty, energetic sex in all kinds of positions. What to do?

Without breaking Marius's stare, I reached out and pulled Max toward me, planting a tantalizingly soft kiss on his mouth. Then I released him and said to Marius, "I'd love to. Only this time, you two are going to have to do a lot more work than you did during the quiz."

Both of them laughed, and we all pulled on our coats to leave. On the way out the door, I dipped my hand into a bowl containing condom-and-lube packets that was sitting at one end of the bar as part of some sexual education promotion, and pulled out a handful of them. Who knew how many we'd use?

I thought we would be going to their apartment, but about two blocks away, we came to another, seedier bar. Marius pulled me in the door and Max followed. "Where are we going?" I asked, getting nervous.

Max answered, "We share our apartment with another couple and they are home right now, so we like to come here to have fun."

The bar looked completely deserted except for a few older guys who leered at the three of us as we came in. We didn't even pause for a drink or to check out the situation before Marius was pulling me toward a door at the very back. As we went through, the lights changed to a dark purple, and I could make out a few shapes that looked like other people in the corners.

I couldn't hear anything over the loud rock music that was playing, but I could see that some dirty, dirty things were happening in there. Suddenly, I realized I was in a dark room! By the time I was out and partying as a young gay man in New York, a lot of the gay bars had closed up their dark rooms as homosexual activity became less and less taboo, so I'd never actually been in one before. Apparently they were still something of a fetish in Europe—even in such a cosmopolitan place as Berlin—and I was going to get my first taste of one tonight.

Marius was the leader and found an empty corner. There was a bench running along the walls. It was padded with some sort of vinyl cushion, probably because it would be easier to clean at the end of the night. Sitting me down between him and Max, Marius began to kiss my neck and cup my crotch in one of his strong hands. Max was stroking my hair and unbuttoning my shirt so that he could slip his hand in and rub it along my hard-packed chest.

I alternately kissed one, then the other, appreciating the difference between Max's soft, pouty lips and Marius's forceful, rough mouth. Every so often the two of them would kiss each other deeply, keeping their hands on me all the while. For my part, I had an arm around Max's slender shoulders, and my other hand was planted on Marius's massive thigh, just about where his leg met his crotch. I could feel the swell of his fat cock beneath the denim of his jeans exuding a cone of heat, and I couldn't wait to feel the weight of that meat stick in my hands.

After a few minutes of getting to know each other like that, Max slipped down onto the floor in front of us and undid Marius's and my zippers. Reaching inside my jeans, he pulled out my semi and began to stroke it to life. Within seconds it was as hard as a steel column and pointing straight up eight inches into the air. I looked down at Marius's crotch to see what was going on there, but in the dim light, all I could see was Max's hand wrapped around something thick and chunky.

Max started by sucking Marius's cock, and I grew even

harder as I watched his head bob up and down in Marius's lap. Marius let his head drop back and his mouth hang open, enjoying Max's blowjob until I leaned over and began kissing his neck and ears. Marius ran his hands through my spiky brown hair and pulled my face farther over so that he could kiss me gruffly, breathing huskily into my mouth as I opened it to accept his moist tongue.

Max, meanwhile, moved over to my cock. Since he had warmed up on Marius's meaty member, he lost no time in deepthroating as much of my rod as he could swallow. I felt a lovely pulse of tingling energy radiate from the tip of my helmet head down to my balls as my cock poked into the moist, fleshy cushion of Max's throat. I grabbed on to his long blond hair and mashed his face down onto my crotch even harder so he would know I liked his technique, and he stayed fully down on me for a minute, working my shaft with his tongue and throat.

Marius had pulled my shirt up over my flat abs to expose my little nipples, and was currently treating them to a thorough licking, kissing, and nibbling at the sensitive circles of flesh so persistently that, between his oral overtures and Max's, I was having a hard time catching my breath.

After a minute or so, I could take no more. I reached down and abruptly pulled Max's face off of me, bringing it level with my own so that I could kiss him. Though his mouth was delicate and soft, I kissed him brusquely and hard, forcing my tongue against his and forcefully mashing our lips up against one another.

Marius let us go on like that for a minute before his giant paw guided my head down to where his cock was beginning to soften. I took a moment to size him up and figured he must have been just under six inches long when erect, but almost as long around. His sausage was compact and squat, but I bet it could get the job done.

I started my licking at the very tip a few times, making Marius spasm with pleasure. He couldn't endure much of that, so he pushed my face farther down onto his cock, forcing me to open my mouth and throat as wide as they would go. Even so, I spluttered as his member invaded my gorge and I concentrated on rubbing it all over with my tongue while I tugged at his hairy ballsack with my free hand.

Max had gotten up and stood on the bench next to where Marius sat. He undid his zipper and whipped out a thin, uncut cock that, though flaccid, was still very long. The skin was so white it stood out even in that barely lit room, though it disappeared almost immediately into Marius's hungry mouth. I continued working on Marius, running my tongue under his rubbery foreskin and around the spongy skin of his cockhead. I rubbed my hands along his burly torso, grabbing hold of his bulky pecs and squeezing when I felt the sharp points of his huge nipples.

With a deep grunt, Marius pulled my mouth from his tool and stood me up directly in front of him. Then he wrenched my pants down around my ankles and pried apart my supple ass cheeks so he could shove his tongue right into the heart of my out chute. Max had hopped down from the bench and got down on the ground in front of me so that he could start blowing me again. He interrupted his slobbery work to tell me how much he loved sucking cut cocks like mine, and boy could I tell as he slurped up and down the entire length, pausing to lick the underside from time to time.

Marius's tongue rammed deeper and deeper into my fleshy pucker, and I unclenched my ass muscles to give him easier access to my pleasure center. His drool covered my entire ass crack, making it dank and moist, and even more sensitive as his rough stubble scratched me lightly with each movement of his head.

With both of them focusing on me like that, I knew I would climax before long, but I was still disappointed when Max disengaged. I didn't have long to feel sorry, though, because he had reached down to pull one of the condom-lube packets from the bar out of my pants. Unwrapping the condom, he slipped it on my eight-incher, then lubed up both my pole and his hole. Marius was still tossing my salad, so Max merely hunched over and sort of backed up into me, navigating my shaft straight into his manhole.

For the first few seconds, the rock-hard head of my cock just pressed against Max's tight sphincter, but when I helped him out with a few short thrusts, I was finally able to penetrate his unyielding sex donut and push deeper inside him. Laying my hands on either side of his narrow rib cage, I slowly rocked back and forth on the balls of my feet, loosening him up to take my entire rod.

I felt his muscles relax more and more, even as my own asshole was getting a tongue-lashing from Marius. As soon as I started pumping with a bit more intensity, though, I felt Max's stubbly head come down between my legs so that his mouth was positioned right beneath my balls and Max's dangling package. Marius started to yank on Max's wand while licking both our balls as they ran over his tongue with each of my thrusts.

Max used one hand to lean on Marius's broad shoulders, and with the other, he reached behind him and slapped my butt, spurring me to ride him harder. I stabbed his hole with my spear, milking his prostate with each prod. I still had my hands on his ribs, and I could feel his breathing grow shorter and more labored. I reached forward and pulled back on his hair, causing him to arch his back and stand up straighter. Even over the thumping music I could hear him cry out with mingled pain and ecstasy before I kissed him.

Marius took the opportunity to slip out from under us, and before I knew what he was doing, I felt his thick meat pole pressing up against my asshole. He had slipped on a condom and doused both of us with lube to make things easier, but I still had to bite my lip hard to avoid crying out as he inserted his beer can cock in me.

Marius stayed still, letting me get used to his heft, and I found that it helped to keep fucking Max, stimulating my pleasure zones while using my humping motion to slide Marius's cock farther and farther into me. Thankfully his cock was not that long, so I could get used to his size faster, and though his girth stretched my anus to its limits, I was still able to handle him. Or so I thought until he started to really skewer me with his club.

Still, by fucking Max's willing hole even harder, I was able to relax and let Marius do whatever he wanted with me. Eventually, I just let his momentum propel me faster and deeper into Max, the three of us groaning and heaving like a well-oiled machine. I reached around to take hold of Max's skinny dick and began to jerk it, rubbing a fingertip back and forth over his head to get him really turned on. It worked, because as soon as I started playing with his cockhead, he began to buck his hips back into me so that my erection plunged into him balls deep.

With Marius's dick ravaging me and punching on my prostate, and my own hard-on gouging Max, I felt I was going to climax at any moment. I shoved Max off my cock, grabbing him by the arm and spinning him around as I ripped of my condom. Then I crammed my pole down his throat and held on for dear life as the surge of semen erupted forth from my balls and shot down my piss tube into his enthusiastic mouth. Max greedily slurped up each spray of sperm I sent his way and milked my cock 'til it was starting to soften in his mouth.

When he was done, I slowly pulled away from Marius, who was streaming with sweat and ready to blow himself. We had clearly determined that Max was our boy toy for the evening, so when Marius pulled his own condom off, he wrestled Max over to himself, clasped his hips and forced his ass down level with that massive piece of man meat of his, and drove his cock up into Max's bare hole. Max stifled a cry but kept still as Marius heaved into him again and again at a furious pace. I could only just make out their shapes, but based on my own experience with Marius ramming me, I knew that Max must be in a world of hurt right now. He seemed to enjoy it even more than I had, though, because within seconds he was smiling, and tossing his head this way and that with pleasure.

Marius gave a few more short, shallow thrusts, and then, with a great bellow, he seeded Max's hole with his wet, gooey cum. Max ground his ass back onto Marius a few more times, milking out his entire load, and then when he pulled off of Marius, he let the whole, messy cream pie slide out of his ass right onto the floor. I could see the steaming puddle shimmer in the low light.

Marius stepped back from Max, giving him an appreciative pinch on the ass, then sat down on the bench. Max walked up to the both of us and shoved his cock in Marius's exhausted face. Marius wasted no time in getting down to work. After all, it was only fair to help Max come to completion after all he had done for us. I joined in by sucking on Max's furry little balls and wiggling a finger into his cum-laden asshole. Using only his mouth, Marius hoovered Max's tool like an industrial-grade vacuum cleaner, leaving Max dazed and weak in the knees as he approached his climax.

Finally, I sat back as Max took hold of Marius's buzzed head in both hands and jammed his slender shaft all the way down Marius's throat just as I had done with Max's face, right as he began to come. Marius's eyes bugged out and the veins on his thick neck surged with blood as he struggled to breathe with Max's tool stifling him like that. I admired his perseverance as he gulped down shot after shot of Max's seed, and after what seemed like a full minute, he was finally able to pull his face away from Max's limpening cock, and wiped his chin clean with a hand.

I kissed Marius softly, congratulating him on a job well done. Max, meanwhile, regained his senses and leaned down to kiss both of us. We all tasted like cum, and we savored the last, lingering drops of salty fluid in our mouths.

I looked around the dark room, suddenly self-conscious and aware that everyone else might have been watching. To my relief, there were still only a few other people in the room, mostly making out or jerking each other off, though a few of them looked up at us from time to time and smiled in appreciation of the show we had just put on. In another moment, the three of us stood up and dressed quickly, making our way back out into the street.

We said a quick good-bye, me giving the boys a last kiss each, then headed off in our separate directions. I never did exchange contact information with them, but at least I can tell you where to find a good bar trivia night in Berlin.

Interview with the Porn Star

After years of working in film production out in Los Angeles, I was feeling burned out. The hours were long, the working conditions were not usually the best, everyone's stress level was sky high, and I just stopped having fun. If the pay hadn't been so good, I probably would have left the field much sooner, but it was hard to quit when I was actually making so much money.

I decided to work on one final movie with the production company I was at, and then I would take some time off. Since I had been working so hard, I had not had time to spend the money I had made on anything too extravagant, so I had a sizeable savings cushion to live off for a while.

For the first few months, I bummed around, taking yoga classes, Italian lessons, hanging out with friends, hitting the gym and the beach, and traveling to some of the far-flung places I had always wanted to visit. I felt like I was reconnecting with the person I used to be before I became a work-obsessed dick who had nothing better to talk about than the weekend box office totals.

I was learning to relax again; I got back into some of my interests like cooking and sports. I started making new friends, and even had more time to date, so I was meeting more guys than I had in years. I felt like I was becoming a whole person again, and I was really enjoying the transformation.

Still, I always had a gnawing sentiment that eventually I would need to regain a sense of direction and find something professionally productive to do with my time. And I would have to start making money again at some point since I couldn't live off my savings forever and it didn't look like I'd be marrying wealthy anytime soon!

So I thought about what I might like to do where I could remain this complete person I'd become again and yet still have a career. After a couple weeks thinking about it and running through all my connections, I decided to try freelance writing for a while and see where that got me.

At first, I wasn't picky at all. I would write about anything for anyone. I just wanted to get a portfolio of clips under my belt, so I accepted low-pay and even no-pay assignments just to get my content out there and establish a name for myself. I was lucky in that I was able to write about a lot of my interests like food and wine, as well as about some of the destinations I'd traveled to during my time off. I got a great response, and soon I was booked with paying gigs all over Los Angeles. My assignments calendar filled up month after month, and I was making a real go of the writing thing.

One of the publications I wrote for was a gay magazine in West Hollywood. Though I mostly did arts pieces for them—reviewing plays, music, movies—I occasionally wrote features and interviews as well. I did not really pitch the longer pieces since I didn't have time to write very many of them, but I rarely turned down an assignment from the magazine because I thought it was good to keep a finger on the pulse of gay life in the city, and I could write the articles pretty fast. Plus, things like that only came up very occasionally, so it didn't usually cause a time conflict for me.

I was surprised, however, when my editor called me up one day and asked if I was interested in doing a rush interview on a local celebrity for the next issue. It had already been booked for a couple days out, so I wouldn't have much time to prepare for it or write it. I looked at my calendar and saw that I had a little free time that week, and I could use the money as a little bonus for the month, so I agreed without even asking who it was with. My editor was in a rush, so he thanked me and said he would be e-mailing me the details when he got a moment.

I wasn't worried about the rush. I wrote quickly, and usually I was able to cobble something interesting together out of the rambling answers I usually got from the subjects. Even rushed, I thought I could do a better job than most of the mag's other writers, so I spent the next day finishing my other articles for the week and waiting for my editor's e-mail so I could prepare some questions.

By that evening, I still hadn't heard from him, and the interview was the following day, so I left a message at the office asking my editor to e-mail me the background information as soon as he got in in the morning. The next morning, I woke up to a new e-mail from him in my inbox, but I had barely had a chance to glance at it before my phone was ringing off the hook.

Another editor of mine in New York was fact-checking an article I'd turned in the week before and needed a bunch of answers and source materials from me. It took me over an hour to get everything together and answer all her questions. When we finally finished, it was already time for me to get ready for my interview.

I liked to shower and change into something dressy like a shirt and slacks before interviews like this just to make it professional, so I took my time getting ready. When I had about five minutes left before I should have left, I finally looked at my editor's e-mail . . . and my eyes went wide.

The person I was to interview that morning was a rising, young, gay porn star named Linus Long. Linus was apparently always typecast as the top in his scenes because he was a huge African-American man, measuring up to six feet five inches, and weighing in at 220 lbs. From a brief Internet search, I could see that he had a . . . prodigious member . . . and that he was a popular figure in light domination films. Not exactly my thing, but still pretty hot. I had to concentrate on a horrible date I'd just been on with a bad kisser to stop myself from getting aroused by the photos I found.

If I had been diligent, I would have rented some of his flicks (purely for research purposes!), but instead, here I was, walking into the interview with barely a clue of who he was or just what I would talk to him about. Packing up my laptop and a notebook, I got in my car and set off to meet Linus at his apartment.

It was only a five-minute drive from my own, and I was surprised at how genteel the building looked with white stucco and a faintly pink trim. I saw several of Linus's neighbors, and they all seemed to be retired Eastern European émigrés. It seemed so strange that I was going to visit a porn star right after making pleasantries with all these nice old folks.

I looked down at my printout of the e-mail, found Linus's real name, and buzzed his apartment. A gentle man's voice answered, and I explained who I was and he let me in. I took the elevator up to the third floor, walked down the hallway, and found the door to the apartment slightly ajar. Knocking lightly, I then opened it and walked in, calling out, "Hello!"

It was a cute one-bedroom, with a kitchen off to the side of the living room and a bedroom farther on down the hall. I heard a voice calling me to the kitchen, so I walked across the main room, taking note of the leather sofas, the huge flat-screen TV with an Xbox plugged in. Clearly porn was paying off. Then I stepped through a swinging door into the tiny kitchen.

I recognized Linus at once. He was just as hot in person as in the stills from the movies that I'd seen. In some of his films he'd had longer hair, but now it was shaved down to the skull, accentuating the handsomeness of his face. His complexion was very, very dark, like those 70 percent chocolate bars I sometimes bought at the gourmet grocery store. The gorgeous color of his skin made his bright eyes and white smile radiate even more intensely, especially his eyes since they were a muddled light hazel color.

In one enormous hand, this behemoth was cradling a steaming cup of tea, and he offered me another. I thanked him and took it, smelling it. It was red rooibos, one of my favorites, with a little cinnamon spice to it. Linus explained that he found it invigorating and calming at the same time. This was his first real interview, so he was a little anxious, but he still wanted to be enthusiastic.

Walking back into the living room and taking up a post on one of the leather chairs, I reassured him that it would be easy since we'd just be talking like friends. That he could say anything he wanted at any time, and that if he had any questions, to ask. He looked relieved, so I thought it was time to start. I asked him all about his background, where he was from, how old he was, and when he had come to Los Angeles.

Linus was born and raised in Detroit. He'd gone to a charter school in the city that was one of the only places a poor kid like him could get a decent education without paying an arm and a leg in tuition. His family life had been decent—his parents were still married, he had a few other siblings both older and younger, and they had never had any real financial problems. His parents both worked at low-wage jobs, as had Linus when he was a teenager and in college, but they had never had any pressing hardship.

Linus knew he wanted to leave Detroit, so he worked hard and got a scholarship to USC, where he studied psychology. To pay for living expenses, he started working various odd jobs. Everything from cleaning houses to working in a psych lab monitoring patient trials. Nothing really interested him that much, and when he graduated (a semester early, he told me proudly), he had not known what to do with his life, so he just kept doing odd jobs and trying to figure out what to do next.

I asked the burning question, "So how did you get into porn?"

He looked thoughtful for a moment, then launched into

a story about how one of his classmates at USC who was also gay had done a thesis on gay porn stars. This guy was trying to prove that, due to the heightened attention and sexual desire expressed toward them, these men had a higher sense of self-worth than the average gay man.

"And what were his conclusions?" I asked, interested by this tangent.

"He was wrong," Linus laughed. "I remember, he was so surprised by the results, but I kept telling him the whole time that he had it all reversed."

"The whole time?"

"Yeah. I was helping him with his project because he had helped me with my thesis—rounding up trial subjects, computer modeling, stuff like that. When he was ready to start collecting his own data, he asked if I could come along on some of the interviews with him and help take notes, photos, you know, all that documentation."

On one of these fact-finding trips, the two had actually gone into a studio to meet with some of the executives there and ask what qualities they looked for when casting their films. One of the producers took a shine to Linus, noting that with his physical attributes, he could probably carve out a niche for himself in the gay porn world. At the time, Linus had laughed it off, but he had to admit that he was still curious about it. Nothing really came of it until the two students were interviewing some of the actors from the studio and Linus developed a crush on one of them named Dmitri.

Dmitri was originally from the Ukraine and had immigrated to the States with his folks when he was a child. He had still managed to market himself as an Eastern European stud, kind of like the boys of *Bel Ami,* and had gotten work in a few films. The two started a brief, torrid affair, but Linus soon found out that Dmitri had a slightly imbalanced personality, and broke it off.

While they were still going out, though, Dmitri had shot another film, and one day when Linus came to set to pick him up (he didn't actually want to see the filming because he thought it would weird him out), Linus ran into the same producer who had suggested he do porn. Long story short (so to speak), by the end of the day, Linus had a part in the film.

There were a lot of reasons for getting involved, he told me. He was having some money problems after graduation. If he didn't start earning some cash soon, he'd have to go back to Detroit and live at home for a while. He'd also been secretly curious about porn—he certainly watched enough of it when he'd been single—and since he was actually gay, he thought it might be fun. He originally hoped he could do a scene with Dmitri, but the producer had other ideas.

He had another actor who was about five foot six—almost a full foot shorter than Linus—and he wanted to do a scene that used their height disparity to full effect. Linus said that some of the mechanics were a little difficult, but the other actor was very experienced and helped him through it. There were a few snags along the way, and it definitely tested Linus's endurance after a couple hours, but eventually the scene came off perfectly and the producer offered to sign Linus to the studio on the spot.

It was a lot of money for the young man to turn down, and he didn't seem to have too many other options at the moment, so he agreed, figuring he'd do a couple of films and then figure out what to do next with his life. Three years later, he was one of the studio's biggest stars, and he had no plans to quit.

I asked how he had gotten into domination porn, and he told me that because of his imposing size, he had been typecast into those kinds of roles almost immediately. He also found that he had a knack for getting into character. That in normal life, he preferred sex to be tender and sweet and unhurried, but that it was fun to be a different person in films and to really take over the scenes. It was sort of like a safe way to act out some fantasies of his. He also thought that because he'd studied psychology, he had a particular insight into what viewers might find sexy about such scenes.

He asked if I'd seen any of his films, and I had to admit that I had not, and told him about the last-minute nature of the assignment, but I also rushed to tell him that I sort of thought it was better this way since we were having a spontaneous conversation that was yielding more genuine answers than the sound bytes I normally got during these things. I told him that I was not really into the domination genre and wondered if he could explain its appeal to me.

He said that he thought it might be better if he showed me. He went over to the entertainment center and perused his shelf of DVDs. He found one of his movies and set it to a scene in which he had tied up another guy with hand-cuffs and was teasing him with a riding crop, slapping at his nipples and giving his ass sharp raps. I have to say that I did find it rather titillating, but I was also a little in-trigued to see that the other actor in the scene bore more than a passing resemblance to myself. He looked to be about six inches shorter than Linus. Had a wiry yoga-gym body like my own, with muscular arms and a rock-hard torso. He had a young-looking, round face like mine, and his hair was dark brown with a wave to it, just like mine was. His chest was speckled with fine dark hairs, and he had a little stubble on his face that made him look slightly rugged.

Linus, meanwhile, was in fine form in the scene. He was wearing a leather Speedo studded with metal buttons, and he had a spiked collar around his neck. He looked positively magnificent, and was so commanding. I was starting to understand the allure of his performances.

As we continued to watch, I asked, "What do you think it is about scenes like this one that are so stimulating for your viewers? Are there any secret tricks you use?"

"No tricks, you've just got to commit to the character. It's a secure environment—everything we do is choreographed, we have safe words, everyone is being very careful. But you also have to enjoy what you're doing or the scene won't work."

"And what is it that you enjoy so much?" I asked, still enthralled.

Linus looked me over with a curious gaze, then got up and turned off the television. "I think it might be better if I showed you. Are you game?"

I was slightly terrified, and more than a little dubious, but I said, "In the interest of journalistic inquiry . . . yes."

He smiled. "Good. I'll be right back."

I stayed on the chair, but I closed my laptop and put it in my bag. I left the notebook out just in case. A few moments later, Linus was back in the room. He was wearing his leather Speedo from the movie. It had a little zipper running up the front that I presumed you could unzip so that he could take his cock out and fuck someone without having to actually take off the underwear. He was carrying a banker's box filled with other accoutrements that I couldn't yet see.

I was about to ask what I should do, when he barked at me, "Get up!" I looked at him, amazed by the switch in his personality. Whereas he'd been gentle and thoughtful before, now he was a striking, imposing presence.

"Did you hear me? I said get up, bitch! Bitch is going to like this!"

I jumped to attention. "Now take your clothes off! All of them." His lip curled in a cold sneer, and I quickly started unbuttoning my shirt. I took it off, revealing my athletic frame, and I noticed Linus eyeing me appreciatively. Then he slapped my chest with an open hand, leaving a red mark on one of my pecs. It wasn't too hard, but it certainly took me by surprise, as did Linus tweaking one of my tight, red nipples in his rough hands.

"Now the pants. Do it!" he commanded.

I whipped my shoes and socks off, followed by my pants, so I was standing there in just my underwear. He shook his head, and pushed me back down onto the chair. "I said *all* of your clothes, bitch," he growled, literally ripping my boxer briefs off my body with his bare hands.

I was completely naked, but I didn't have time to think about it because Linus grabbed me by the shoulder and forced me into a kneeling position right in front of him. "Stay there, and don't even move," he ordered.

He pulled a flogging whip with leather tendrils from his box and asked me if I knew what it was. I said that I didn't, and he used it to slap me on the shoulder. It stung, but I didn't flinch, staring into his flinty eyes, daring him to do it again. He did, and it stung even more, but I could take it.

Linus grabbed a handful of my hair, pulling my head back so that I was staring up at his face. "So you like that, huh? You like it when I slap you? Answer me!"

I only nodded my head, not breaking eye contact with him as he reached back into the box and grabbed a leather collar out of it, which he then snapped around my neck. Now he could drag me wherever he wanted, using a metal ring on the back of it.

He made me crawl on all fours, like a dog, and every time I didn't perform a trick fast enough, he slapped my ass with the flogger. Hard. I could feel the blood rushing up into the faint welts he was creating on my backside. Every so often, he would lean over to pinch my nipple or cup my pec. He would run a hand along my face, poking his fingers roughly into my mouth for me to suck.

He told me to stay on all fours, and I felt something cool and slippery slide down my ass crack. In another moment, I felt a slight pressure as something small and round and hard pressed against my sphincter. Linus didn't even bother preparing me beyond that as he pushed an anal bead into my ass. I yelped in pain, but he gave me a sharp donkey punch on the back of my neck to shut me up and slid another bead into my ass. Then another and another and another. I lost count, but I think he was up to seven. By that time I was gasping uncontrollably. It hurt so much, but every time he spiraled them around in my ass cavity, it gave me arpeggios of sensations that played on my every nerve.

He was no longer slapping or pinching me, but actually rubbing my back and the taut muscles of my gluts, calming me down. I felt elated, like I'd earned this comforting from him, and I found myself wanting his approval even more.

So that's what this was all about. Just giving up control completely to someone else and placing your sexuality entirely within their power. It was heady to think that he'd found me attractive enough to practice this upon as well, and I felt like that conferred a power of its own upon me.

"Yeah, you like this, bitch? Does this make you feel good?"

I grunted my assent, but he continued, "Yeah, master likes it. Master likes it a lot. He likes controlling you. He's gonna make you feel real good soon."

I couldn't take much more of this, though, and I was relieved when he started pulling the beads out, one by one. When they were all out, he yanked me up by the collar into a kneeling position. "You did well, bitch, but I don't need any help dominating you. I got this with my own hands," he chortled, chucking his implements back in the box.

He stood directly in front of me, one hand on my shoulder, squeezing it hard. My shoulders were bulky from all the fitness activities I'd been enjoying since my career change, but his hands were so large, they completely dwarfed me. His feet must have been size 14, a good few inches larger than my own, and he was forcing me to look down at them. Then with his other hand encapsulating my skull, he forced my face down to the floor, right next to his enormous foot. I stayed there, with my head on the ground, as he straightened back up.

"Sniff them," he directed me. I obliged immediately so he could hear me. They didn't smell one way or another, I was glad to note, but that relief was short-lived. "Now suck my pinky toe."

I set to work immediately, sucking and licking that toe like there was no tomorrow. I thoroughly cleaned each toe in turn, ending with his big toe. He squirmed a little bit, so I could tell he was ticklish, and when I finished with his toes, I ran my tongue back along the top of his foot, then under the arch, where there are lots of nerve endings. He grunted his approval, but when I started working my way up his ankle to his calf, gently kissing his leg, he pulled it back.

"Bitch thinks he's ready for the big time? Let's see if he is then!" he yelled, whipping my head back by the hair and dragging me part of the way up so my face was level with his crotch.

I was pleased to note that I must have been doing a good job since he had a semi that was straining the vinyl of his Speedo. For a first timer, I was catching on fast. I reached up to take down his underwear, but Linus pushed my hands away, telling me not to use them. Improvising, I rubbed my stubbly face along his bulky package, and when I got to the top of the zipper, I used my teeth to slowly undo it, staring right up at Linus's stony face.

When I had unzipped it all the way, Linus whipped out his donkey-sized dong and his big, black balls. He was under control now, so that while the cock was still swollen with extra blood and was a good six or seven inches, he wasn't hard, and his balls were hanging low and relaxed. I started to open my mouth to suck him, but he gave me a small slap on the face with his cock, stunning me momentarily. He slapped me a couple more times and told me I wasn't ready to suck him just yet, I hadn't earned it. All I was allowed to do was sniff his balls.

I sat back a moment, but he grabbed my head and jammed my face into his balls so I was instantly enveloped in their musky, sweaty odor, and their rough, hairy texture. He rubbed my face around, covering it with his scent, marking me. He told me to suck them, and I took one, then both in my mouth at the same time, opening it as wide as it would go to accommodate their huge volume.

I sucked them hard, hoping to pay him back at least a little for his rough treatment of me, and I could tell that he liked what I was doing. His cock started hardening again, ticking up and up with each pulse of his heartbeat. He was no longer barking orders at me but just grunting as his breath grew shorter and I continued to work over his gonads.

I knew he would be ready for a blowjob in a second, but I had a thought. Just as his hand was starting to guide my head north to his waiting jackhammer—extended by this time to its full ten inches—I pulled away quickly, stood up, and pushed him hard so he fell onto the couch.

He looked up at me, registering shock, but I didn't let even a second pass before I said, "I'm starting to understand, but I need to get both sides of the experience. It's my turn."

He started to protest and rise, but I shoved him back down and slapped his chest with my open hand, then took a ball gag I had seen from his box of tricks. I jammed it in his mouth when he opened it to speak again, and I threw my body over his, pinning him to the couch. As I snapped the straps of the gag in place at the back of his head, I whispered in his ear that it was going to be okay, but that I just needed to see. I explained that it would help him be better in his scenes, too, since he'd understand the other side of things. I would be gentle, but he'd better do what I say.

I was exploring a side of myself that I had not really opened up to before, and I loved the feeling of dominating a much larger man. I punched him in the chest, reveling in the feel of tenderizing his solid muscles with the power of my fist. I punched him again and again, not full force, just to knock the wind out of him a little; then I let my hands knead and pinch the contours of his abs and hip flexors. I looked down to see how he was taking it and saw that his cock was still at attention. Clearly Linus was enjoying this new experience as well. I flicked the tip of his cock with my fingers, causing him to wince in pain with each strike. I asked him if he wanted more, and each time he nodded, little tears forming in the corners of his bright hazel eyes.

Then I decided to let him have a little taste of what he was missing. I gently suckled the tip of his gargantuan hard-on, really giving my full attention to pleasing him. He started moaning almost immediately as I stroked the sheath of his cock and got his dark mushroom cap all worked up.

I went down on him for about a minute, methodically bobbing my head up and down, getting him relaxed. Then I got rougher, using my teeth to trace the edges of the top and bottom of his shaft, and sending jolts of mixed pleasure and pain through his man root. On my last swallow, I bit down harder, really running my teeth all the way up and down his cock, doing my best not to gag as I deep-throated his giant. As I withdrew, I practically scratched his skin, making him groan even louder. But to his credit, he stayed completely still and let me do it.

When he was completely aroused, I sat up and went back over to the box of fun, telling Linus to stay still or he'd regret it. I found lube and some condoms in the box, as well as a leather restraint. I showed them all to him and told him that we were going to get a lot of use out of all of them. I grabbed him by the strap of the ball gag round his face and pulled him to his feet. I handed him the condom and gel, telling him to lube up my cock and put the condom on me.

He obediently did as he was told, and I loved watching him submit to my bidding as he stroked my cock to a full erection, which, though smaller than his, was still a pretty substantial eight inches. He handled it impeccably, and I had to struggle not to show how good his handiwork felt.

When the condom was on, I took the leather restraint, turned Linus around, and he let me bind his brawny arms behind his back. I tightened the restraint until Linus cried out, then loosened it a little. I didn't want to hurt him per se, I just wanted to be in complete control so that he knew it. I made him bend over the back of the sofa and spread his legs.

"They told me you'd never bottomed in a movie before. Well, I'm going to get a sneak preview," I told him. All he did was grunt dumbly back at me.

I liked the view of his cock and balls that I was getting, but it was his clean-shaven ass that I was anxious to get a taste of. I spat several times into his ass crack, getting it wet with my hot saliva and rubbing my spit all over with a few fingers. Linus clenched his powerful ass closed, but as I massaged and kneaded the muscle, then started lashing him with the flogger, which was still at hand, he started to acquiesce, and I was able to lick his puckered hole a couple times.

I squirted some lube onto my fingers and slid first one, then another of them into his anus. He was unbelievably tight. No wonder everyone was excited to see him bottom. Every time he tensed up at my manual intrusions, I only got rougher, really banging my fingers in and out of him until I had broken down his resistance.

When I finally thought he was ready, I stood up behind him and took hold of the arm restraints. I pulled him down so that his legs bent and his asshole was level with my crotch; then I nudged my joystick against his manhole. He tightened up again, but I was as solid as a piece of granite, so I just forced my way in, using the arm restraints to pull him painfully back toward me. He had no choice but to let me penetrate him.

I felt momentarily bad when he started to whimper, so I stayed still to let him get his bearings, but when he started to buck his hips up and back into me, I knew he was ready for his pounding.

Taking a firmer grip on the restraints, I kept him still, and I started to plunder his ass with long, searing strokes. I made him take my entire length, shoving up and into him until my balls slapped against his taint. His own balls were still hanging low, and each time my pelvis hit his juicy ass, they jiggled with the impact. I was really going to town now, looking down to see my huge white prick bury itself in the luscious darkness of Linus's black ass. He was starting to sweat with the effort of holding it together for me, and his muscles were bulging from the restraints. But he was going to have to do a little of the work himself.

"You didn't think I was going to do all the work, did you?" I asked him. "You're going to have to show me you can bottom any way I want."

I pulled out of him and then led him over to one of the chairs by the head strap of his ball gag. I was getting the hang of this. Sitting down in the deep armchair, I ordered Linus to lower himself down onto my cock, but not to sit on me. I mean, he was a huge guy, he would crush me. He had to straddle me, one leg on either side of my hips on the large chair, his arms bound behind him. It took him a second to get his balance, but he managed it, and quickly took my cock into his ass while I guided it into his anus.

He lowered himself almost completely onto me so that his ass rubbed against my thighs, but he was careful not to put any weight on me. I made sure of that by jerking his arm bindings as a warning. I used them to help him balance so he didn't fall off the chair as he raised and lowered himself up and down on my rod. As he got into the rhythm of it, he began to go faster and harder. His cock got completely hard again and would alternately slap his stomach and mine with the force of his springing. He had closed his eyes and let his head roll back, but I jerked him back to attention so that he was looking into my eyes as he fucked me.

I noticed a pool of drool forming at the edges of his mouth thanks to the ball gag, and I wiped it away with my hand, then rubbed it on my chest in a big wet mark. I made to take the gag off so that he wouldn't have that problem, but he shook his head. He liked being my bitch, and if that's what he wanted, that's what I was going to give him.

I let him fuck me like that for another few seconds; then I stopped him and made him spin around on my cock so we were screwing reverse cowboy style. I loved the sight of his huge back curving away from me, and the clear vista I had of his ass on my tool.

Holding on to the arm restraints, I kept him still, and I began to buck my hips, sending my cock farther and farther up into him. I was really thrusting with all the force I had, making a huge slapping noise with each movement of my hips. Linus was having a hard time keeping still while I kept up my assault, and he started to groan with what I thought was pain and also arousal since his cock was still stiff as a tire iron.

With my free hand, I reached around his huge leg and started to jerk him off, not taking care to be gentle, just trying to keep him excited. He responded intensely, jerking his hips and gyrating round and round on my pumping cock. We were a full-force fuck machine, and we were going full steam. Both of us glistened with sweat, but I hung on for dear life and just kept laying into him.

By the time his head started lolling, I realized that maybe he had had enough. I slowed my pace, then eventually stopped. I pushed him off of me, a little roughly, and walked around him so I could grab on to one of his nipples and pull him over to the couch like that. He winced in pain, and there was a fire in his eyes that unnerved me, but like he had said himself, I was committed, and I wasn't going to stop now. I showed no weakness, staring right back at him and daring him to try something.

"You've done a good job so far, but there's one last position you'll need to get in before I believe you can be a convincing bottom on film."

He nodded slowly at me, the drops of sweat standing out on his forehead. We were both flushed from all the sex, and I was surprised at my own stamina, but there was just something about the situation that made me rise to it.

"Because you've been so talented, I'm going to fuck you in a very special way," I told Linus as I started to get him into position. "You're going to be upside down, with your ass in the air and your head on the ground."

Immediately without my asking, he got into position so that his ass was supported by the edge of the sofa, and his shoulders were bearing his weight on the ground. I stepped up onto the sofa so that I was standing directly above him. His legs were spread apart so that I could have clear access to his abused fuck chute, which was pink from all the wear it had gotten so far. I asked him, "Do you need some more lube?"

He nodded his head like I knew he would, but I laughed cruelly and spat in his face, shouting, "Too bad! You're going to take it like it is, and you're going to like it."

With that, I abruptly turned around so that my back faced him, pointed my dick straight down, and squatted until I had entered him again. Then I started to dip and raise myself, fucking him slowly but brutally. The position was intense for both of us. My dick was being pulled downward, contrary to its usual upward curve, and getting rubbed all along the top, creating a concentrated sensation all along my genitals. That also meant it was prodding all kinds of places that Linus wasn't used to having reached, and he was shuddering with the new experience.

While I was fucking him like that, Linus had a front-seat view of my ass bobbing up and down. I had a great little ass—like that of a high school lacrosse player, all soft, white skin and tough, toned muscle. I started to fuck him faster so he could enjoy the performance even more.

My legs began to ache with the effort, but I was not giving up yet. I was so turned on, and I kept slapping Linus's ample buttocks, really getting into the act. Every thrust brought me closer and closer to ecstasy, and I could hear from Linus's whinnies that, though he was uncomfortable, he was coming to the edge as well. It was no small matter of pride to me that he was going to get off without having fucked me at all, or jerked himself off. I had plans for him, though.

With a few, final, frenzied drives, I was ready to blow. I pulled out of Linus, whipped off the condom, and jumped down from the couch. I kneeled next to him, asking him, "You want my cum, bitch? Is that what you want?" He nodded again, more energetically this time, and I said, "Good, 'cause you're gonna get it. You earned it."

Then I unleashed the floodgate and let wave after wave of orgasm overtake me, sending spumes of white jizz all over Linus's face and colossal chest. I kept jacking off, getting every last drop out of my balls, and shook them off onto Linus's face before rubbing my shaft in the pond of goo I'd poured on his face and neck.

I only took a moment to enjoy it, though, since I didn't want to lose momentum. Linus was still hard, and I quickly latched on to his cock with my hand, asking him, "You wanna come, too, bitch?"

Again, the nod, accompanied this time by a few hip thrusts, forcing me to jack him off faster. He tried to reposition himself, but I wanted to see his cum mingle with my own on his face, so I grabbed the arm restraint again and kept him pinned like that. He resisted for a moment, then realized it was futile, so he became docile, and his eyes rolled back in his head as I coaxed his orgasm from him.

I set to work on his ten-incher with both hands, using one to rub his knob and the other to work the sheath. Every now and then, I'd smack his balls to wake him up a little, but that only made him harder.

Within a minute or two, his cock started twitching on its own. I kept jerking, but as soon as I saw his perineum contract, I stopped jerking him, letting his body do the work as arc after arc of hot, white semen flew down from his dick and onto his face. One shot hit him in the eye, and he was forced to close it, but he just kept coming. Whatever I had done to him, it had worked out a bucket-load of cum.

I could smell the salty, creamy odor of our sperm all over him, and I could no longer distinguish between his load and mine. When he was finished shooting, a strand of the white goop hung tantalizingly from his cockhole, and I gently lapped at it with my tongue, just to take a taste. It was as good as I'd imagined, and I smiled down at him.

He started breathing more slowly and relaxing, so I gently undid the ball gag from his mouth and the restraints from his arms. We didn't speak as I turned him right side up so that he was sitting next to me on the ground. He rubbed his wrist, and I massaged his shoulders, restoring the circulation that had been cut off by the restraints. I wiped his face with my hand, removing our semen while he looked at me and grinned.

I grinned back, saying, "You're going to be a great bot-tom, you know? The film is going to be awesome."

"You want a role in it?" he asked me. "You were amaz-ing. I thought you'd never gotten into domination before."

"I haven't, this was the first time."

"I don't believe that. You were a natural."

"I had a good teacher," I replied.

"None of this is going in the interview, right?" he asked, laughing.

"Well, you never said 'off the record,' so . . . ," I began, joking.

He punched me on the shoulder, lightly, but still with some force. I raised my eyebrows and challenged him, "What, already up for round two?"

With that, he sneered, and grabbed my head to guide it back down toward his already reviving cock. . . .

What an in-depth interview that turned out to be.

Subject to Interpretation

There is an episode of *I Love Lucy* where Lucy gets arrested in Paris, and in order to explain herself and get out of jail, she has to tell her story to a police chief who only speaks French. So she tells Ricky her story in English and he translates it into Spanish for another man in jail who was arrested that night for drunkenness. The drunk speaks Spanish and German, so he tells it to another French policeman in German, who then tells it to his chief in French, sort of like an interpreter daisy chain. Well, I got stuck in a similar situation while trying to help my friend Barrett hit on a hot Brazilian guy named Rafael at a party.

If I'd had my druthers, I would not have even been at the party that night. I had just broken up with a guy named Dennis that I'd been dating for a few months, and I was down in the dumps big time. I had met a few nice boys out in Los Angeles since I'd moved there a few years earlier, but I had really thought that this one was something special. At the beginning, he had been so sweet, kind, and considerate. The sex was amazing at first, too. He was very flexible, so we got into all kinds of fun positions. Plus, he had a little thing for role-play, so we were always acting out kinky scenarios.

We had really seemed to connect quickly, and I thought things were going well until I left town for a short trip without Dennis, and when I came back, he started pulling away from me. I wasn't sure what was up, and I tried to have a conversation about it with him several times, but he said I was imagining things. I'm not the jealous type, and I completely trusted him, so I wasn't afraid he had cheated on me, I was just concerned that something had happened he wasn't telling me about.

As the weeks drew on and his behavior got more and more erratic, Dennis shrank away from me even more. By the end, we were barely even talking on the phone every other day, and we hadn't had sex in weeks. Finally, I had had enough. I told him I needed to see him immediately, and that we were going to talk.

I went over to his house that night with a bottle of wine and sat him down to discuss what had been going on. At first, he used all his same excuses—that I was imagining things, that he had been under a lot of stress at work, that sometimes he got scared of commitment. But I knew there had to be something else. The change had been so sudden and total that I had a feeling he was keeping something from me. I dreaded to learn what it was, but I had to find out.

After a couple glasses of wine and the threat of walking out of his life forever, I finally got Dennis to confess what had been bothering him. It turned out that while I was away on my trip, he had met someone else. I nearly dropped my glass, and I just stared at him in an inarticulate haze of anger and incredulity. What did he mean?

"Met someone else," was not exactly the right way to describe it. While I was gone, he had made plans with a bunch of his friends to keep busy and distract himself from my absence. One evening, he had one of his oldest, best friends in the city over to his house for dinner. I had met this friend before and gotten along great with him. He was funny, sweet, and obviously cared about Dennis a great deal. I secretly thought he might have a crush on Dennis, but I kept my opinion to myself, not wanting to interfere in their relationship. Things had been great between Dennis and me, so I didn't want to wedge myself between him and his friend.

Turns out my suspicions were dead on. Dennis's friend had come over for dinner, and before the evening was over, he had pled his undying love for Dennis. At first, Dennis hadn't known what to do. He thanked his friend and asked him to leave. When I got back to town, Dennis was still trying to sort out his feelings. On the one hand, he thought I was fantastic, but on the other, he had always wondered about being with his friend.

He had started treating me strangely because he was just unsure of what he should do. As time went on, he thought more and more that he would like to try things with his friend, but he did not know how to break up with me. A big part of him still wanted to be with me and not ruin things, but if he stayed with me, he would lose his best friend.

Finally, he had made his decision. His relationship with his best friend was just too valuable to him to lose. He had always wondered in his heart of hearts if the two of them could make a go of it, and he wanted to try. The only thing left to do was figure out how to tell me, and he had messed that up royally. He hoped that I could forgive him and understand why he was doing this. He did not want to lose me, but he knew that I would probably not want to be around him anymore, and he completely understood. He had been horrible to me, and I would be completely in the right never to have anything to do with him again.

I sat through this entire explanation in steely, disbelieving silence. When Dennis finished his speech, I just stared at him, daring him to say something else. I wished this was a bad dream that I would wake up from at any moment, but I knew it wasn't.

My mind worked furiously trying to figure out how to react and what to do next. Part of me wanted to ask if there was anything I could do to change Dennis's mind. Things had started so well for us, and I'd had such high hopes, I didn't want to let our relationship go after all the work I'd put into it.

Unfortunately, I was too proud to do that. After all of this and the way he had treated me, I could not bring myself to beg, so I got up without a word, grabbed my keys, and walked out the door. Dennis ran after me and tried to grab my arm before I got in my car, begging me to say something, but I shrugged him off and shut the door in his face.

I drove all the way home before I let myself feel the pain. I threw stuff all over my apartment and slammed my fist into the wall. I didn't cry—I was still too angry—but I could not believe this had happened. I spent that night and many after tossing and turning.

My friends slowly found out what had happened—we had a few acquaintances in common—and dutifully came over to comfort me and called me up all the time to make plans. My funk lasted several weeks. I just didn't want to see anyone, but my friends were too good to let me sit and wallow. They invited me out places, took me on weekend trips, or just out to dinner. One of them even tried to set me up on a date with a cute coworker of his, but I just couldn't go there quite yet.

One weekend about a month after all this happened, my friend Barrett called me up to ask me if I wanted to go to a friend's birthday party with him. I reflexively said no, but Barrett wasn't having it. He complained that he hadn't seen me in weeks, and that the party would be awesome. It was at someone's house way up in the Hollywood Hills, and there would be lots of good booze and hot boys.

I still tried to get out of it, but Barrett said he'd be over in an hour to pick me up, and that I should be groomed, dressed, and ready to go. Then he hung up. So I guessed I had no choice.

Barrett was a good friend of mine, and he had been entirely supportive of my relationship with Dennis. When it ended, he was the first person I told about what had really happened, and he had said all the right things to make me feel better. Maybe he was right, maybe a party was exactly what I needed. At the very least, I needed to get out of my apartment, and it had been ages since I'd shaved or given myself a mini-facial or anything like that, so it was a good excuse to primp.

An hour later, I looked at myself in the mirror and liked what I saw. The stress of the breakup had taken away my appetite, and I'd been logging long hours at the gym trying to work off the angry energy. The result was that I was as skinny and muscular as I'd ever been, and I was looking fucking hot. I only wished I'd had time to get a haircut since my straight brown locks were getting a little shaggy and falling in my hazel eyes, but I was pulling off a Beatles sort of thing, which looked messy and cool. I put on a cute Ben Sherman polo and my skinny jeans, and I was ready to go.

Barrett came a few minutes later, and wolf-whistled at me. I smiled appreciatively as I bounced into his car and off we went. Barrett was looking pretty good himself. He was a head taller than me, and had a long, lanky swimmer's frame bookended by big, manly hands and feet. His hair was straight like my own, but lighter, and much shorter. It contrasted dramatically with his big, bright blue eyes.

I lived pretty close to where the party was, but it took us a while to navigate the winding roads up into the hills and then to find a parking place anywhere near the house. When we had finally parked and taken one last look in the mirror, we flounced into the party.

It was already in full swing by the time we walked in, and we immediately saw several people we knew. Barrett was a trouper and ran interference so no one would question me about the breakup, and I made my way to the kitchen where everyone seemed to be emerging with drinks.

I explored the house a little on the way. Whoever's it was, it was one of those gorgeous mid-century modern stunners that seem to hang off the hillsides overlooking the entire panorama of Los Angeles. I really wanted to take our drinks out to the back patio where everyone was crowding around the pool and soaking in the nighttime view of the city. I poked my head into the three bedrooms, each more tastefully furnished than the last, and the home office, which was fully set up as a writer's oasis with several computers, a fridge, and a sofa and chair for lounging.

In the kitchen, everything was stainless steel and granite. It was as though I'd found my own dream house. Even the wineglasses and corkscrew I found were exactly where I would have put them myself. I felt like I was home.

I found Barrett on my route back to the living room and we made our way outside. Somehow we managed to score a couple of sunning chairs at one end of the pool, and took turns watching the city and the newcomers to the party. One of the reasons I loved hanging out with Barrett was that he rated every guy who passed through view, saying hilarious things and conjecturing who each of them was in real life. When we went out together, we often played a game making up back stories for people we thought looked interesting.

At one point, his constant stream of hilarity paused for a moment, and I looked around to see who had stunned him into silence. It didn't take long to zero in on the culprits. They were just Barrett's type. He was staring at two beautiful men who looked like they had just stepped off the plane from Rio. One was about my height with wavy dark brown hair lightened here and there with honey-colored highlights that looked natural and not at all tacky. His eyes were as dark as coal and looked vaguely sinister in a sexy, smoldering way. His tan was the color of mocha, and he seemed to smile a lot, which was charming. He had the hottest little body I had seen in quite a while, his ass filling out the back of his linen pants with a supple, firm roundness, and his arms were knotted with muscles that contracted every time he clapped his friend on the back or raised his drink to his lips.

His friend was a lighter skinned, more of an olive complexion, though with longer jet-black straight hair that was slicked back. His eyes were also some of the darkest brown I had ever seen, and he had some fur on his forearms and little chest hairs poking out of the collar of his polo shirt. I guessed that he was Italian. Both were in their mid-twenties.

I turned to Barrett and saw that he was still mesmerized. I feared he was in love already, and I joked so to him. He laughed, but continued to look at them until the first guy, the Brazilian (as I called him), looked back. The two of them played the eye-flirting game for a few minutes until it became clear that they were both interested. The Brazilian and Italian kept looking over at us and then conferring clandestinely. I thought they were both very handsome, but it still felt too soon to hit on another guy, so I tried to keep my gaze disinterested as I looked around the party.

A few minutes later, the game was still going on, and Barrett was trying to figure out whether he should go talk to them or wait for them to come to him, but I had had gotten sick of hearing about them, so I urged him just to get up and go over there. Fortifying himself with a gulp of his drink, he set down his cup and marched around the pool to where they stood.

I tried to watch as covertly as possible, but I was too interested in what was going to happen not to stare. I also just wanted to be aware of what was going on in case Barrett needed some backup or a little wingman action.

At first, he seemed to be doing really well. They all

shook hands and laughed at something. There was some pointing back and forth, and some gesturing, but after a minute or so, Barrett hadn't made any progress that I could tell.

They all seemed to like each other, but there was some sort of block to the conversation. The three of them weren't talking very much, and the two friends chatted a little between themselves but not to Barrett. He looked a little desperate, and looked around for me. When he caught my eye, he waved at me to come over. I tried to give him a reassuring nod to get back in the game, but he was having none of it, and only insisted more emphatically that I come over there.

I reluctantly left my lounge chair, skirted the pool, and stepped up to the spot where the three of them stood. Barrett looked relieved as he introduced me to the group, telling me that the first guy actually was Brazilian (good guess!) and that his name was Rafael, while his friend's name was Paolo. Paolo was also from Brazil, but as I'd find out in a few moments, his parents were actually Italian (another good guess!).

I shook hands with them, and then I realized that apart from a few words, neither of them spoke English. I grimaced at Barrett—what was he going to do? We conferred for a few seconds while Rafael and Paolo talked in Portuguese. Barrett knew I spoke several languages, so he asked me to try out a few on the boys. I almost groaned. Was it really worth the effort?

"Please, Brad, I need your linguistic...cunning," he said with an arch smile. Barrett had been such a good friend to me, I felt I owed him something.

Turning back to the Brazilians with a hopeful look, I

asked if they spoke Spanish. No. French? No. Italian? I braced for another no, when I heard *"Sì!"* instead.

As I mentioned, Paolo's parents were Italian and that is what they spoke at home. Within a moment, I got their whole story. The boys were friends just visiting California on their way to New York for vacation. Rafael had another friend from Brazil who lived in L.A. and had brought them to this party, only he had disappeared a little while ago and wasn't answering his phone, so they were just waiting around for him to show up again.

I relayed the information to Barrett and he got a hopeful grin on his face as he took it all in. He asked me to ask Rafael if he had a boyfriend. I blushed—what a bald question! But something about the booze and how nice the Brazilians were (and how hot they looked with their tans, and how good they smelled with their cologne) made me feel a little brash, so I asked Paolo. Paolo said no, but I told him to ask Rafael so he understood. When Paolo did so, Rafael looked faintly surprised, then smiled at Barrett and said, comprehensibly enough, "No."

Barrett smiled back at him, and the two stayed like that, grinning like idiots, for a couple seconds. I took the initiative and told Paolo to tell Rafael that Barrett didn't have a boyfriend either. He did so, and Rafael sidled over to stand next to Barrett.

Over the next few minutes, we all talked about where we were from, how old we were and all that. Rafael was twenty-five and Paolo was twenty-six. Both were from Sao Paolo, and this was their first time in the U.S. It was a shame they were leaving the next day for New York because they had not gotten to see much of Los Angeles. I said that next time they were in town we would be happy to show them around. Paolo and I were able to converse rapid-fire despite my rusty Italian, but I was always sure to check back in on Barrett and Rafael to see that they weren't getting bored, or to lend a helping ear if they wanted to exchange pleasantries . . . though after a few moments, it became clear that the only thing those two wanted to exchange was bodily fluids.

Paolo and I continued chatting, letting Barrett and Rafael flirt and get a little touchy-feely. Despite myself, I was having a good time chatting up these two handsome foreigners, and I had definitely gotten the more interesting one in Paolo. He was well educated, interesting, and despite not having traveled much, very cultured. We talked about all kinds of things, and I was fascinated to hear more about his life in Brazil. I had had no intention of getting physically involved with him when we'd started talking. I was doing this solely for Barrett. But as time wore on and we got deeper into conversation, I felt my inhibitions fading away, and I found myself wanting to kiss Paolo's wide, smiling mouth.

By this time, the party was starting to get a little rowdier. More people had shown up, and a lot of them had brought alcoholic reinforcements. People were swimming in the pool—some of them fully clothed—and the music was pumping. It got more and more difficult to hear one another, which was fine for Barrett and Rafael, because they were making out now as Paolo and I continued trying to talk.

Finally, Barrett came up for air, looked around, and said, "It's getting pretty crazy!"

I agreed, and he suggested we go somewhere quieter. I told Paolo, who told Rafael. They asked where we could go, and Barrett pointed to the guest cottage that was along a flight of steps farther down the hill. He started to lead the way. I was going to let Barrett and Rafael go alone since they were the ones who were interested in a little more intimacy, but Rafael grabbed Paolo's hand, and Paolo, smiling at me, took mine. I hesitated a moment, and in that moment, he leaned in and gently kissed me. When he pulled away, he brushed away my shaggy bangs to look straight into my eyes and smile. My heart pretty much melted, and I took his hand and followed the others down the hill.

We were all disappointed to find that the cottage was locked. I didn't blame the guy throwing the party. I wouldn't have wanted strangers ransacking my guesthouse either, but it definitely put a damper on our plans for the evening. Barrett was ready to turn back, but I stopped him and took a look around. Under one of the bushes, I spotted it: one of those fake rocks you hide a key in.

I had just felt like I knew where everything in the house was, I figured the owner would have the same idea I had about hiding the guesthouse key, and I was right. I opened up the rock and brandished the key triumphantly. When everyone was duly impressed (Paolo even gave me another peck on the cheek), I inserted the key in the lock, turned it, and . . . nothing.

The key fit, and it worked, but the door was stuck somehow, like the locking mechanism would not fully release. I embarrassedly tried the door again, but no luck. Each of us took turns trying to force it open, but it was stuck.

Biting his lip, Rafael pulled out his wallet and took out a credit card. Then he did that thing that burglars do in movies where they slide it along the door jamb and use it to jimmy the lock. I couldn't believe what I was seeing. More than that, I couldn't believe when it worked!

The door swung open and Rafael replaced the card in his wallet and sauntered in. I looked at Paolo quizzically and he explained that Rafael had a checkered past even though he was completely successful and legit now. I repeated this in English to Barrett, but he just shrugged his shoulders and followed his conquest in the door. Paolo went in next and I followed, closing the door behind us.

The cottage was a simple affair, just a large studio with a big bed, a kitchenette, a chair and love seat in the little living room area, and a bathroom. It was decorated in the same minimalist chic style as the rest of the house and felt like we'd rented a hotel bungalow somewhere in Hollywood. We left most of the lights off to avoid being noticed, but I turned on one of the bedside lamps and the light in the bathroom so we could see each other.

Barrett and Rafael lost no time stationing themselves on the bed, though they kept all their clothes on for the moment. Paolo pulled me over to the love seat and sat down next to me, his leg touching mine, and his hand curled around my own; then his tongue was in my ear, tickling me and turning me on all at the same time.

I closed my eyes and relaxed into it, letting him nuzzle my neck and massage my thigh with his strong hands. He rubbed the flat muscles of my stomach and the firm roundness of my pecs, all while whispering sweet nothings in my ear in Italian. Verses rolled off his versatile tongue with the slickness and sweetness of a gourmet chocolate.

I looked over to where Barrett and Rafael were going at

it on the bed. They already had their shirts off and were rolling around so much, it looked like they were in a wrestling match. I was mesmerized of the view of those two, with Barrett's creamy flesh entwined around the darker hued Rafael's sprawling limbs. Barrett used his size advantage to pin Rafael underneath him, and with his arm snaking down to Rafael's crotch, he soon had the Brazilian boy's pants unzipped and halfway off.

I could feel Paolo's hands taking an interest in my package at the same time. The blood was surging into my salami, and the more he squeezed it, the harder I got. I was wearing my skinny jeans, so there wasn't much latitude for my cock to maneuver, and it remained plastered to my inner thigh, running from my crotch eight inches down my leg. Paolo fondled it appreciatively as he brought his warm mouth up to my face, where mine was waiting to be kissed. Sucking gently on my lips with his, he bit my lower one lightly and smiled even as he kept kissing me. He smelled of Acqua di Gio and cocktails and hair product, and though I didn't normally find the Eurotrash aroma combination terribly sexy, in the moment, it drove me crazy with lust.

I'd had enough of this gentle foreplay, especially in contrast with what was happening between Barrett and Rafael on the bed. They had somehow both managed to get naked without us noticing, though one of their pairs of underwear (I'm guessing by the bright lime green color and skimpy cut that it was Raf's), came sailing through the air at one point, narrowly missing mine and Paolo's heads. Barrett and Raf were going full force, tongues down each other's throats, blazing erections frotting, backs arched as they dry-humped, hands groping each other's every inch of skin. Paolo had been good at taking charge so far, but I was going to show him how it was done.

Flipping so that I was on top of him on the sofa, straddling his lap, I broke off from kissing him to whip my shirt off over my head and placed his hands on my bare torso, encouraging him to rub me as hard as he wanted as I fell back upon his mouth and shoved my tongue into it. He seemed shocked at first, but only for a moment. Within seconds, he was kissing me back as hard as I was, and he had wrapped his strong, lean arms all the way around me, pulling me into a crushing but comfortable bear hug.

After a few moments, I was out of breath from our frenzied kissing, and I pulled away from him for a little pause. I took the chance to unbutton his shirt and slide it off his shoulders before slithering down his body, using my mouth to create a trail of slobber from his perfect but thin chest, down his tan stomach, to the furry patch surrounding his navel. I looked up to see how he liked it, and he was looking back down at me, smiling with those charcoal-dark eyes and silently urging me to go even further. Within another moment, I had his pants and underwear down around his ankles, and had placed a hand on either of his furry thighs while taking in the sight of his erect member.

Like I had noticed with Rafael on the bed, Paolo was uncircumcised, and his dark cock looked like a fat cigar. He rivaled me for length, measuring at least eight inches, even with the thick, loose foreskin fully pulled back from the pinker, squishy head. His dick was just the right girth so that I could only barely close my hand around its middle when I started to jerk him, producing a milky drop of precum at his tip almost immediately. His penis wasn't one of the prettier ones I'd seen. In fact, it was slightly gristled, covered with rubbery skin that was cross-hatched with big veins. His dense snarl of black pubic hair was only slightly trimmed, and hairs ran halfway up his enormous shaft. I usually liked a guy who was a little better manscaped, but I found his manliness so sexy that I couldn't wait to get that monster in my mouth.

We were still running behind Barrett and Rafael on the bed. Rafael was on his back, his legs pointing at us and spread so that I could see his huge donkey dong. It looked positively gigantic on his compact frame, and I guessed it to be at least nine inches of uncut meat. Barrett had assumed a push-up–like position toward Raf's head, his cock pointing directly down into Rafael's eager mouth, which Barrett was fucking with the consistent strokes of an oil derrick drilling for black gold.

Not to be left behind, I set to work on my man, knowing I was successful as soon as the first moans escaped his open mouth. He laid a hand on my head as I dipped it farther and farther down onto his hard piece of meat. When I pushed my mouth downward, his foreskin retracted and I was able to curl my tongue around Paolo's triangular glans. When I sucked back up, his foreskin followed the line of my mouth, pulling all the way back over his cockhead. It was a thick ring of rough skin, and it felt so different from the glossy smoothness of his little helmet head. I loved playing with it, seeing just how far past the tip of his cock I could get it to extend just by using my mouth, then how far down his shaft it would withdraw.

Running my tongue down the entire length of his shaft, and then sending my closed lips back and forth along the underbelly and sides of it, I teased Paolo into an ever higher state of excitement. His dick was twitching and jerking with a mind of its own. I concentrated my efforts on his hairy balls, like two brown coconuts hanging low and loose between his legs. They must have been two inches long each, and they lay relaxed next to each other like bronze door clappers until I sucked them each in turn into my mouth. That made Paolo groan even louder, and I looked up to make sure he was okay. His eyes were closed, his mouth agape, and he was pinching his dark nipples until they were an angry red color.

I looked over to see what Barrett and Rafael were up to, and found that they had switched positions, too. Rafael was on all fours, his ass presented for all the world to see. Barrett was directly behind him, his face buried in Rafael's luscious crack, and his head bobbling all over the place as he ate out the Brazilian. Rafael was apparently enjoying everything that was going on because he kept pushing his ass farther and farther back onto Barrett's face, and was jerking off his cock with abandon, his tan arm muscles flexing with each movement. I had never seen Barrett naked before this evening, but I got a perfect view of his thin little ass and the pink donut that it concealed, as well as of his tight round balls and his pale erection, which had to be at least nine inches long, but narrow and curved slightly downward like a watering can spout.

My own cock, meanwhile, was aching for some oral action, so I unbuckled my pants and pulled my underwear over my bulging erection and off. The band of my underwear caught on my dick, though, so when I pulled them even harder, as soon as they cleared my length, my meat sprang back up and slapped against my stomach. Paolo opened his eyes to see what I was doing and smiled as soon as he caught on. He reached down and grabbed hold of my instrument, using it to gently lead me to a kneeling position on the love seat; then he began to return the favor I'd just done him.

He was a talented cocksucker, alternating vigorous suction with daintier tongue twists. He didn't use his hands at all, as I had. Instead, he used his mouth to full effect, creating a warm, spongy, wet piece of heaven in his mouth. He made these nasty, hot burbling noises, like he was choking on my cock, and that only made me want to shove it even deeper down his throat. As far as I rammed it in, he could take it, and even seemed to like deepthroating me more than just blowing me. After cocking my hips a few times, I relaxed and let him take over at his own pace, just closing my eyes and enjoying all the sensations and shivers he was making shoot from the tip of my dick to my fingertips and toes.

I was brought out of my reverie a minute or so later by a muffled cry. Paolo and I both looked over to Rafael and Barrett to discover the source of this new noise. Rafael was on his back again, his legs thrown high in the air, resting lightly on Barrett's freckled shoulders. Barrett, meanwhile, had slipped on a condom and was kneeling in front of Rafael's ass, in the perfect position to penetrate his tropical love slave. Raf had angled his ass up in the air slightly so Barrett could have easy access. Even so, Barrett's long, thin prick was no easy thing to squeeze in, so Rafael was whimpering and gasping in both pain and rapture. Barrett helped ease the struggle by jacking off Rafael's enormous tool. That seemed to make Rafael relax, and in one swift, fluid motion, Barrett had managed to bury his sword up to the hilt in Rafael's sumptuous inlet.

I didn't realize it, but I had been holding my breath, waiting to see what had happened. When I looked back down at Paolo, I saw that he, too, had been spellbound by the unfolding sexual drama. But then he looked back up at me and smiled, waggling his eyebrows at me like he'd just had an idea. He raised himself up so we were eye level and planted a sensual, long kiss on my lips. Then he stood up and extended a hand to me. I stood up, too, taking it, and followed him over to the bed.

I had a twinge of trepidation as we approached our two friends. Barrett and I often talked about sexual things, but we'd never been in a situation like this before. Neither of us was interested in dating the other, so I thought this might be okay—something we laughed about later on—but I still looked at him questioningly as I took up the position to which Paolo guided me right over Rafael's open mouth. Barrett grinned and gave me a friendly nod to let me know that whatever I did was okay, then went back to ramming Raf with his shaft.

Paolo had me sit on my knees just above Raf's head, facing Barrett. Then, just as Barrett had done earlier from the other direction, I pointed my still-hard cock straight down into Raf's mouth. Rafael immediately started suckling the sensitive tip of my meat, making me moan and squirm with pleasure as I looked on to see what Paolo was doing. He had taken up a stance directly in front of Barrett's face. Barrett looked past Paolo's narrow hips to where I squatted over his lover, and I gave a little shrug and a smile to let him know that it was okay with me. So Barrett started sucking Paolo's leathery man muscle while continuing to nail Raf.

For his part, Rafael had started pivoting his head up and down like he was doing some kind of demented impression of a pigeon, giving me a totally upside-down blowjob that was rocking my world. His tongue was hitting all the right nerves along the topside of my dick, while the underside of it cradled cozily in the bowl of his hard and soft palates. Then he relinquished my hard meat, sending it slapping back up into my belly as he began to lick playfully at my balls. They were hanging low and tender, like ripe cherries ready to be plucked, and Rafael was having fun running his tongue into every little groove of the smooth scrotal skin that covered them. My favorite part was when he would moan every so often at the ass-slamming that Barrett was delivering farther down the bed. It would make Rafael breathe hard onto whatever part of my anatomy he was sucking on at the moment, and the vibration of his vocal cords sent shivers down my spine each time he uttered a sound.

I couldn't see much of what Barrett was doing with Paolo's cock, but his head was in constant motion, and Paolo's ass kept clenching, then relaxing, so whatever it was, it must have been good. Personally, I was just enjoying the view of Paolo's olive-toned buttock's suspended directly in my face.

I'm not sure who initiated the position change, but before I knew it we were all in different places. Barrett was lying on his back and pointing his cock straight up in the air like a bare flagpole. Rafael quickly plunked himself down on it to ride Barrett in a reverse cowboy, setting the pace himself this time. I just watched for a moment as he ground his hips back and forth over Barrett's crotch. His lower back and tailbone looked so limber as he used them to hump Barrett's disco stick.

Paolo wasn't done using Barrett's mouth yet. He had positioned himself sort of like I had been in our last configuration, his package dangling right over Barrett's face. But he wasn't interested in a blowjob this time. Instead, he slowly lowered his ass crack right into place over Barrett's mouth and nose. Not having to concentrate on fucking Raf in this position, Barrett eagerly went to work tossing Paolo's salad, lubricating that jungle of black hairs with copious amounts of spit.

I had stood up on the bed, and Rafael pulled me by the hips over to stand in front of him to start blowing me again, but I knew that if he kept going, I'd blow my load too soon, so instead, I crouched down on the mattress in front of Rafael and set to work sucking his massive tool, then alternately licking his balls and Barrett's. Raf's tasted like the familiar, musky aroma of a nutsack that has not had a bath in a few hours, while Barrett's tasted pretty neutral, with just the faintest trace of soapy scent to them. They were getting saltier by the second, though, as all four of us worked up a sweat.

It was no easy task to keep my mouth glued over Raf's banana. Like I mentioned, it was huge, especially for his size, so I had to open wide to be able to swallow it. He was also riding Barrett like a pro, gyrating his hips all over the place, lifting almost all the way off Barrett's cock, then slamming himself back down. It was all I could do to stay in place, but then again, I wasn't at that difficult assignment too long before I saw Paolo raise himself off Barrett's mouth and come up beside me in a position on all fours.

Barrett looked over at me and said, "I've gotten him all ready for you. Condoms are in my back pocket."

"Thanks," I answered, grinning stupidly. I reached down to grab Barrett's pants and found a condom packet. While I was getting into position behind him, Barrett and Rafael assumed the same pose as us right next to me. Since they were already warmed up, Barrett had slid himself back into Rafael and was pounding him apace. I took my time unrolling the condom onto my dick, then rubbed it for a couple seconds with a wad of my slippery spit so that I would not chafe Paolo when I penetrated him.

He had relaxed his back so that his asshole was pointing straight at me, giving me a clear route. I scooted up behind him, then ever so gently, I pushed the tip of my cock directly into the center of his furry bull's-eye. Paolo grunted as the thick crown of my wang pushed past his sphincter, but after that, it was a straight shot into the cavern of his ass, and my shaft pushed forward with relative ease.

Almost immediately, Paolo started grinding his ass on my cock, and I let him have his fun getting himself anally aroused before showing him the real hammering he was in for. His grunts got louder as he pushed himself back onto me harder and harder, and I got so turned on watching his ass cheeks spread to swallow my cock down to the balls. His arms were flexed as he leaned on them, and his back muscles were all knotted and glistening with a sheen of sweat.

Reaching around to hold on to the front of his hairy thighs, I hunched my back so that my torso leaned over his, and I could feel his sweaty body warmth and smell his manly scent wafting up from his pits. Slowly at first, I started pumping my hips up and into him, aiming directly for where I knew his prostate should be. I must have hit it on the first try because he started to groan loud and long, and rather than trying to fuck me, he had enough trouble just staying in place on his knees as I poked all the way into him. Now that he knew who was boss, it was time to give him what he had coming.

I straightened back up and started to fuck him with straight, simple strokes. As soon as he had gotten used to that, I extended them, pulling all the way out of his ass, then penetrating him all over again. Each time I exited him, he moaned, but each time I crammed my cock back into his ass cavity, he positively whinnied. When he was properly tenderized, I shortened my strokes only slightly so that I would not have to reenter him each time, but I kept up the same force.

Paolo laid his head down on the mattress, unable to concentrate on anything else but the ass battering I was giving him. I chipped away at his resistance from every angle, swirling my hips in circles, varying the trajectory of my strokes, sometimes punching up and into him, sometimes crouching in a squat and digging my dick into his very depths. I was out of breath and dripping with sweat, just like Paolo, but I was smiling and having the time of my life.

I looked over at Barrett and Rafael to find Barrett eyeing me with newfound admiration. He was giving Rafael a pretty good pounding, and the two of us settled into a pace, watching our Brazilian buddies take everything we had to throw at them. We kept at that for another minute or so, mirroring each other, and I even threw my hand over Barrett's shoulder for balance. We were both damp with perspiration, and our camaraderie was sort of like that of teammates fresh from a big victory. I wanted to try one more thing before we all finished, though, so I told Barrett to follow my lead.

Pulling out of Paolo, I arranged him so that he was lying on his side along one of the long edges of the bed, his head toward the top of the mattress and facing the middle. He was far enough from the edge so I'd have space to lie behind him. Then I placed Rafael the same way, only in the opposite orientation, with his head toward the foot of the bed but also facing the middle. I placed the boys right next to each other so that, if Barrett and I weren't there, you'd think they were 69-ing, and in fact, that is exactly what they started to do. Rafael swallowed Paolo's prick all the way down his dirty little gullet, while Paolo went to work squeezing his mouth around Raf's monster.

Barrett and I, meanwhile, took up our positions behind our respective boys, hoisted their top legs in the air, and burrowed our snakes into their welcoming ass caves. I loved that position, kind of like you're spooning your lover, and I wrapped my arms around Paolo's lithe body. He was using one hand to jerk of Raf's penis, but with his other, he reached behind me to clasp my ass, sending me into himself more vigorously with each hump. Barrett was kissing Raf's neck and back as he pummeled his hole. We each sent our boy's cock farther into the other's throat as we plugged their holes harder and harder, pushing deeper and deeper with each thrust.

We were all packed together in one tight, sweaty, breathless cluster, and we were all fast approaching the finish line, but I had no idea who was going to go first. Raf won that race. I saw him go completely rigid and his jaw slacken around Paolo's meat. Then his hips were bucking and twitching even while Barrett kept up his pace, squeezing every last drop of semen out of that boy's innards. Raf's dick engorged several times as he sent his load into Paolo's open mouth.

I heard Paolo gulp mouthful after mouthful of Rafael's juice down, and smiled when I saw that he had managed to keep his mouth glued to Raf's colossal cock the whole time. I nailed him with even more enthusiasm, sure that he was going to be next. Turns out I was right, because just after Raf had finished his own orgasm and had begun to suck Paolo off again, Paolo's ass muscles tightened and began to spasm around my cock. He grabbed hold of Rafael's wavy brown hair and crammed his eight-incher all the way into it as he shot his wad. I kept up my pounding and hit every fiber of pleasure in his body as he emptied his balls into Raf's mouth.

When he was finished, he went limp with one last moan. Like Barrett already had with Raf, I pulled out of him and snapped the condom off my dick. Barrett was on his knees jacking off over Raf's prostrate body, and in seconds, he was turning a bright red as he held his breath for the last sprint toward ejaculation. When he blew out his lungful of air, I knew he was about to shower us all with his cum, and he exploded all over the bed. He had always told me he was a big cummer, but I had no idea of the scope until that moment. He must have shot almost a half cup of his man juice that time, and he sent it as far as eight feet away, arcing high across the mattress and onto the floor. The following shots drizzled over all of us but landed mostly in white splotches and spurts on Raf's tan body. I felt a few of the warm drops hit my shoulder and arm but didn't care much because I was going to cum any second myself.

Paolo had regained his senses and scooted around so that his face was beneath my undercarriage as I sat back on my knees and jerked myself to completion. I could feel a massive surge rising within the pit of my stomach that intensified as Paolo began to lick at my constricted ball-sack. His tongue tickled the hairs that lined it, sending tingles up my entire shaft. Suddenly, the vague, deep itch that had permeated my body concentrated to a single point at the tip of my cock, and the first wave of semen pumped up from my testicles, down the length of my shaft, and out my piss slit. It was hot, thick, and as white as heavy cream, but it flew almost as far as Barrett's cumshot had, landing on the floor past the edge of the mattress with a loud splat. I was seeing stars as the next swell of gratification overtook me, and I had to lean forward on one of my arms as I continued to discharge my jizz. It landed in viscous white lines up and down Paolo's dark torso, and even on his legs and feet. Finally, I gingerly wrung the last, thick blobs of it down my cock to the tip, where they hung like heavy raindrops.

Paolo inched forward so that he was right under my cock tip, and he curled his tongue up to taste the last few drops of my essence. I shivered as his rough tongue rubbed the sensitive end of my knob, and nearly fell over when he swallowed the whole crown and sucked out my very last dregs of fluid.

After another moment, I collapsed on the bed between him and Raf, who was cuddling with Barrett. I turned to face Paolo, and with a *"grazie,"* I began to kiss him, tasting my own saltiness on his lips.

We all relaxed for a few minutes, cleaning up in the bathroom one by one and then getting dressed. I straightened up the guesthouse and we all managed to sneak out without being noticed.

Back up at the party, it had gotten a little calmer, though not much. Paolo and Rafael still couldn't find their friend, so we told them we'd take them back to his apartment. As we made for the door, I saw someone familiar out of the corner of my eye. I turned to look and saw Dennis standing there. He was with his new boyfriend, and neither had noticed me, but they were standing directly in our path to the exit.

I had a minor panic attack, fixing my hair and straightening up my shirt. Barrett saw Dennis and exchanged a worried look with me. Paolo had picked up on my anxiety, too, though, and asked what the problem was. I quickly explained the situation to him and told him that my ex was by the door with his new boyfriend and that I was embarrassed to see him. Paolo understood what I told him and relayed it to Rafael, who glanced scornfully at Dennis; then he smiled back at me with a mischievous look in his eye.

In mile-a-minute Portuguese, he hatched a plan with Paolo, and before I knew it, both of them had their hands wrapped around my waist and were guiding me to the door, right past Dennis. He turned to look at the two handsome strangers, and as he saw me, he got a surprised look on his face.

"Brad! I . . . how are you doing?" he asked, looking curiously at my two new friends.

"I'm fine," I said curtly, barely taking the time to stop in front of him.

"Good, I'm glad to hear it. Who are your new friends?"

he asked, now completely confused. His boyfriend had also turned to look and was blushing a bright crimson.

Understanding that Dennis was talking about them, Paolo and Rafael just smiled at him, then each in turn, they planted a delicious, lingering, wet kiss right on my lips. I nearly popped another boner right then and there, but I kept my wits about me, and as soon as Paolo had withdrawn his mouth from mine, I just shrugged my shoulders at Dennis, and said, "No time to explain, the boys and I are on our way out for the night. Have fun."

And with that, we were out the door, Barrett giving Dennis one last sidelong glance as he followed us out and shut the door behind us.

"Man, that felt good!" I told Barrett as we all got in his car. I thanked the boys, and Paolo said Dennis must have been an idiot to break up with me for that other guy. I said that I realized it wasn't the fact that he had broken up with me, but the way he had done it.

"After all," I said with a little chuckle, "communication is the most important thing of all. Even if you don't speak the same language . . ."

The Casting Session

When I moved from New York to Los Angeles, it was to start a job in film. I was lucky in that I'd put out the feelers before I had moved, and by the time I got to California and found an apartment, I had also landed a job at a small production company. I thought it would only be temporary and that I'd move on to more companies to work on different projects and learn other sides of the business, but as it turned out, I stayed at that same production house for several years.

During my time there, I did everything from mundane tasks like running the office administratively to chauffeuring producers' kids around to after-school activities to being an on-set gofer, as well as more advanced work like developing scripts with writers, meeting with studio executives, and even trying to set up my own projects. I knew that eventually I wanted to be a screenwriter, but the job seemed like a great opportunity to learn about the elements of how a film comes together.

As time passed and I'd worked for my company for more years, I became increasingly responsible and senior within it. My bosses started letting me do things independently as I worked on more films with them, and eventually, they were letting me run meetings and be the on-set point person.

One of my biggest new responsibilities was running casting sessions for our films. Over the years, I had forged relationships with the casting directors who worked with us, and eventually, I was so good at that part of the job that my bosses left it in my hands to do preliminary screenings before we brought in actors for the directors of our films to see and audition for real.

We worked on all kinds of films from period pieces to black comedies to family dramas to musicals. Often, we had several projects going at once, so everyone had a huge amount of responsibility, and I took over as the main contact on a few of the projects.

During one of those busy periods, we got the green light from the studio on a teen comedy we had been developing for years. Since I was the person at the company who had put in the most work on the script, was closest with the writer, and had really lobbied for it with the studio, I was given the go-ahead by my bosses to start setting up the production office and bringing in people for auditions.

The pivotal role in the film was that of the high school quarterback. This kid needed to be handsome, sympathetic, intelligent, and funny. Basically, the character was the guy I'd always wished I could have found and dated in high school. He was the emotional and comedic heart of the film. Once we found an actor for that role, the rest would fall into place.

I went ahead and called one of the casting directors we worked with a lot to set up the initial screen tests. I fully trusted them to bring in some great unknown actors looking for a break. The film did not have much of a budget, so we couldn't go for a big star, but I knew there were enough hot young male actors (and had dated a few of them!) out there that it should not have been hard to find someone appropriate.

Little did I know the difficulties we would have. Though the film was a generic teen comedy, the role did have some meat to it, so we couldn't just hire a handsome bonehead. We needed an actor who exuded confidence and smarts as well, though he also had to look like the gorgeous boy next door.

Day after day of screen tests passed, with each actor coming off more horribly than the last. Sure, they were pretty to look at, but after five minutes with each of them, I was ready either to fall asleep or shoot myself. Then I would have to review their auditions for my bosses, which was even more painful since they came off even worse on film, and it was making me look bad.

Those days reminded me of why I had a rule not to date actors. They were either self-absorbed egomaniacs or clueless airheads . . . or a combination of the two. It takes a special kind of person to go into acting in Hollywood, and being a successful actor requires a single-mindedness that I found off-putting.

What was even worse was when these straight guys who spent all their days in the gym working one muscle group or another would have zero personality but, trying to be charming, would flirt with me anyway in the hopes it would help them land the part. In my personal life, I might have had a thing for the straight-acting, wholesome boys, but as a professional, I was all business, and I did not have time for these games.

As the days wore on and we still hadn't cast the quarterback, I was starting to feel the pressure to find the right actor. Time was running out. We would have to cast the rest of the roles and start the transition from pre-production to actual production. Our start date was fast approaching, and I needed to do my job.

At the end of another long, miserable day of casting, cooped up in a tiny room at the production offices instead of enjoying the fresh air and sunshine of a California spring day, I was ready to call it quits. There was one more actor on the docket for the day, but he had called to say he was running late. I was working with the casting director's assistant, but I told her I could handle filming a single screen test and sent her home for the day.

While I was waiting for the actor to arrive, I went over my notes from the day and tried to figure out what I would tell my bosses when I called them for an update that evening. I prayed that the next actor would be *the* one for the role, but I knew that it was unlikely.

As I was reading through one of my reviews, I heard a knock at the door.

"Come in!" I yelled, still looking down.

The door opened and I heard someone walk in and clear his throat. When I finished reading, I looked up.

"Uh, hi. I'm Owen, I'm here to read for the part of Billy, the quarterback?" he said hesitantly.

I didn't answer immediately because I was dumbstruck. In a good way. Owen looked *perfect* for the part. He had big blue eyes, curly brown-blond hair, and a perfect smile that stretched from ear to ear. He had a cute button nose with freckles on either side of it, though the rest of his fair skin was completely blemish free. His forehead and eyes were unlined, though he looked like he was maybe in his early twenties. He had a relaxed, easy way of moving, and he was wearing dark blue jeans, black Chuck Taylors, and a tight (but not too tight) white V-neck T-shirt that showed off the hours he had clearly been logging either at the gym or on his surfboard. The white of the shirt set off his modest tan beautifully, and I noticed a few little blond chest hairs poking up from the collar of his V-neck. He was the boy next door you were always in love with. So far so good.

I told him to come in and take a seat. I filmed him as I asked him a couple questions about himself. He had just moved to Los Angeles a few months earlier to start a career in modeling but had already gotten a film agent and was being sent out on auditions for roles like this one. Originally he was from a town in Michigan on the shores of Lake Superior, and his family owned cherry orchards. Best of all, he had actually been the quarterback of his high-school team! Though he admitted with a blush that they hadn't been very good.

I was instantly charmed. Unlike the sullen one-word answers other actors had given, Owen spoke volubly, coloring his stories with amusing anecdotes and factoids that revealed a playful but focused personality. He seemed a little nervous—fidgeting and running his hand through his hair every now and again—but I didn't blame him. This was a big audition for him and he wanted to do well.

After a few minutes, during which I laughed at most of the things he said, I ran lines from the audition scene with him. His first reading was already leaps and bounds above what I'd seen so far from others, but I needed to see how well he took direction. I set the scene for him, talked about his motivation and what his character was trying to accomplish; then I told him to try it again. He furrowed his brow in the cutest way as he concentrated on what I was saying, then launched into the scene again and nailed it.

I gave him another direction to go in, telling him to pretend that this scene was with another character—a girl he wanted to convince to get into bed with him, and that every line had a subtext with that motivation. I described a gorgeous woman to him to give him a good image to have in mind, and I saw him blush and bite his lip as I was talking. I reassured him that he was doing great; then we started the scene again.

His performance was so understatedly sexy and beguiling, I nearly forgot to say some of my lines. It was hard concentrating on the lines and filming at the same time, but I was getting great footage of him to show my bosses, and I was sure they were going to love him. He pulled off the sexual subtext perfectly, and seemed so confident and suave, but when we finished the scene, he was back to his nervous self, smiling anxiously at me and asking if there was anything else.

"That's it!" I said, hitting the "Pause" button on the camera and looking up at him. "That was really good. I'm sure everyone is going to love the screen test."

"You think so?" he asked, breathing out heavily as though he couldn't believe he'd done well.

"Absolutely. You're definitely the best I've seen so far, and I'm going to pull for you. I think you'd be perfect for the role."

He was biting his nails now, so I decided to say something. "But I'm only going to give you a little piece of advice. You have the acting skills to pull this off, and you obviously have the looks to be a movie star, plus you're outgoing, so don't be so nervous."

He immediately stopped biting his nails, suddenly aware of his bad habit. He also stopped fidgeting. "That's better," I said. "The bottom line is, your acting skill level doesn't have much to do with whether you get a part anyway. You're talented, so you're already there. It all comes down to whether or not you look like the person a casting director pictures in the role, and there's not that much you can do about that."

"Yeah," he said. "Thank you. I was just really nervous. I'll try not to be if you decide to bring me back in for a callback."

"But you did a great job. What were you nervous about? The scene? The directions? Are you afraid you can't pull off the part?"

"No, that's not it," he began. "It's just, most casting directors are dumpy older women, so it's easy to act natural around them and just sort of perform and get out of there, but you're . . . you . . ."

"I what?" I asked, both ready to be flattered, but also dreading a clumsy attempt at flirting to curry my favor.

"Well, you know how I got flustered when we did the scene the last way? With the, you know, the girl?"

"You blushed. Was I too graphic or something? Did I embarrass you?"

"It's not that," he said, his lovely eyes still downcast as he fidgeted with his hands in his lap. Each time he moved them, it made his beautifully veined biceps and forearms flex, making it hard to concentrate on what he was saying, but he continued, "When you were describing how to do the scene and telling me to picture a girl I was trying to get into bed . . . well, I wasn't picturing a girl." He looked up at me, unsure of whether he should go on.

I wasn't sure where this was heading, so I said, "No? What were you picturing?"

Taking a deep breath, he said, "Well, I was actually imagining that you and I had met somewhere else and started talking, and that it was you I was having that conversation with." He watched me to see how I would react. I myself wasn't sure. I didn't like to mix business with pleasure, but I could see that he was being honest and not just trying to get into my good graces.

"I see," I said, walking over to him and standing very close. "And what else would you have done to accomplish your objective in the scene?"

"I might do this," he said, running his fingers through my long brown hair. "Or this," he said, then pulling my face toward his and lightly brushing his lips against mine.

"I think you can do better than that," I said, grinning. "You really need to commit to it, make it convincing."

He smiled back at me, then pulled me in again, this time really kissing me with his full, pink lips and running his tongue into my mouth for a second as a nice little tease. I embraced him and felt the ripped muscles of his back relax into my grip as we pressed our bodies into one another's. He had the physique of the high school quarterback he was auditioning to play, with broad shoulders that were muscular but not too beefy, and a narrow waist that was trim and toned from hours of doing crunches each week. His pert little ass fit perfectly in my hands, and I loved the feel of his hard chest against my own as we made out.

When we pulled apart a few moments later, I tugged at his shirt a little and suggested, "That was much better, but let's see how you do with taking even more directions."

He looked puzzled, and I wasn't sure he was going to go for it, but I had always fantasized about this very situation, and I wasn't going to let it go unfulfilled. Stepping back from him and walking over to where the camera waited paused. I took out the audition tape and put in a new one so he could see this was for fun; then I pushed the button to record, looked him with half-playful, half-sadistic smile, and said, "Let's get started."

"What would you like to see?" he asked, suddenly his smooth-talking onscreen persona again.

"Everything. But we'll get to that. First, I want you to take off your shirt like you've waited for this moment your entire life."

His face took on a smoldering expression, but I could see a hint of vulnerability that made part of me feel bad for taking advantage of him like this (though he was the one who'd made the first move, after all), but that thrilled another part of me so much that my heart started racing.

Keeping eye contact with me, and pouting slightly in a defiant, sexy way, he ever so slowly pulled his shirt up, revealing the hard knots of muscle of his six-pack one by one. Then he raised the hem of the shirt level with the grooves where his pecs stood out from his rib cage, then an inch farther so that I could see his bright pink nipples standing erect from the surrounding tan skin of his chest.

He deliberately removed one arm and then the other

from his sleeves, and finally, he pulled the shirt over his head, ruffling his curly hair. Owen balled up the white cotton in his hands, then held it straight out from his body with one arm and let it fall to the floor. When he was done, he stood there facing me, hand on his hip, and asked, "How was that?"

I swallowed, then responded coolly, "That was very good. But it's just a start."

Arching an eyebrow, he asked, "What next?"

"I want to see your underwear."

Without saying a word, Owen unbuttoned his jeans and then played with the zipper between his two fingers. Looking back up at me behind the camera, he smirked and said, "But I'm not wearing any."

With that, he unzipped his fly about two inches so that I could see a small nest of light brown pubic hair. Turning so that his back was to me, he unzipped his pants even farther and let the waistline fall slightly over the subtle curve of his ass, revealing a tan line on his bare skin.

"Show me what you'd do if you were thinking about me alone in your room tonight," I directed him.

Looking back over his shoulder at me seductively, he began to run his hands all over his body, raising goose bumps on his skin. He flexed his various muscles, first his shoulders, then his triceps and his back. Turning around to face me, he slipped a hand into his pants so that it covered his crotch, though it could not hide the fact that his bulge was getting bigger by the second.

Still cradling his package with a hand, he began to rub it and massage it, coaxing it to life while swiveling his hips suggestively. With his other hand, he groped his own pecs, pinching his nipples repeatedly and kneading the muscles of his chest before caressing his throat and neck, then rubbing his washboard stomach.

Kicking off his shoes and socks, he continued to play with himself without revealing what exactly he was packing under those jeans, and I began to get hot and bothered, both wondering what I would find when he removed his pants, as well as trying to restrain myself from ripping them off myself.

In another moment, he had his pants down around his ankles, and he kicked those off as well, then stood facing me. Still, he wouldn't show me his cock, but I knew that would come soon enough. Instead, he turned most of the way around again, though he kept his face turned toward me. I stayed exactly where I was, and he could tell that I could not see his dick from my perspective, so he decided to tease me. Still staring at me, he went glassy-eyed as he began to stroke himself with his hand. Watching his arm motion back and forth along his dick—what I imagined it to look like, at any rate—was almost too much for me. I wanted to jerk him off myself, but I was getting so turned on just passively observing that I could feel my own member growing turgid in my shorts.

He flicked his tongue across his lips to wet them, then bit the lower one as he moaned softly. Clearly, his manual session was going well and he wanted me to know it.

"That's very good," I said softly, "but I'm going to have to see how committed you are. Show me."

Smiling coyly at me, he turned back to face me, letting go of his cock and placing both hands on his hips so that I could see him in all his glory. He looked like a porn star who could headline all my dreams. His athletic body, rock solid from head to toe, was perfectly muscled, while his all-American face was a stunning combination of whole-someness and sexy allure. In truth, though, my eyes darted immediately to eye the treasure that had been hidden from me thus far.

His filigree-thin happy trail of dark hairs led down to a carefully tended trapezoid-shaped fluff of pubic hair. It narrowed down as it descended toward his genitals but was completely shaved above his stalk, as was the stalk itself and his low-hanging balls, the right one drooping farther down than the left. He had shaved it that way to give himself greater visual impact, but he didn't need much help.

His erect penis was lean and long, a good eight inches, and maybe four in circumference. It was slightly darker than the rest of his fair skin, as were his balls, but every so often, the tan skin was punctuated by a freckle or two, and there were several dotting the spongy head. I found it so cute, and I just wanted to suck it.

But this wasn't about me. I wanted to see how he could perform. "Now show me how you get off when you're alone."

Without questioning me, he began to rub his cock with his right hand while fondling his balls with the left. He didn't have any lubrication, but that didn't seem to bother him. He simply left his hand loose and limp as he ran it back and forth along the length of his shaft, the friction making the skin rosy and pink within a minute or so.

His balls reacted to his attentions by curling up tight into his body, but he kept them hanging out by tugging down on them every so often. He changed up his jerking technique from time to time, first using both hands to stimulate his rod like he was rubbing a twig to make fire, then like he was rolling a cigar. He would spend a few seconds concentrating on just the head, twirling his hand round and round it. Sometimes he would tickle his skin just with his fingertips, and others, he would squeeze his cock hard enough that I saw the veins pop out on his arms.

Meanwhile, his eyes closed to slits and I could tell that he was fantasizing about something. "What are you picturing?" I asked him.

Opening his eyes slightly, he looked straight at me without blinking and replied, "You. Naked."

"Let me see if I can help you with that," I told him, more than flattered. Mimicking his earlier performance, I slowly removed my shirt to reveal a torso that had turned to sinew and muscle thanks to countless yoga classes, morning swims, and hikes in the mountains outside L.A. I was lean and wiry but still solid, and I flexed in a few different positions to give him some eye candy.

With each of my movements, Owen's jacking became more intent, more hurried. He liked what he was seeing, and it was translating into his work. He spat down onto his right hand and rubbed the natural lube onto his cock so that each time he stroked it, it gave a little squeaking sound. He was masturbating so hard now that he was growing short of breath, and his skin had started to splotch red here and there from his body heat. A trickle of sweat dripped from each armpit down the side of his rib cage.

I wanted to see just what I could make him do, so I had one more request for him. "Sit down on the chair again," I ordered him, "your back to me." He did as he was told, sitting backward on the chair.

"Good, now lean back until your head and shoulders are on the floor and your package is hanging right over your face."

Getting the idea, Owen grinned at me, then did as he was told. "How does that feel?" I asked him as he resumed his duties. "You gonna come for me soon?"

"Oh yeah, anytime you want it," he answered.

I could see he was telling the truth. Where his trail of precum had been a mere dribble before, now it was oozing steadily out of the cratered hole at the tip of his cock, and it would be only a matter of minutes before he was spewing his whole load all over.

"Good, you just work it up nice and good, and when you're ready to shoot, I want you to aim for your mouth. Understand?"

"Uh-huh," he gasped out as he continued to yank furiously. His breathing came quicker and quicker, and he emitted sporadic moans and whining sounds. This boy really knew how to get himself off. I wanted to help him finish, but I stood transfixed behind my camera, recording it all.

When he was ready to blow, he announced several times, each louder than the last, that he was going to come. Finally, he went completely rigid, his legs straightening and toes pointing toward the ceiling, his stomach tightening, and his balls pulling up into his body. His hand squeezed more firmly around his flesh rocket, and he began to send jets of white goo arcing down onto his face. The first few shots hit his forehead, ear, and cheek, but he managed to get a few huge gobs of his juice into his mouth, and he licked eagerly at the drops that landed near his mouth and chin. With each shot, he went rigid, then relaxed, then seized up again to send another volley of jizz down onto himself.

Nearly a full minute later, after a dozen loads, Owen concluded his performance, giving his softening prick a few last strokes to wring out the dregs before slumping down on the floor and breathing in deeply.

I picked my jaw up off the floor and approached him warily. Kneeling on the floor next to him and smiling, I used my fingers to wipe at the drips of cum still on his sweaty face, scooping them up and dropping them into his waiting mouth, which was smiling back up at me.

"You like that? Does that taste good?" I asked him.

"Uh-huh," he said.

"Good. You want to eat my cum, too?"

"Mmm, yeah," he said, licking at my finger and then sucking the whole thing into his mouth. "Just tell me what to do," he said, sitting up to kiss me so that I could taste the salty lees of his ejaculate still on his tongue.

"You're gonna have to earn it with that pretty mouth of yours," I told him between kisses.

I pulled away from him, leaving him on the floor while I walked back across the room and detached the camera from its stand. Coming back to stand above Owen, and pointing the camera down to film him, I said, "Go on, feel what I've got waiting for you."

Owen lost no time in squeezing my package, which was already as hard as an iron rod beneath my pants and drawers. Even through the camera lens I could tell by his expression that he was impressed by what he felt, and I let him bury his face in my crotch as he used his mouth to trace the outlines of my cock through the fabric.

Within moments, I was sporting a woody that ran from the center of my crotch out to nearly the outside edge of my right leg. Owen gently kneaded and rubbed it, getting it from semi to fully hard instantaneously.

"Can I?" he asked, his pretty blue eyes looking up at me expectantly.

"Yeah, go ahead," I said gruffly, looking back down at him through the camera.

Owen unbuttoned and unzipped my pants, pulling them down around my ankles, but he left my boxers on. My hard-on was tenting them out dramatically, but it still hadn't popped through the fly. Owen started kissing my thighs and then darted his tongue up between the fabric of my boxers and the skin of my leg, landing a few wet swats on my left testicle.

He pushed his mouth even farther up into the fabric until his was able to lick my entire testicle and even suck it into his mouth, rolling it around with his tongue before releasing it again. I lost my breath when he did that, and I didn't regain it by the time he started poking his nose through the fly of my shorts and licking at the base of my shaft.

In a swift motion, he pulled my cock out of my fly, then set to work in earnest coaxing it to its full erection. Just as I'd guessed from the skillful way he'd used his hands on himself, Owen was truly gifted with his mouth, sending shivers of pleasure up and down my body almost as soon as he started to blow me.

Like he had with himself, he slipped a hand up the leg of my boxers and used it to fondle my balls while his mouth got busy with my thick mushroom head. My cock was as long as Owen's, so he was used to the size of it, but I'd say it was slightly thicker than his own, and his hand couldn't fully close around it. He sized it up appreciatively between suck sessions, clamping his mouth back on with more gusto each time.

While stimulating the tip, he swirled his tongue around the plump lip of sensitive skin that separated my cockhead from my shaft; then he opened wide and sucked farther down my sheath until he reached my carefully groomed pube topiary. Though not as . . . geometric as Owen's trapezoid of hair, my pubic area was very well maintained, with just a little patch of hair taking shape a half inch above the root of my cock.

I had trouble holding the camera straight as Owen slid his mouth all the way down my dick, deepthroating me like that for minutes at a time and making the sexiest gagging noises as he struggled to take in my whole length. When he finally released me from his mouth, my cock was shiny with his slippery spit, and he jerked me off for a little bit while regaining his composure and taking a moment to suck on my balls.

I caught all of his actions on tape, zooming in on his best work while also taking moments here and there to film the rest of his body as it was thus engaged. I was enthralled by the rigid muscles of his shoulders as he leaned on one arm for balance. His ass was round as a ripe apple when he clenched it, and his legs were thick but shapely from the squats he must have done day after day at the gym.

What I loved best, though, was the view of his curly mop bounding back and forth as he played with my dick, running his tongue down one side of it, then back up the other; fluttering his tongue on its underside, then gently grazing the top with his teeth. Each move was calculated to heighten my gratification, and it was working. Already I could feel those telltale tingles beginning to fire up in my abdomen, signaling that my balls were amassing a huge load of spunk to shoot down his gorge.

"Keep going, faster!" I told him, zooming in on where his full, thick lips were wrapped around the darker skin of my shaft. He swallowed me whole, making my knees quiver, then began to jerk me off with his hand as his mouth continued to suction my rubbery skin harder and harder. Almost as riveting as his handiwork was the sound of spit sloshing in his mouth and throat around my rod. It was like listening to an erotic washing machine as Owen kindled that orgasmic fire within me.

Soon he was stoking the embers and bringing flame to life as he sucked and pulled on me harder and harder. I had trouble standing up straight as he continued to add fuel to my fire, and I had to reach down and lean on one of his strapping, sweaty shoulders to maintain balance as my rocket finally ignited.

"Open up, you're about to get seconds," I told him, jerking his chin up so that he was looking into the camera as the first spray of my semen shot from my piss hole right onto his chin.

While Owen jacked me off to completion, the second shot was no better aimed and arced right over his head onto the floor, though some of it landed in his hair. The next few loads all got him on the forehead and nose, while the last ones actually hit their target, landing square in his hot, waiting mouth. Owen didn't wait for me to finish shooting on my own, but fastened his mouth back onto my dick again and sucked out the leftovers of my orgasm. My tip got very sensitive and felt like volts of lightning were passing over it with each swipe of his tongue, but I didn't stop him until I knew that every last drop was out of my body.

When I was sure that I was finished, I shut off the camera and placed it down on the floor, then pulled Owen to his feet so I could kiss him and taste my cum on his lips. Mine was saltier and thicker than his, landing as it had in huge white squirts all over his face. I tenderly wiped away the blobs I had spewed on him and held out my hand for him to get another taste, then continued kissing him until all I could taste was his tongue and his lips, my own salty essence long since having disappeared.

We broke apart, both smiling, and began to dress again. As Owen slipped on his shirt, he turned to me and asked, with a self-satisfied grin, "So how did I do?"

Smiling slyly, I told him, "That was definitely the best audition I've seen so far, but I'm going to have to study your performance again and again to be sure."

"Anything to get the part," he told me as he wrapped one of his strong arms around me and pulled me into another kiss.

Louis in the Library

By the time junior year of college rolled around, I had become an English major, and was looking forward to immersing myself in Romance poetry, Shakespearean dramas, and modern novels.

Unfortunately, I had to fulfill a few general course requirements in a variety of subject areas first. My university was one of those stodgy East Coast institutions with a few centuries of first-class educational history behind it, so they felt the right to impose strict (and numerous) liberal arts background classes on their student body.

Luckily, I had already completed most of my requirements by the time I had declared a major. That was the one advantage of being indecisive about what department to settle on. All my science labs and philosophy courses were out of the way. The one subject area I still had to fulfill was in history.

Because of my standing as a junior, though, and the fact that I had already completed my coursework not only in about ten departments, but was deep into English history as a result of my literature major, I was eligible to take a seminar rather than a huge survey course filled with freshmen.

The class I decided on was a European Renaissance history class that tied in perfectly with my own interests in Shakespeare and Elizabethan literature. Ordinarily it was open only to history majors, but I pled my case to the professor, and he told the department to let me in. It helped that the professor was a relatively young gun with a *New York Times* best seller under his belt that the faculty had hired to attract more interest in the department. He was also interested in having me voice an outside perspective in the history-major-heavy seminar setting.

I did my best to fulfill my obligation, often bringing primary literary sources into the discussion. The rest of the students seemed to be by-the-book history majors. There were five girls and six guys including me. The girls all fell into the usual categories: There was a crunchy hippie girl, a preppy cardigan-and-pearls-wearing girl, a butch field hockey girl, an evangelical church youth group girl, and a few of the other stereotypes that haunted the campus.

As for the guys, most of them were straight-arrow preps I had seen around but never talked to. A few were in fraternities. I felt like I knew everyone in my year since we had all been at school for two years now. There was one guy, however, whom I had never seen before, and as soon as I met him, I felt a connection with him.

His name was Louis, and he had shaggy black hair and bangs that strayed so that he would have to brush them out of his wide-set light gray eyes flecked with brown markings. His creamy skin was punctuated by a few freckles here and there, and his thick, pink lips were often twisted into an impish smile that made it look like he was thinking of something naughty. He played soccer, so he had powerful legs and a round bubble butt that stretched his tight jeans, but his torso was all lean muscle. Combined with the button-down Oxford shirts he wore under cardigans and crewneck sweaters, along with an occasional jauntily looped scarf, the entire effect was to make him seem like an East Coast aristocratic scion.

I hadn't seen him around campus before because I was more into the arts. Plus, we were in different colleges and different majors, so it made sense that our paths had not crossed. Still, I thought he was so handsome in an offbeat kind of way, I was surprised that I had never noticed him before.

It was not long before I got the chance to rectify the situation, though. The first day of the seminar, everyone went around and introduced themselves. I listened to everything Louis said with great interest since I planned to Facebook stalk him when I got back to my room that night and wanted to remember all the details. He was a junior like me, but he was a history major.

I was the odd man out in the class since I was the only one taking it from outside the department. I could tell that a few of the other students pretty much wrote me off, but Louis seemed intrigued by what I had to say, and that first day, I spotted him eyeing me a couple times when he thought I was taking notes or looking at the professor.

The other students soon learned that I was not a waste of time either, especially since the professor kept asking for my contributions to the discussion and my take on the readings. He encouraged me to participate, and once I got over my initial hesitation, I was soon debating ferociously with the other students. I did not want to become a teacher's pet, but I sort of reveled in the attention. It was nice to stand out, and the professor always thanked me for my comments.

Louis also stood out to me. He seemed a little shy and did not speak out much in class, but when he did, I found myself surprised by the profundity of his statements and arguments. I thought I could listen to him for hours, ruminating on each syllable of his resonant tenor voice.

More often than not, Louis would be the last to show up for class, rushed from lunch, and slightly flustered, with just the faintest hint of a blush reddening his fair cheeks. Since it was a small seminar, there were plenty of empty seats, but as week after week passed, I noticed that he kept sitting next to me, giving me a timid smile as he bashfully slid into his seat. I usually smiled back. One time I lent him a pen, and another time our legs brushed under the table, but that was the extent of our interaction.

I didn't know what to make of him—if he liked me, or if he was just a really nice, cool guy. I couldn't blame him for being shy since I was trying not to give him any clues as to how I felt. It would just be awkward if I flirted with him only to find out he wasn't into guys. And since he was a jock, he probably wasn't into guys. Still, I had to wonder . . .

I got the chance to do some more in-depth research on the situation thanks to a big midterm project our professor assigned us. We would be working in teams to present a paper on one of the topics we had covered in class. Randomly, the professor just assigned us with whomever we were sitting next to at the time, and I happened to be sitting next to . . . Louis.

Both of us smiled brightly when we were assigned to be partners, and we made a plan to meet for lunch at my college the next day to discuss a research plan. We had only two weeks before the paper was due, so that would mean putting in a lot of hours in the library working together. I couldn't wait.

The next day, I went to the cafeteria for lunch at the time Louis and I had arranged. He wasn't there. I began to get nervous, but then remembered that this was Louis I was waiting for, and I had never seen him get anywhere on time, so I grabbed a soda and cracked open a poetry book I had to read for one of my English classes.

Several minutes later, a hand swiped it away from me, and I looked up to find Louis grinning down at me. He looked at the poem I was reading and recited out loud, "That he might gaze and worship all unseen; Perchance speak, kneel, touch, kiss—in sooth such things have been."

I blushed. It was a pretty racy poem. I rushed to explain, "It's for one of my poetry classes, it's called 'The Eve of St. Agnes' by . . ."

"Keats," Louis said, finishing my sentence for me. "I know. It's one of my favorites."

My eyebrows rose in surprise.

"What?" he asked. "You're not the only one who likes to stray outside your major."

"Fair enough," I said, "and it's a good thing you can relate since we'll be deep in history land for this project."

"I was actually hoping I'd get you as a partner," he continued.

"Really?" I asked, genuinely surprised.

"Yeah," he replied. "You always make the most interesting comments in class, and I'm dying to read a little lit.

It's been all history all the time for me this year, and I could use a change of pace."

He said that with a smirk, so I could not tell if he intended it as a double entendre, so I only smiled and responded, "Well, I'm glad you're my partner, too. You're much more insightful than the other guys, and clearly you appreciate a fine mind when you come across one."

Louis laughed, and we headed into the cafeteria, first swiping our meal cards to get in and then choosing from the mediocre selection of entrées waiting under heat lamps. Louis followed me out into the dining hall, where we found a table in a secluded corner with windows overlooking a picturesque quad. It was late in the lunch hour, so we had the area all to ourselves.

We started out by talking shop, discussing our ideas for the project, and eventually settling on a topic: the royal succession in England during the Renaissance. It was a turbulent time in English history, though also one of the most artistically productive, and I suggested that we could make our paper really interesting and idiosyncratic by bringing in Shakespeare's history plays to talk about how the ruling class used the arts as propaganda to further their agenda. I anxiously stole a glance at Louis as I mentioned my idea, thinking he would shoot it down in favor of using strictly historical sources, but he loved it and even gave my shoulder a quick squeeze in his excitement. I beamed with satisfaction.

Once that was decided, we divided up some of the preliminary research tasks and then made a plan to get together at the end of the week to start writing the paper together. Our work done, we started to chat informally.

I told Louis all about myself, and when I said I was sorry for talking so much, he smiled back at me and asked me to tell him more. In return, he told me about himself as well. He was from New Hampshire and had been recruited by the university to play soccer. He really loved it, but he wanted to study history in Europe after college, which was why he was a history major, and why he was concentrating on his studies rather than prioritizing sports.

Neither of us had an afternoon class that day, so we just kept talking, and eventually went back into the cafeteria for some frozen yogurt. When we got back to the table and started eating, I wasn't happy with my combo of strawberry yogurt and peanut butter Cap'n Crunch, so I set it aside. Louis offered me a taste of his, but before I could reach for my spoon, he scooped up a bite with his own spoon and gently fed it to me. I was too stunned by the intimate gesture to do anything besides accept and chew.

"Good?" he asked, with that impish grin.

"Mmm-hmm," I answered, my mouth still full.

Reaching over again, he swiped his thumb across my chin, where a drop of the yogurt had dribbled, then sucked it off his thumb, still smiling. By that time, I was smiling, too.

I could barely concentrate on the assignment for the rest of the week. I was so nervous about seeing Louis again and working on our paper that I could not think about anything else. Unfortunately, I had the rest of midterms to distract me, so I eventually forced myself to do my school-work and spent only an idle moment here and there thinking about him. Okay, and maybe I jacked off once or twice before bed imagining how hot his naked body would be lying next to mine.

I also went and talked to a couple of my English professors about my paper for the history class. They were full of insights about the literary aspect of what Louis and I were discussing, as well as the historical context, so that by the end of the week, I had a copious stack of notes and leads, as well as several pages worth of quotes and footnotes.

The day before our final seminar of the quarter, I e-mailed Louis my notes and he e-mailed me his. I was impressed. He had done as good and thorough a job as I had, and he brought up some really interesting points. I was still a little afraid of dorking out in front of him, but I was really looking forward to writing this paper.

We had our seminar as usual that week, and sure enough, Louis shambled in late. I managed to catch his eye and noticed that he was flushed. He shot me a furtive grin, and I flushed, too. I didn't hear another word the professor said until the very end of class, when he made the following announcement: "I want to remind you all about your group papers. They will be due on Monday. If you haven't already started writing them, I would suggest dedicating the whole weekend to them because they are worth forty percent of your grade . . . and there will be no extensions."

The whole class groaned, but there was not much to do about it. I slowly put away my class materials as the other students and the professor left, waiting to say something to Louis.

He seemed to be taking his time, too, and soon it was

just the two of us. I stood up with my bag and said casually, "I'm glad we already started on our own, it sounds like this could be a killer paper. At least we have all weekend to work on it."

Louis's pale, freckled skin blushed even more crimson. "Yeah, about that," he started uncertainly. "I have an away game on Saturday."

"What?" I started, panic already rising in my chest. "How . . . when are we going to write the paper?"

"I'm sorry, I know—" he started.

I cut him off, "You heard the professor; there are no extensions, and it's forty percent of our grade!"

Louis stood up and took a step toward me. Our chests were almost touching. I thought he was going to take my hand . . . or kiss me. Suddenly I forgot about the stupid paper and just wanted him to kiss me.

"Don't worry. I get back early Sunday. We have all day . . . and night . . . to write the paper," he said, half smiling at me.

"It's not funny!" I said, still uptight.

Louis turned serious again. "I know it's not," he conceded. "But it's the best I can do. Besides, we've seen each other's notes, and we've got our entire angle covered. It's just a matter of fitting it all together."

"But . . ." I started.

Then he put his hand on my shoulder and gave me a quick squeeze. That quieted me down. "Listen," he told me, "we can do this. You're brilliant. We're going to work hard, and we'll spend all night in the library if we have to, but we're going to do this paper, and we're going to get an A."

I breathed in deeply, smiled at him, then said, "Okay."

"Okay," he said, also smiling, and giving my shoulder another squeeze.

That Sunday morning, I rose early and quickly showered and got dressed, throwing on a peacoat and scarf against the autumn chill in the air. The campus was practically deserted at that hour, everyone still sleeping off the parties of Saturday night. I drank in the silence, broken only by my own footsteps, and admired the leaves changing colors on the trees.

After a few minutes' walk from my dorm, I arrived at the library to find Louis waiting for me. He was early for once. And miracle of miracles, he was holding two huge, steaming cups of coffee. He did not see me for a second, so I stared freely. He looked so cute in his tight jeans, loafers, a corduroy jacket with arm patches, and a cashmere scarf. He must have just showered, too, because his mop of hair was a mass of wet strands.

His face lit up when he saw me, and he stepped forward, offering me one of the cups. "I know it's unfair to make you get up early and work all day on a Sunday, so I brought a little morning present."

"Perfect," I sighed, breathing in the invigorating steam. "Did you win your game?"

"Yeah," he said, seemingly delighted that I asked. "And I even managed to score."

"Lucky you," I said, fully intending the double entendre.

We went inside, greeting the security guard. He must have felt sorry for us being the only ones there on a Sunday morning because he let us bring our coffees in with us. We made our way up to the top floor, where the history section was, and found a corner alcove with a big table where we could spread out all our books and notes.

And that is where we stayed for the rest of the day, working intensely, putting our arguments in order, debating with one another, and finally typing up the paper we came up with. We only took short breaks to get up and walk around, check our e-mail, and grab a bite to eat.

Before we knew it, night had fallen, and we still had a ways to go, though the paper was looking good. It was Sunday, so the library was closing early, but we still had a lot of work to do. When we heard the closing bell, Louis and I looked at each other. I was nervous. We had to find a way to get our books out and finish the paper tonight. It looked like it would be an all-nighter.

We could hear a security guard climbing the stairs, telling stray students it was time to leave.

"We'd better go," I said. "Grab as many of the books as you can and let's find a classroom somewhere."

Louis looked at me a second as if trying to make up his mind, then grinned and said, "I have a better idea. Grab your stuff."

I did not know what he intended to do, but we had to get out of there before security kicked us out, so I gathered all my stuff and followed him. He led me down a few hallways on the floor, past the rows of grad student offices and studies, until we came to the end of the corridor. Looking surreptitiously around, he pulled a key from his pocket, opened the door, then pulled me into the dark room behind him.

Just as the door closed behind us, I heard the security guard yelling to a colleague, "Just going to do one last round up here; then we can lock up for the night!"

I held my breath, hoping we wouldn't get caught. Almost without realizing it, I sensed someone's body heat behind me and felt their warm, nervous breath on my neck. Louis must have been standing right behind me, completely tense like me.

I wanted to lean back into his warmth, to take in his smell of clean soap, old corduroy, and after a day spent in the stacks, musty books. I leaned imperceptibly toward him and could swear that he came closer to me. It seemed like we were almost touching.

The guard shouted, "All clear!" and shut off the lights on the floor, and just like that, the spell was broken. Louis pulled away. I took a deep breath, and we sat down at the tiny desk in the cramped room to begin working.

"Whose office is this?" I asked.

"One of my T.A.'s," Louis replied. "He lets me use it sometimes when he's off on a research project."

We got back to work, and spent the next few hours drafting and re-drafting the paper. It was like our minds worked at the same speed, and after a day spent together talking and writing, we were completing each other's thoughts.

We flew through the work, and at about 3:00 A.M., we finally finished the paper. I typed up the last footnote, and hit "Save" with a flourish, basking in our accomplishment. Louis was standing behind me, and as soon as I'd finished, he gave my shoulders a little back rub.

I tossed my head back to look up at him and could see

that he was smiling down at me with sleep-deprived eyes and a mischievous arch to his eyebrows.

"Phew!" I said. "Finished with hours to spare."

I stood up and stretched, feeling the bottom of my sweater come up above the waistband of my pants and revealing the last little bit of my happy trail and belly button. I saw Louis steal a glance at it before looking back at the computer screen. I let out a little "whoop!" in celebration—for being done with the paper and for attracting the notice of this completely adorable guy. Punch-drunk, Louis joined in, and soon we were hooting it up, just enjoying being done. Then, without thinking, I hugged him.

Louis tensed up, and I knew that I had made a mistake. I started to mumble an apology and let my arms drop as I pulled away, but then I found that Louis had put his arms around me, too, down near my hips, and was holding me to him.

His nose was next to my ear, and I could feel him breathing in the scent of my hair and my nape. I, too, was breathing in his smell again, reveling in my bookish companion, and wrapping my arms back around him, my hands on the middle of his back.

I pulled my head back and looked into his soft gray eyes. They were completely serious now. I looked down at his rosy, moist mouth and wanted to kiss it more than I'd ever wanted to kiss anyone.

Slowly, hesitantly, I moved my mouth toward his. He did not flinch or move, he just kept staring at me . . . and then we were kissing. His lips felt supple and sweet as they caressed my own. He tasted like coffee and mint gum and plain old spit. I touched his cheek with my thumb, holding his face close to my own, and the traces of dark brown stubble scratched lightly at my fingers.

Louis was still holding me by the waist, but he slid his warm, soft hands up under my shirt, squeezing my rib cage and tracing the long muscles of my svelte torso before coming to a rest on the small of my back again.

We kissed long and sweetly, absorbing each other's mouths, surreptitiously daring each other with our tongues, smiling between pecks. We had both been waiting for this for months, and now that it was happening, we were in no rush. We had the whole place to ourselves, and the dusty smell of old books was more of an aphrodisiac than anything else.

Louis's hands delved beneath my belt, cradling my buttocks and rubbing them gently. My cock began to stir within my corduroy pants, tenting out the fabric slightly as it brushed against Louis's own hardening crotch.

I lifted my arms up in the air so that Louis could hoist my sweater off me, and I stood bare-chested in front of him, letting him grope every inch of my torso. I was still young, and so my chest had only a few stray hairs here and there, with a sprinkling around each of my round, red nipples. They grew harder as Louis's hands passed over them, and soon his mouth was all over them, suckling them 'til they were pointy and sensitive.

Louis trailed down my body 'til he was eye level with my belt, which he unbuckled and then removed before unfastening my pants. He pulled those down, too, but left my underwear on, nuzzling against the growing mound of my cock and balls as he inhaled my scent and wetted the front of my briefs with his saliva.

His tongue darted under the fabric at the bottom of my

briefs, tickling the skin between my balls and my thigh. Stretching the cotton there, Louis pulled out one of my testicles and licked at it, getting it all moist and tender with his tongue before stretching the fabric even more to reveal the swelling head of my cock. I was getting more and more erect by the second, but I hadn't nearly reached my full length or hardness yet, so Louis was able to pull my cock down through the bottom band of my underwear and suck eagerly at the still semisoft helmet head and piss slit. I am so sensitive right there, and each swipe of his tongue was electrifying. When he'd decided I'd had enough, he pulled my underwear down, having a hard time getting them over the massive tent pole of my cock, then started blowing me in earnest.

I knew he had a smart mouth, but I had no idea just how talented that mouth really was. The lips that curled into the impish grin I loved put just the right pressure on the skin of my shaft as his mouth bobbed up and down on me, while that tongue that made such erudite arguments swirled back and forth with each movement of his head. By the time he'd sucked me for a minute, my whole cock was glistening with his saliva and my balls had pulled up tight to my body from the stimulation.

He didn't even use his hands, instead swallowing me deep down into the back of his throat and spluttering as my rigid rod poked into his soft palate. I felt him relax the muscles of his throat as he stretched it wide to accommodate me, the fleshy softness of his cheeks cradling my girth when he sucked them in to provide more delicious pressure on my shaft.

After a few minutes, I pulled his face back up level with my own, wiping stray drops of drool from his upper lip and chin, and kissing him deep and hard to thank him for his excellent efforts. I reverently lifted his shirt up over his head and threw it onto the desk so that I could take a good look at his wiry frame. His skin was milky fair all over, with freckles here and there, and the reddest little nipples I'd ever seen. Like the hair on his head, his patch of chest hair was dark and thick, though limited to a little diamond that stretched between his nipples to the middle of his chest, then reappearing again between his belly button and his crotch.

I kissed my way down his rippling abs and swiped my tongue a few times in his belly button, making him giggle. Despite a long day in the library, his skin still smelled soapy and fresh, like the fabric softener on his clothes. I ran a hand along the thick shaft I could see running sideways from his crotch to the right side. His dick looked pretty impressive, and even longer than my own. I unzipped his jeans and reached through the fly of his boxers to unleash it and have a look.

It, too, was fair and smooth, with a round, pink mushroom head and a narrow hole. His pubic hair came halfway up the shaft, though it was very sparse. I started to tug at his cock with one hand, making him moan, and unbuttoned his jeans with the other so I could pull them off. That's just what I did before opening wide to swallow Louis's monster. He tasted clean but a little sweaty, with the same funk I imagined his soiled jockstraps to have after a long game that went into overtime. I loved the way he smelled—like a real athlete with the odor of the locker room following him. It drove me crazy and I slurped away at his dick with abandon.

Louis started to shudder with each suck, his knees buckling from the intensity with which I was working him over. I made sure to concentrate on his glans, hitting every last neuron as I swirled my tongue around it. I made my way down to his balls, which smelled tangy and sharp, and tasted even more so as I sent my tongue slithering into every last little nook and cranny among the folds of skin. I took one of his nads into my mouth and sucked at it like an everlasting gobstopper, really tugging at it with my tongue and making Louis moan even louder.

I had him at my complete mercy now, so I stood up and bent him over the desk. Sidling up behind him, I began to frotte my still-hard meat against the hot, dank skin of his taint and asshole, getting him used to the friction that was about to come. I spat wads and wads of mucousy saliva down into that dark vale, getting us both lubricated at the same time. Louis started to move his ass in time with my own, wiggling it this way and that against my crotch.

When I thought he was ready, I rubbed one last loogie onto my cock and I ever so slowly pointed it directly into his fuck button. At first, his sphincter didn't give way at all and I couldn't slip inside him. But as I stood still and kept the pressure on, I could see him take a deep breath and relax the muscles of his anus so that I could slide inside little by little.

My spit was doing the trick, and we were both comfortable and well oiled, so it wasn't long before I could take longer and longer strokes, shoving my dick in up to the hilt, then withdrawing it to just past the lip of the head. I got such a thrill watching his asshole stretch to fit my cock, seeing its length disappear completely inside him, then reappear in its entirety a second later. His hold was so tight, it gave me the best feeling as it suctioned the skin on my cock with each of my thrusts, rubbing every square inch of my sheath.

Within a minute, I was picking up speed and shortening my thrusts. We had both become out of breath—me from the exertion and Louis from the effort of withstanding my assault. His pale, muscular ass cheeks were turning red where my thighs slapped into them, and I could feel my balls bouncing against his own as both our pairs dangled beneath us. I reached around his thigh to feel his cock and was surprised to find it was as rock hard as before. Apparently he liked what I was giving him and didn't require any manual stimulation. I still gave him a few tugs anyway, causing him to wriggle his hips up and down and push back harder and harder onto my cock.

Before I finished with him, I wanted to act out a fantasy I'd always had. I was a nerd, after all, so library sex was always within the realm of my naughty daydreams. I pulled out of Louis, then turned him around and sat him down on the desk, spreading his legs on either side of me. Holding his tackle to one side, I bent my knees and penetrated his fuck chute again.

Louis might have been the soccer player, but my arms were definitely the stronger of us two since I'd put in long hours at the college gym and constructing theatrical sets for the plays I was in on campus. Reaching under his legs and holding on tight, I had Louis sit up; then I lifted him off the desk and walked over to the bookshelves that lined one of the walls of the office. With each step, I impaled Louis farther and farther on my cock, but he just gritted his teeth and ground down onto me even harder.

I backed him up into the bookshelf with a thud so that his ass was half-resting on one of the shelves and he could grab another that was higher up to balance. Then I just started tearing into him. I wanted to make the walls tremble. I wanted to break the shelves. Books started flying everywhere as the force of my pounding shook the walls. The only sound that was louder than the quake I was causing were Louis's gasps of pleasure. I launched into his ass again and again with the force and precision of a piston. I fucked him on all cylinders, ramming into his prostate, so that each of my thrusts elicited an uninhibited yelp from him.

His cock and balls were jingling from my motions. I wanted to jerk him off while I fucked him, but I needed both my free hands, and the muscular heft of my upper legs, to support him while I went to town. Louis managed to balance himself pretty easily, despite my forcefulness, so eventually he was using just one hand to hold on, while urging himself to orgasm with the other.

He was an intense masturbator, grabbing on to his shaft with a death grip and pulling hard all the way up and down its length in slow, powerful strokes. He pleaded with me to fuck him harder and faster, and I forgot everything else as I punched into him like a jackhammer. I was giving it all I was worth, all in service to making him ejaculate. I forgot about my own orgasm, so concentrated was I on bringing him to his.

I couldn't keep up my furious pace much longer, but I didn't have to. Louis's breathing became shallower and his strokes became shorter. The muscles of his stomach all contracted and he held his breath, making the veins pop out on his neck and forehead. He was completely flushed from the sex, so when the first spray of cum hit his stomach, it glowed white against the rosy tone of his hot skin.

With each spurt of jizz, Louis's ass muscles closed around my cock, holding me inside him. It was like his ass was giving me a blowjob, and I knew I was going to cum any second. I wanted to let him finish, though, so when his jerking finally slowed and he opened his eyes again, I quickly withdrew from his tender hole and put him down. I was about to reach down and jerk myself off, but Louis beat me to it. His hand was covered with his own semen, and it made the perfect short-term lubricant to get me to the finish line.

He only had to work my cock with a few quick strokes before I exploded with burst after burst of cum. It arced as high as my shoulder, splashing the bookshelf a good three feet in front of us. Louis just kept jerking, and I just kept coming. More and more flowed out of me, marking the dusty spines of the books, splattering the shelves, Louis's stomach, and finally drizzling over the floor. Louis gently milked me until he was sure I was done. Then he pulled one of the volumes I'd hit and licked the line of cum off of it with that lovable impish grin on his face.

I brushed his sweaty black bangs from his forehead as I pulled him in for a kiss, rubbing his cum-drenched stomach against my own sweaty one. When we had sufficiently thanked each other for a job well done, we used a box of tissues to clean everything up, then snuck out of the library for the night to get at least a little sleep, parting ways when we got to Louis's dorm.

The next day, I brought in our paper to the seminar, and Louis and I handed it in together. The professor told us he was looking forward to reading what we came up with.

"We worked up until the last minute on it," I told him.

Louis added, "Yeah, we really put everything we had into it. It was a whole new experience for both of us."

"College is about learning and trying new things," responded our professor. "I'm glad you two made a good team."

"Definitely. I can't wait to work on another assignment together," I said, eliciting a smirk from Louis.

Henry the Hotelier

I was standing in the lobby of the hotel waiting for someone named Henry. That was all I knew. I had not written much about hotels up to that point, so this was all new to me. An editor had called me asking if I was interested in taking a tour of a new hip boutique property that had just opened in Los Angeles that was already attracting a celebrity clientele thanks to a scene-y restaurant and a spectacular rooftop bar, not to mention palatial and private suites. Intrigued, I had said yes.

So there I was, feeling conspicuous in my surroundings as beautiful people wandered in and out of the chic space around me, and I stood there in a shirt and tie with my messenger bag strapped across my chest, waiting for Henry.

Henry was the general manager of the hotel, and had been working for the chain for several years, my editor told me. He specialized in opening new properties for them, so he was a tried-and-true veteran.

I didn't know what to expect. Usually with hotels like this, you'd hear ambiguous catchphrases like "retro-chic" and "minimalist-mod." Sure, those descriptions fit, but they didn't really tell you anything about the place.

From what I could see, the lighting was low to emulate a bar or nightclub, the space was all pared-down décor with dark woods and burnished mirrors, and orchids haphazardly placed here and there. There was just a touch of '70s cool thrown in, too—shag carpeting, gold-framed mirrors, that kind of thing. It felt a little odd hanging out there in the middle of the afternoon, but it was good to come at a less busy time so I could get some photos without people milling through the shots.

I figured Henry would be some PR queen who was going to shuttle me around for five minutes, then kick me to the curb so he could get to his next appointment. Nothing against PR people, but they only allocate the time for you that they think your usefulness deserves, and no one (not even me) was sure how useful I would be, this being my first hotel feature and all.

I looked around for a moment, then approached the front desk, where a coiffed young guy dressed all in black (I think he might even have been wearing a mock turtleneck!) was talking into a Bluetooth headset. He looked at me pointedly as he continued his conversation, and I just stood there trying not to snicker at his insolence. Finally, when he'd hung up on his call, he turned to me with a simple, sneered, "Yes?"

"Um, I'm looking for Henry? I'm a writer, he's supposed to . . ." I didn't even have time to finish before the receptionist had somehow connected to a call and told someone to send Henry down.

"I think he's a writer or something," he said, barely glancing my way.

He hung up and simply said, "He'll be right down," then picked up another call. I was left, once again, to my own devices.

I was just turning around to find a seat in the lobby when I saw someone walk down the staircase that led to the mezzanine. The man was dressed in a simple gray suit that must have been hand-tailored because it fit him that well. He had broad shoulders and a powerful frame, but he was not barrel-chested or stocky, just worked out, and his girth suited his six-foot frame. His arms were long, and even through the sleeves of his suit, I could make out the slight contours of his muscles. The crisp blue-gray shirt matched his bright blue eyes perfectly, and both were set off even more by the tanned tone of his skin. His hair was a thick mane of straight, fine salt-and-pepper, though cropped close and neat. I guessed he was about fifty, though he looked closer to forty.

You could just tell, looking at him, that this man was cultured and worldly. He had been places, he had seen things, and yet he was relaxed, confident, and utterly, devastatingly handsome. By the time he stepped down into the lobby, I had practically melted into a puddle at his feet.

I hadn't realized I was staring until he was standing right in front of me, extending a hand in introduction.

"I'm Henry," he said, smiling. "You must be Brad."

"Yeah, um, yes," I stuttered. "Thank you for taking the time to show me around. I hope this is still an okay time."

"Of course, of course, we're glad to have you. I'm just going to show you the restaurant, a few of our different rooms, and then maybe we'll check out the rooftop pool," he said, leading me to the elevator bank.

"Sounds great!" I said, a little too enthusiastically. To be honest, the rooftop pool bar was what I had really come to see since it was supposed to be the next celebrity hotspot in Los Angeles, but I figured the more time I got with Henry, the better.

We started in the restaurant that was just off the lobby. It was some sort of sushi-fusion too-cool-for-you-so-don't-even-try-to-get-a-reservation kind of place with exposed wood, steel beams, and polished wooden tables.

When I had snapped a few pictures and dutifully asked some questions about the food, we took the elevator up a few floors to see a standard guest room. As soon as we stepped from the dark hallway into the room, I could tell this hotel was all about being sexy. That's the only way to describe the room. It had black floors, black furniture, a black bed, and even the mirrors that lined the wall behind the bed and continued as jagged shards on the ceiling were tinted darker, so that if you were making love there, you would only be able to catch fleeting, voyeuristic peeks at the action.

I said as much, and Henry chuckled. "I think you've pretty much got it," he said, lightly placing a hand on my bicep to guide me toward the bathroom for a few more room photos. As he passed me, I could smell his cologne. It was light and fragrant, with just a hint of citrus and spice to it. I could bathe in that scent.

After that, we went up to one of the suites, which was pretty much like the regular room, only there was a sitting area as well, and the bathroom had a Jacuzzi tub for when you didn't want to bathe alone.

While we were looking at the rooms and Henry was telling me about the hotel and its design, I managed to slip in a few questions about Henry himself, and he told me his story. He'd been in the hotel business for a long time, and had worked at several of the world's larger chains before shifting gears and going into boutique hotels. When I asked what had precipitated this change, Henry hesitantly explained that he had been in a long-term relationship with another man, and that when they had broken up eventually, he had decided to overhaul his life.

I didn't ask a follow-up for fear that I'd already been too nosy, and I went back to taking notes and reference photos of the suite.

Then it was time to take the elevator to the roof to check out the pool. Henry produced a special key card from his breast pocket, explaining that only hotel guests and people who either bought or were invited to be members of the hotel "family" were allowed to access the roof. It all sounded snooty, or "exclusive," as I was going to call it in my article, but I was still eager to take a look at what they'd done on the roof.

When we got up there, I could see why they were going to such lengths to keep the roof off-limits. The view was simply breathtaking, with 360-degree views of the entire city from the ocean to the mountains. The deck was covered in dark wood, and the bar was a bright, creamy marble shaded by specially imported palm trees. On either side of it were two cabanas that could be turned into private outdoor dining rooms, and the rest of the space was filled with little bar tables and booths.

On the other side of the roof, behind the bar, was the pool. Though it wasn't big, it was also quite beautiful, carved out of marble shimmering aquamarine in the late-afternoon sunshine. Surrounding it were lounge chairs, and at the far end of the deck, another set of cabanas.

"Wow," was all I could say as I leaned against the glass railing and took in the view.

"I know," Henry laughed, taking a place next to me. "It hasn't opened yet, even for guests, so sometimes I come up here alone just to take it all in."

"Well, thank you for sharing it with me," I said, eagerly taking pictures and thinking up catchphrases to use in my article. "When is it opening, by the way?"

"Tonight, actually," replied Henry. "The opening party starts at nine. You should come by." As he issued this invitation, he stepped closer and placed a hand on my shoulder.

My heart was racing. Was he hitting on me? I felt myself blushing, but looking at Henry out of the corner of my eye, I saw that he was still gazing out at the city, so I relaxed a little bit and explained, "I can't tonight. I have another story I'm working on."

"Busy guy!" Henry said, turning to look at me with a new interest.

"Always in demand," I said, smiling and hoping my surfer-shaggy hair was looking good blowing in the light breeze.

"I feel that way, too," he confided. "There's always something, or ten somethings, demanding my attention."

"It must be a really stressful job opening up a hotel, so much can go wrong, you have to be on top of everything," I conjectured, trying to relate to him.

"That's right. It doesn't leave much time for . . . well, for anything else."

From what he had left unspoken, I gathered that the pressures of his job might have been the major factor contributing to his breaking up with his partner. I kept mum, though, not wishing to make him uncomfortable.

After another moment of wistful gazing off into the mid-distance, Henry seemed to flip a switch, turning back to me and smiling. "Tell you what. If you can't come to the party tonight, why don't I fix us a drink now to enjoy up here. I can answer any questions you have. That is, if you're not in a hurry." He gave my shoulder a little squeeze.

My heart started racing again. "That sounds great," I said, trying to sound casual and not grin like an idiot.

"Great," he said, letting go of my shoulder and leading me back to the bar. As he went behind the bar and started getting out mixers and bottles, he asked what I'd like. I told him to make me a French 75. He looked surprised.

"You know how to make that, right?" I asked. Then, embarrassed, I backpedaled, "Of course you do, sorry, some people don't, though, you know?"

"Yes, I know how to make it. It's one of my favorites, actually. It's just, not a lot of guys your age order it. It's kind of old-fashioned."

"Well, I'm almost thirty," I said, puffing out my chest. Most gay guys would hate to admit that, but I wore my age like a badge of pride. Especially since I looked a lot younger. Getting older meant I'd done things with my life, and I didn't care who knew it. "Besides, they're nice and cold on a hot day, and vintage cocktails are huge right now. What's old is new."

"Then I must be very, very new," Henry replied, not meeting my eye.

If I was reading the situation correctly, I thought that that was Henry's way of gauging my interest in him and whether I cared about our age difference. I decided to keep the conversation a little abstract, saying simply, "Most of the things I enjoy the most require a little aging—wine, cheese, art. All the best things in life get better with age."

I was staring straight at him, willing him to look up from the drinks he was mixing. I smirked a little bit so he would know I was being playful, and sure enough, as soon as I said that, he met my gaze and smiled back at me.

"That's a refreshing perspective," he said, handing me the drink. "And this should be a refreshing cocktail. Enjoy."

He poured the rest for himself, and we took our glasses to one of the poolside cabanas, which was basically a tent that could be closed off for privacy. Inside, there was sort of a large sectional with cushions that ran around the entire interior, and in one corner were a cocktail fridge and a flat-screen TV for entertainment. Henry and I didn't need those, though.

We sat down next to each other at one corner of the sectional, looking out over the pool. Clinking glasses in cheers, I toasted, "To meeting new people." We drank, and then Henry proposed a toast of his own: "To a beautiful view." I clinked glasses again with him and took a sip, pausing to look out at the city, but when I turned back to him, I found that Henry hadn't taken his eyes off me. Now I was really blushing.

Putting my glass down on the side table, I slid closer to Henry, placed a hand lightly on his knee, and asked, "So, is there anything else on the tour that I should see?"

Without a moment's hesitation, he leaned in and started to kiss me. His skin was completely clean-shaven and so smooth, I worried that my own stubble would scratch him, but Henry seemed completely unconcerned about that as his lips drank deeper and deeper of my own.

I inhaled deeply through my nose, trying to place the amber-laden scent of his cologne. Tiffany for Men, I thought, as I breathed in again. He smelled like a real man, not like the Acqua di Gio–sporting boys I always found at the West Hollywood bars. It was a heavier, more herbaceous, clean-smelling fragrance, and I found it intoxicating (or maybe that was the drink I'd gulped down) as I ran my tongue deeper into Henry's open mouth.

While I kissed him, I wrapped one hand around the back of his head, enjoying the fuzzy feel of his close-shaved hair. I inched the other one up from his knee along the contours of his thigh to his package. I could feel his cock beginning to stir, gradually getting harder and harder even though all I was doing was cupping it with my hand.

Henry, meanwhile, had unbuttoned a few of the buttons on my dress shirt and snuck a hand through to grope my chest and then rest on my taut abdomen. He was gently petting my furry abs while wrapping his other arm around my back.

I pressed myself against him, feeling up every square inch of his solid torso and thick arms with my roving hands, slipping off his jacket, and getting more and more impatient to taste his cock in my mouth. I was in such a rush, in fact, that I didn't even bother to take off his shirt or mine. I just knelt down on the deck in front of Henry and without bothering to undo his belt or unbutton his pants, I simply unzipped the fly to unleash his still stiffening prong.

Henry's cock was rather like him—tan and solid, with

some heft to it. It was one of those beer-can cocks that can tear you up (in such a good way), but that you can deepthroat with ease because it's not that long. It had a huge vein running along one side of it and another forking around it from the top. I couldn't wait to wrap my mouth around it and bury my face in his immaculately groomed sprout of pubic hair. Those, I was relieved to see, were still completely black, unlike the hair on Henry's head. I think that otherwise it might have freaked me out a bit, but I was trying to get in touch with my more mature-leaning side, and I was ready to say, "Hello, Daddy!"

Milking Henry's cock gently with my hand, I smiled back up at him to let him know how much I was going to enjoy this, then I swallowed him inch by inch. His sausage was so thick, I had to stretch my lips as far open as I could and be careful about not biting down with my teeth. I took it slow, though, and used every spare second to work my tongue around Henry's shaft. Even his cock smelled good, like he'd bathed it with extremely expensive shampoo. I was loving every second of sucking him off.

I used only my mouth to suck him, running one of my hands up under the hem of his pants and feeling the cut, hairy muscles of his calf. With the other, I caressed his belly and chest through his silky dress shirt. I reached up to his face and stuck a finger in his gaping mouth. He started suckling at it between the moans I was producing with my talented oral ministrations.

Within a minute or two, his cock was freely leaking pre-cum, sending drop after drop of the sticky, salty liquor down my throat. I sucked at his prong harder and harder, trying to milk out even more of the stuff, greedily swallowing every iota of it he poured out. My dick was rapidly engorging, getting to full erection within seconds. I felt a small wet patch forming in my underwear where my piss slit was oozing out a film of my own precum. I hadn't even touched myself at all, and I was already as stimulated as if Henry had been the one blowing me.

Henry started to undo his tie and unbutton his shirt, but I stopped him. "Leave it on," I said, interrupting my blowjob to keep him from taking his clothes off. In any other situation, this might have seemed counterproductive. And I did want to see Henry naked. From what I could feel through his clothes, he had a really sexy, worked-out body. But there was just something so aphrodisiacal about a powerful man in a suit—and the fact that I had him at my complete mercy—that I didn't want him to get undressed at all. I wanted him to fuck me while we were both wearing our dress clothes.

He must have felt the same way because he instantly complied, letting his hands drop before placing them on top of my head and grabbing a handful of my shaggy hair. Holding me tight, he forced my head to bob up and down on his cock as he started to thrust it up and into my mouth, deeper and deeper. The facefucking left me breathless as I tried not to gag while accommodating the huge circumference of his meat. My eyes started to water from the effort, but I didn't stop him, relishing the animalistic grunt he uttered with each pump of his hips.

After another minute, I knew Henry wasn't going to get any harder, and I wanted to feel that monster ripping apart my ass before he came, so I took his hands off my head, stopped sucking him, and stood up. I quickly undid my belt and pulled down my pants and underwear, releasing my erection so Henry could get a prime view. I left my own shirt and tie on, just like him, though.

He started to stand up, but I pushed him back down onto the daybed. I worked up a huge gob of saliva and spat it onto my hand, then turning around, I let him watch as I worked the natural lube into my ass, first with one finger, then with two. I kept at it for a minute or two, trying to loosen myself up for what I knew was going to be a painful penetration, and spitting repeatedly into my hand to try to get as much lubrication as possible to help.

I turned around and saw Henry was enthralled by the show I was giving him. He had pulled down his own pants and underwear to facilitate what was going to happen next, and he was idly tugging at his dick to keep it hard. That didn't look like it was such a problem, though, since it was still as rigid as a rock, and his fur-covered balls were scrunched up tight to his body.

Though I was almost thirty, like I said, I looked a lot younger, and my ass was as pert as it had been when I was a teenager. Henry had the look of a starving man who has just sat down at a banquet. I watched as he sent a big wad of spit down onto his waiting monster and rubbed it in, getting it nice and glistening with moisture.

Turning back to face front, I gradually lowered myself onto Henry's lap. At first, I could feel the massive roundness of his mushroom head pressing against the tense, pink skin of my anus. I had worked up a good bit of spit into it, though, and after I took a deep breath and relaxed my perineum, I could feel the crown start to poke through into me.

Inch by inch, the hardened knob of Henry's rod impaled

me, straining at the fleshy walls of my ass and ripping into me with a mind-blowing mixture of sting and stimulation. He hadn't even started to fuck me yet and I was already aching. I could tell I would be sore as hell the next day, but I knew that the orgasm I was going to have was going to be worth it.

When Henry's cock was all the way in—thank goodness it wasn't that long—I began to gyrate on his lap, trying to loosen myself up even more before I started to fuck him for real. Henry leaned back on his elbows and moaned as I swirled around counterclockwise on his penis.

I was feeling a lot better after a minute or so, so I began to bounce slowly up and down on his cock, enjoying the sensation of it pulling, then pushing the walls of my anus each time I went up and down. It seemed like Henry's little soldier hit every mark along the line of fire, sending tingles of electricity throbbing up and down my entire body.

Gaining speed, I rode Henry like the prized bronco at a state fair, leaning forward so that I would have more of a range of motion, and could use the muscles of my legs to squat and rise more quickly. Every time Henry's penis stabbed up into me, I felt my knees go weak with the searing twinge of pain, but he was hitting all my pleasure zones with his impressive girth, and I couldn't stop myself, quickly picking up tempo.

Henry was grunting again by this point, matched in volume only by my own muffled groans of pleasure. I had forgotten we were outside in a public space, and who knew if anyone in the surrounding buildings could see our lovemaking, but I didn't care. This was just too delicious, and the threat of exposure only heightened the thrill of it. I leaned back, placing a hand on Henry's square chest to give myself some more purchase, and I dipped up and down on top of him even faster.

My member was throbbing from the intense hammering Henry was giving my prostate, and I could only yank it for a few moments at a time before I felt an orgasm rising up within me, so I knew I didn't have long before I would erupt.

I gingerly eased myself off Henry before he could stop me, kicked off my shoes and pants, and then turned around to face him. I pushed him farther up onto the daybed so that he was reclining full-length on it, then I pulled his pants off, too. He lay back, fully extended, and waited for me to mount him. Both of us were drenched from the adrenaline rush of our tryst, and our shirts clung sweatily to us.

I threw my tie over my shoulder and climbed onto the daybed, straddling Henry's hips by planting one knee on either side of his body. I grabbed hold of his bludgeon, pointing it skyward so that I could sit back directly on it. Again, I felt a fiery pain as he pressed up into me and I saw stars for a moment, but by the time I had regained my composure, Henry had started thrusting up into me, plundering my manhole with his battering ram.

Soon I had picked up his rhythm and started to flex my hips in time to his ass-drumming so that each stroke became a symphony of mutual stimulation. My eight-incher was practically spewing precum now, and I got a thrill watching it pool onto the edge of Henry's expensive silk tie. Dry-cleaning wasn't going to get that out.

Each time I swiveled my hips, my balls rubbed against Henry's bespoke shirt, tickling the hairs on my nutsack and bringing me closer and closer to my limit. I barely even touched my cock now, knowing I would shoot at any second. Every time his dick hit my G-spot, I felt another load of sperm working its way up from my balls. I was going to detonate.

Henry's fuse was clearly coming to its end, too. He was staring up at me with glazed-over eyes, and his jaw was slack as he breathed harder and harder. I leaned over to kiss him, shoving my tongue deep into his open mouth while continuing to hump away at him. When I pulled away, I told him I was going to come any second.

"Do it," he begged me, "shoot all over me."

At that point, I couldn't hold back any longer. I spat one last loogie onto my palm, jerked my cock once or twice, then let go as I felt the muscles in my penis start to pump uncontrollably, and a body-wrenching orgasm overtook me.

I had no idea how much juice Henry's fuck tool had worked up in me. I torpedoed glob after glob of white-hot fluid onto him. The first shot reached his chin, causing him to jerk back reflexively. The second hit him square on his upper lip and nose, hanging there like a huge wad of creamy snot. The third got to his hairline, like a leftover bit of gel, and the fourth arced all the way over his head, past his right ear and onto the daybed cushion.

That was the farthest trajectory. The next five shots landed all over his shirt and tie, making a Jackson Pollock-like pattern, and it just kept coming. I didn't think I'd ever produced this much semen in my entire lifetime, let alone one fuck session, but I shot a whole reservoir of baby batter onto my handsome hotelier.

As soon as I had finished, Henry quickly pulled out of me, issuing a throaty growl as he jerked himself to completion a few seconds later. I felt a jet of his semen land on my shoulder—and I thought that I'd shot far—and another drop land on my ear. Then the rest must have hit the back of my shirt and run down along Henry's dick and thighs. I stayed on top of him, rubbing his chest and bending back down to kiss him as he wrung the last drops out of his sperm gun.

When he had finished, I rolled off him, leaving an arm draped over his chest. We stayed like that for a few minutes in the waning sunshine, drying off and calming down from our unexpected romp.

I sat up after a while and reached over for our drinks. We both guzzled down the icy slush that remained, thirsty from our exertions.

As we pulled our clothes back on, Henry joked, "That was certainly the most in-depth tour I've ever given."

"I have a way of getting deep down to the real story," I replied, chuckling. "I'm just sorry I ruined your shirt before your opening night."

"Not to worry, I keep a set of clothes here," he explained. "Though I've never had to change because of anything like this before."

"I hope you've got a full closet, then, because I'm probably going to have to come back for some follow-up looks," I told him.

"Anytime you want."

"And after the opening? What next, are you heading to another city to oversee another new property?"

Straightening his tie and throwing on his jacket to cover up the stains I'd caused on his shirt, Henry looked back at me, raising an eyebrow. "Actually, we've been thinking about renovating another hotel here in Los Angeles. I was going to argue against it, but the property is looking more and more . . . attractive every moment. I might just stay on to help them launch it."

"I'll look forward to taking that tour, then," I said. "I'm sure there will be all sorts of fascinating features to . . . poke around."

Henry led me back to the elevator and slipped his card into my hand when we parted at the valet stand. As I waited for my car, I thought, *I really like hotel writing, I'm going to have to look into doing a lot more of this.*

Simon the Sommelier

Sommeliers are usually old men. Stodgy old men with big noses, a hint of disdain, and notes of boredom. Or so I thought until I met Simon, who was twenty-seven, sharp, lively, funny, and energized about sharing his passion for wines with the diners who patronized the fancy restaurant where he worked in San Francisco. Not only that, but Simon was very cute, with short blond hair, friendly gray eyes, and a compact little body that was all muscle. In fact, the only big thing about him I could see was his aquiline nose—perfect for detecting the tasting notes of wines.

I was lucky enough to meet Simon while up in the City by the Bay visiting friends at the end of a long tasting trip to Napa. Though I was practically pickled from all the wines I had drunk over the course of the previous few days, I figured that one more evening of epicurean indulgence couldn't hurt. Though I was a food writer at the time, and every meal meant the possibility of more work, I left all the plans in the capable hands of my friend Derek.

He was one of the only people I would implicitly trust to make a great choice for a dinner out. I always made sure to schedule a dinner with Derek whenever I was in San Francisco.

The first time I met Simon I had just gotten back into the city only a couple hours earlier, with barely enough time to shower, primp, and make it to the restaurant in time for the reservation. I did have time, however, to admire the nice tan I'd acquired tromping through vineyards during my week up in the beautiful sunny summer weather of Napa.

When I got to the restaurant, Derek was already there, having a cocktail at our table. Derek and I had met through mutual friends when he still lived in Los Angeles, but he had since moved to San Francisco, and we saw each other only occasionally when we were in each other's city. We had never dated, though he was around my age and a successful designer. There just wasn't that spark, though he was very cute, with a lanky body, wavy blond hair, limpid blue eyes, and a funny little smirk. The thought had definitely crossed my mind, but at a certain point, it was clear we were just going to be friends. Still, I always looked forward to my evenings with him.

We fell easily into conversation, and I helped him finish his French 75 while we decided on what to order. One of the best things about Derek was that he and I shared similar tastes, so we always agreed on what to order, and we always ended up sharing everything. It was like having two meals in one. The food chosen, it was time to look at the wine list.

Now, this restaurant was famous for having one of the most extensive wine lists in the city, and in San Francisco, that's really saying something. There were, of course, the choices from nearby Napa and Sonoma, as well as Mendocino and Santa Cruz, but there were also pages and pages of vintages from such far-flung places as South Africa, Tasmania, Austria, and even Japan. I had been feeling pretty good about my wine knowledge after my Napa jaunt, but now I realized just what a neophyte I still was.

Just at that moment, our white knight arrived . . . in the form of Simon. A white knight wearing a crisp, navy blue suit, a white shirt with French cuffs and wineglass cufflinks, and a gorgeous pale blue silk tie. I was smitten. I was also pleased when I got an extra moment's smile from him, but that was probably calculated to get me to order a more expensive bottle, right?

But how could this be the sommelier? He was far too young. I made a point of saying so, though I wasn't much older than him. He explained that though he was just twenty-seven, he'd been working in restaurants for years and had just received his sommelier certification, with several tasting awards under his belt. I was duly impressed and gave him a shy grin . . . which he returned.

Derek, dutiful wingman that he was, noticed what was going on and excused himself to go use the restroom, saying that he would be fine with whatever we decided on. I shot him a grateful, silent thank you and returned to the wine list with Simon, who had sat himself down in the booth next to me so we could discuss the options.

I pushed for a New Zealand Sauvignon Blanc because I wanted something light and crisp, but Simon kept suggesting Austrian Grüner Veltliners. I wasn't familiar with the wine and I was hesitant, but Simon firmly took the menu out of my hands, placed one of his strong paws over my own, and said that if I didn't like the wine, he would bring me something else, free of charge.

In return, I smiled charmingly and said that I was sure to like whatever he thought was best, and that I enjoyed trying new things. At that, I arched my eyebrow slightly, just to be a little puckish but not slutty. Simon caught my meaning and laughed nervously before regaining his composure, asking, "So, do you and your . . . dining companion live here in San Francisco?"

Aiming to clear everything up at once, I explained, "My friend Derek lives here, but I'm just passing through on my way back to L.A."

Simon looked elated at the news that I was not with Derek, then disappointed that I was not local, so I added, "But I'm up here pretty frequently, and now that I've seen this wine list, I'm going to have to come back every time I'm in the city, just to try everything!"

"I'll look forward to it," said Simon, rising again as Derek returned to the table. "Let me get your wine."

Derek raised an eyebrow in question and I winked at him in response. Maybe this was the start of something?

Over the next few months, I happened to be in San Francisco a lot, in addition to traveling all over the country and even the world for my work. I had made sure to hit a lot of wine regions because I was so interested in the subject, but every time I was back in San Francisco, I made sure to eat at Simon's restaurant. I almost became a regular, and I always called ahead to make sure that Simon was working. At a certain point, he and I exchanged contact information so I could just ask him directly, and we would compare notes on wines we tasted. Every time I took a trip, I consulted him about the best wineries to visit, and he, in turn, consulted me about changes he was making to the restaurant's wine list.

At a certain point, my visits to the restaurant almost became tasting trips in their own right, because as soon as he saw me, Simon would come over and start pouring tastes of different wines that were open, and new ones he had gotten in and was trying to decide whether to add to the wine list. In return, I started bringing him fine bottles of wine I picked up on my travels that I thought he would like.

Our tastes were pretty different, with me favoring French reds and him going more for exotic whites. Our conversations could get pretty heated, but it was a pure pleasure having someone to talk to who was as interested in wines as I was. Not to mention the fact that I thought he was just plain dreamy, like my own little professional pocket gay.

Sometimes when he was pouring me a glass, his hand would envelop my own. Or he would brush a stray wine drop off my face or wipe a smudge from my hand. I loved watching him strain to open a stubborn bottle, his compact muscles flexing and heaving.

Most of all, I loved the expression he got when he first swirled a wine and smelled it, trying to parse out the different scents and components. His look was so concentrated yet faraway, as if he was both extremely focused and yet daydreaming. His steel-gray eyes would look right through me, then quickly refocus and turn warm again as he smiled at me and asked what I tasted. I would have to bury my nose in the glass to keep from smiling too obviously.

*   *   *

On one trip, I got into San Francisco much later than I was supposed to. Luckily, I managed to call Derek ahead of time and warn him, so he changed our reservation at Simon's restaurant until it was almost closing time. By the time my plane landed, I was exhausted and considered canceling dinner, but the thought of seeing Simon again reenergized me, and I quickly showered and changed at my hotel, hustling to get to the restaurant in time.

When I arrived, Derek was already there. Again. Enjoying a cocktail. Again. But Simon was sitting with him, looking debonair as usual and having a glass of wine himself. I checked myself in one of the mirrors, straightening my shirt and making sure my pants looked just right, before ambling casually up to the table.

"Sorry I'm late," I said, not really apologizing at all.

Simon practically jumped up. "You made it!"

"Of course," I replied. "I never miss dinner here."

"Welcome back," said Derek, rising to give me a hug. "Simon was just telling me about some of his new wines."

"Exciting! I can't wait to try one with dinner tonight," I said, turning to Simon and extending my hand for a shake.

Simon took my hand, but used his other one to grasp my shoulder in one of those hearty old-man half-hug kind of gestures. He pulled me close enough so that I could smell his light, citrusy cologne. I wanted to lick it right off his skin, but pulled back again, smiling.

"In fact," Simon said, "there's one in particular I want to show you and get your opinion on, if you wouldn't mind."

"I'm flattered," I said, completely honestly. "What is it?"

"Ah, that's the thing, I have to show you later. Can you stay 'til closing?" he asked, suddenly nervous and hopeful.

I looked at Derek, questioning. He shrugged. "I don't mind," I told Simon, looking at my watch. "Besides, that's not long from now, and it doesn't look like you have too many customers left."

"Excellent!" Simon exclaimed, a little too excited. "I'll come get you when it's ready, then. Enjoy your meal."

When Simon had gone and I'd taken a seat at the table, Derek looked at me with that smirk of his, and said, "You're going to be tasting more than wine tonight, buddy."

Blushing, I objected, "Oh, stop, he's just excited, and you know we like to argue about this sort of stuff. It'll be interesting."

"I bet it will," said Derek, returning to his menu. "But I'm going to have to leave a little early, so that should give you every opportunity," he said, pausing dramatically before concluding, "to concentrate on the wine."

I snorted a little laugh and thought about what to order for dinner.

True to his word, Derek left after giving me some cash for his portion of the bill. The restaurant emptied out as I enjoyed the last few sips from our bottle of wine and looked around for Simon, who was nowhere to be found. Reluctantly, I paid the bill and got ready to leave as the rest of the staff started to clear all the tables and get them ready for the next day's lunch service.

I was just about to head for the door when I felt a hand on my shoulder. "Brad, don't go," was all I heard as I turned around to find myself face-to-face with Simon.

"I thought you'd gone home for the night!" I said in surprise.

"No, sorry, I was just finishing up." He waved off some coworkers who were leaving for the night, his hand still grasped tightly on my shoulder. "You don't have to go yet, do you?" he asked, anxiously.

I made a show of looking at my watch, just to make him nervous, but then conceded, "No, I don't have to go. What did you want to show me?"

That luminous smile of his was back, and I couldn't help smiling in response. We were the last two people in the restaurant by now, and he unself-consciously ran his hand down my arm and took my hand, leading me to a staircase in the back that led underground.

He had never shown me the restaurant's cellars before. They were a thing of legend in San Francisco, rumored to hold millions of dollars' worth of rare vintages. In fact, they had a rather involved security system that was put in place after several alleged burglary attempts.

Leading me deeper into the bowels of the cellar, past rack after rack of bottles, Simon held tight to my hand, entwining his fingers in my own. We were deep in the heart of the cellar now, and the air was palpably cooler and damper, with dark streaks of mold lining some of the dripping walls.

Finally, we turned a corner at the end of a row of racks and came to a fancy dining room. The room was dimly lit with candles in sconces lining the walls and a chandelier fitted with those special light bulbs that spark and flicker to emulate candlelight. It was so beautiful . . . and romantic.

Pushing through the glass doors, Simon beckoned me to follow him and pulled out a seat for me at the large, round table. This must be where the restaurant threw private dinners for important customers, and I looked around the room admiring the labels of various wine chateaux that adorned the walls. Simon, meanwhile, rushed over to a corner of the room and busied himself at the bar there doing something I could not make out.

When he turned around, I saw that he was carrying a tray with an empty wine bottle, a crystal decanter full of beautiful garnet liquid, and two glasses standing ready. He set the tray down right in front of me and took the seat next to me, waiting to see my reaction. As soon as I read the label on the bottle, I heard myself suck a sharp intake of breath. I could not believe what I was seeing, and my incredulous expression told Simon so.

"Yes, it really is," he said, practically hugging himself with glee.

What he had poured into the decanter was a very rare vintage of Bordeaux—made in the 1940s—from one of my favorite chateaux in France.

"Where did you get this?" I asked him.

"I have my sources. I got word that a big block of this was going up on the auction block in a few weeks, and they sent me a sample to entice us to buy it."

"Ah, the economy," I sighed, staring at the decanter. Thanks to the economic downturn, formidable wine cellars were being liquidated every day in order to pay off debts. Once-mighty wine collections were being decimated, and Simon was definitely going to benefit from the carnage thanks to a hefty wine-buying account.

"Have you . . . ?" I started to ask.

"Without you? Do you think I'd dare?" he replied, chortling.

"Thank you, I . . . don't know what to say," I said, my eyes imploring him to tell me how I could make it up to him.

"Just tell me what you think. Honestly," he told me as he started to pour some of the wine from the decanter into the glasses. "I decanted this about an hour ago, so it should be settled. Let's taste."

We both examined the color of the wine, then gave it a few swirls and several deep inhales to take in all the complex aromas. Though the wine was older than my parents, it still had such a youthful, lively vigor to it. You could smell the balanced acidity and herbaceous notes just as strongly as the flavors of summer berries and darker fruits. Sharing a look, we both raised our glasses to our lips and tasted, swishing the wine around in our mouths, gargling with it, splashing it on every last taste bud in our mouths.

When we had both swallowed—normally I would spit, but this was special—we both took a moment to gather our thoughts and compare notes. I thought the wine was incredible. It had lost none of its vivacity or lightness, and the tasting profile was as rich as any Bordeaux I'd ever drunk. I told Simon so and said he'd be a fool not to buy it, whatever the price.

He listened carefully to what I had to say, nodding from time to time in agreement (for once!) and said he still wasn't sure whether it was worth it. I said he was crazy and that I'd do anything to get my hands on the lot.

"Anything?" he asked, lasciviously raising his eyebrows.

My heart popped up into my throat. Was it the wine

giving me this sudden indigestion or just my nerves? Was this really going to happen? Keeping my gaze firm and looking him square in the eye, I replied simply, "Anything."

I felt my cock begin to stir imperceptibly beneath the wool of my pants. It was already a step ahead of me and preparing for action.

"Even if you don't buy it, this was very special. How can I repay you for sharing it with me?" I asked him, replacing sardonic flirting with genuine gratefulness. If we were going to have a fling, I wanted it to be based on our honest attraction to one another, not the ratcheting up of plain old sexual tension (though that was good, too).

"I'm just glad I know someone who would appreciate it as much as I did," he told me, laying his small, strong hand over my own.

I looked down at his hand on mine, and with my other, I lifted my glass up for a toast. "To mutual appreciation," I said, holding out my glass for Simon to clink. He did so and we both took another sip of that gorgeous nectar, and when I'd swallowed, I leaned in for a kiss, planting one right smack on Simon's full pink lips that were tinged with the reddish hue of the wine.

I thought I had taken him by surprise and that he might pull away, but he met my lips with even greater pressure from his own, and before I knew it, the glasses were out of our hands and he was sitting on my lap with his face planted on my own.

I loved the feel of his compact torso on my legs. He was a few inches shorter than me, but must have weighed just as much, and I could feel why with his buttocks clenched on my crotch and my arms wrapped around the brawny muscles of his back. His arms, too, I could feel through the light fabric of his suit, were like huge cords of rope that felt like they could lift a wine barrel.

I ran my hands through his short, thick blond hair, relishing the smell of his gel as it crackled between my fingers. I petted his smooth cheek with my thumb and dipped a finger beneath the tight collar of his dress shirt, feeling the heat emanating off his bare skin beneath.

Without knowing what I was doing, I started to untie his tie and unbutton his shirt while Simon shrugged off his coat jacket. My shirt came off next, and I basked in the warmth of our bare chests pressing against each other's as we came back into a close embrace to continue our fevered kissing, Simon still on my lap and clutching me tight.

Whereas my chest had a diffuse dusting of curly dark hairs that, though extensive, were not too thick, Simon had a few concentrated areas of chest hair near his collar and in the middle of his chest, and then a happy trail that ran all the way down his stomach and past his belly button. I tickled his chest, feeling his hair with my fingertips, then branching out to pinch one of his elliptical pink nipples. Simon, meanwhile, had reached behind me and was in the process of shoving his hands as far down my pants as they would go so that he could get a firm grip on my toned little ass.

I broke free of his mouth and started to kiss his ear, sending shockwaves of pleasure down his spine and making him rub my butt even harder as he squirmed on my lap. The feeling I got as his solid hiney rubbed against my crotch made me want to bend him over right then and there and go to town on him, but I knew that if I exercised a little restraint, it would be worth the wait.

I reached under his butt and lifted him so that he was sitting on the edge of the table right in front of me. I planted my face on his belly, taking a big sniff of his clean, manly scent, and distracting him while I undid his fly. As soon as I'd accomplished that, I reached into his boxers to free his cock.

It was already swelling with blood, though not hard yet, and plastered with body warmth to the cushiony cradle of his balls. Both cock and balls were sprinkled with little blond hairs, I saw as I started to coax his hot dog to full plumpness, pleased to see how round and fat it was getting, even if it didn't grow much longer.

I'd say Simon's man meat was a full six inches long, but over five around, making it more of a beer can than a wine bottle, but that was okay by me. I had enough length for both of us, and I was going to use every inch of it on that athletic little ass of his.

When I'd gotten Simon to a semi, I lowered my face teasingly, tantalizingly, agonizingly slowly onto him. Before opening my mouth to receive his flesh rocket, I hovered millimeters above it, taking a good long look, and blowing lightly over it to stimulate his more sensitive nerve endings and ratchet up the anticipation. I could smell Simon's natural odor—it was musky and slightly sour, but also spicy. I just wanted to lick every square inch of his genitals and get that taste all over my face. So that's what I did.

I decided to detour from his dick, and started by licking lightly at the fleshy warmth of his balls, savoring the scent he was giving off and getting them slick with my moisture. Then my tongue delved farther into the space between his testicles and his thighs where the pubic hair turns downy and light, and where the sweat from a guy's balls gets trapped and amplified. I licked every skin cell there, eager to lap up each iota of his odor while making him squirm more and more on the table's edge.

When I turned my attention back to his cock, I noticed that my efforts had produced a steady trickle of precum from Simon's narrow hole. I locked my mouth over the pink ring around the head of his cock and sucked out every last drop of the watery stuff, swishing it around in my mouth and coating the inside of my cheeks with it.

Simon moaned, and pressed my head farther down onto his sausage, forcing me to open my mouth as wide as it would go and relax my throat muscles when his cockhead poked into my soft palate. I took back the lead and started to bounce my face up and down on his crotch, taking every inch of him, then sucking all the way back up to the tip of his bulb. I didn't use my hands except to tug on his balls occasionally or give his taint a little rub to heighten the pleasure I was inflicting on him.

Every few seconds, he would flex his dick, causing it to thicken even further with the extra blood and making it nearly twice as firm as the arteries stretched his cock skin as far as it would go. The first few times I thought he was getting ready to shoot, as I felt the urethra swell up on the underside of his shaft, but then I realized it was just an involuntary reaction to what I was doing, and I relaxed, hoping that would relax Simon, too.

As his moans increased in volume, duration, and frequency, I thought again that he might be getting ready to shoot. My pants were still on, though, and I would be damned if he didn't get a little taste of me before the evening was through, so I popped his penis out of my mouth, gave his balls a little suck, and butterflied his legs on either side of my head, forcing his asshole up in the air where I could get at it.

Simon's crack was mostly smooth, but it did have a light trail of blond tendrils on either side of it and a swath of them around his tight little milk dud. The skin of his hole was pinker than the surrounding pale skin, and it made the cutest, smoothest pucker I'd ever seen. Easing Simon into it, I began by licking up and down either side of his crack, pulling out a hair here or there with my teeth to give him a fun shock every so often.

He was so fit and packed with muscle, I had to pull apart his perfectly spherical ass cheeks in order to get to the prize, but it was worth it. I rubbed the broad expanse of my entire tongue over his fudge pucker over and over and over again, eliciting sighs and groans from Simon, while achieving my desired affect of loosening him up. I knew I'd succeeded when the previously contracted anus slackened and dipped into his body slightly. That's when I decided to go for it, following my strategic victory with a punishing full-on oral assault. I rammed my pointed tongue into his rose bud repeatedly, forcing it deeper and deeper into his flesh vault while holding his sporadically flexing cheeks as far apart as they would go. Despite Simon's initial resistance, I slowly wore him down, and after a couple minutes of consistent pressure, his back door was swinging open and ready for someone to pay a visit.

Keeping Simon in position, his legs spread-eagled on either side of my waist, I quickly stood up and undid my pants, letting them and my underwear fall to my ankles. Sending a glob of spit down onto my shiny knob, I rubbed it in, then immediately started to press my cock up against Simon's manhole.

After all the attention I'd given him, he put up barely any resistance as I worked my corkscrew deeper and deeper into his bottleneck. His ass muscles stretched to take me in, and I was gentle . . . at first. My eight inches sank farther and farther into his moist depths, and I pushed until my pubes brushed up against his spit-covered balls and the base of my shaft could go no farther.

Then I began to push in and out of him at half-tempo, getting him ready for the real treat that was to come. Simon began to flush with the effort of taking me into him, with red splotches rising sexily on his cheeks, his throat, and his chest. I balanced myself as I fucked up and into him by holding a hand on his chest. I loved the outline of my hand that was becoming visible from the pressure I was putting on him, and I could feel how his heart was beginning to beat just as fast as my own. With my other hand, I held on to one of his burly, hairy, short legs, and wrapped it around the back of my torso so that my strokes would be quicker and shorter as he held me close to him.

With the power and steadiness of a chugging locomotive, I rammed myself into him, building steam and making us both groan with the sweaty effort of our lovemaking. I clocked him again and again, slamming my legs into his ass, my balls flapping against the bottom of his crack, and sticking there momentarily before following the rest of my pelvis for the course of the next stroke. I hoisted a leg up onto the tabletop in a kind of standing-kneeling position so that I could delve even deeper into him with greater speed, setting all the muscles in my lower back to work.

I was so aroused, my cock turning to a melting-hot rod

of iron inside Simon's fuck chute, but I wanted to connect with him, to kiss him, as I fucked him, so leaning over him, I wrapped my arms around him, lifted him for a moment, and came to rest sitting on a chair with him in my lap.

Because he was shorter than me, when he was sitting on my lap like that, he was perfectly at eye level with me, and we kissed and caressed each other tenderly as he jiggled his hips and ground his ass all the way down onto my cock. I let him ride me like that for a few moments, easing himself up and down on my staff, but then when he held himself slightly aloft and started kissing me more urgently, I began to lift and lower my hips so that I was the one in charge again.

His muscular arms wrapped themselves across my shoulders, over my neck, pulling me into an ever-closer embrace, Simon's breath hot on my face as we gave up kissing and merely concentrated on fucking each other. Both of us were out of breath, sweat pouring everywhere, and as I pried apart the muscles of his ass so that my cock had an easier time gliding in and out of him, I could tell we were coming to the delicious end of our time.

I continued my efforts, pulverizing Simon's fuck hole with a renewed vigor. I relaxed into it, letting my eyes drift closed as I concentrated on hitting Simon's prostate with each new thrust. Simon hadn't uttered a word in a while, so it surprised me when he whispered in my ear, "You want to repay me for the wine? I have a way."

"Tell me," I groaned, pulling him into a sloppy, sweaty kiss.

Hopping off me, he knelt in front of me and began to give me a blowjob. Apparently he'd known I was getting close as my eyes glazed over, and he had something he wanted from me. I looked down at his thick head of blond hair bobbing up and down on my furry cock, loving watching him work with such intensity, the sweat glistening on his broad shoulders, and the feel of his forehead perspiring as it tapped my pelvis with his every suck.

My stomach muscles began to tighten involuntarily, my balls wrinkled up into themselves, and my cock became as hard as a crowbar. I announced that I was getting ready to shoot, and without losing a beat, Simon whipped his wineglass level with my cock while continuing to jerk me off. I didn't have time to puzzle out what he was doing, though, before my dick erupted with a gut-wrenching orgasm that mustered every last drop of semen I had produced and sent it ricocheting around the wide-mouthed crystal glass that Simon was holding. Rope after rope of my juice accumulated where his wine had been minutes earlier, filling a good third of the glass with my essence.

Simon was very talented with his hands, and sending one last shiver from the top of my head to the tip of my toes, he milked out a final, fat drop of semen from my distended cockhole and let it fall slowly into the glass. Then he started to jack his short, fat cock with a fury I have never seen paralleled. He was beating off so intensely, I thought he was going to yank his dick off, but it was only a matter of seconds before he, too, was shooting his own, paler fluid down into the glass to mingle with my own.

Simon's orgasm was more protracted than my own but produced less cum. After nearly a minute of continued manipulation, he had finally finished, and then stuck a finger in the glass to mix our two issues together completely. He took his finger out of the mixture and licked it clean, pronouncing it delicious; then he took a big sip of the jizz.

Because of its viscous consistency, it smeared on his lips and chin as he drank it in. At first, I didn't know what to think, but he seemed to be relishing it so much that I reached down and pulled him up to sit on my lap again, my softening dick and wet balls sticking to the sweaty skin of his ass. Swiping my thumb across his chin where there were several drops of our mingled goo, I wiped it away, and then brought my thumb to my lips and tasted for myself. I thought it must be Simon's jizz I was tasting since it was sweeter than what I normally produced. I decided I wanted another taste, so I pulled Simon's mouth down to my own and drank deeply of his lips, letting his tongue push its way into my mouth and share the residual semen that coated it.

After a couple moments, I pulled away, smiling. "Delicious," I started, "but I have to say, I prefer the wine."

He laughed, and answered, "Not me. I could drink this every night."

So naughty, but so sweet! Half of me wanted to spank Simon and half wanted to move up to San Francisco to be with him. I settled for kissing him again. I couldn't wait to see what other treasures he had hidden away down in his cellar.

Diego the Designer

My writing career was really taking off in Los Angeles. Of course, that's what every writer in Los Angeles will tell you. Everyone is trying to sell themselves . . . or rather, to promote themselves, and everywhere you look, you'll see people tapping away at computers working on their next screenplay.

Luckily for me, I was not a screenwriter. Instead, I had stumbled upon an opportunity to be a restaurant reviewer, and that led to more and more work writing about the city's dining scene, as well as other fun topics like wine and travel—all things I thoroughly enjoyed. Sure, I still had dreams of being a big-time screenwriter some day, but in the meantime, I was well fed, well traveled, and well rested.

Life as a food critic was fun. There were always new restaurants opening in Los Angeles, and thanks to the fact that I was a freelancer and could work for several publications at once, I was able to get assignments for every place

I wanted to check out. Not only that, but it kept my social calendar full, and it was a big perk to be able to take friends (and yes, dates) out to wine and dine them on someone else's dime.

Every so often, however, one of the publications I worked for would ask me to write content for some of their different sections if they were in a pinch for an article or if I had a particular contact or "in" that would be useful to get a story.

That is how, one winter day, I got an assignment from a local magazine to interview an up-and-coming young interior designer named Diego. I did not know much about design in general, and even less about interior design. If I'd had more disposable income to spend on my shabby little apartment, I suppose I would have been more educated, but as it was, I was content with my bohemian lifestyle, so I left that aspect of review to other writers.

My editor was adamant, however. One of the PR firms I dealt with regularly represented the designer, and none of the magazine's other writers had any sort of connection. They wanted an interview with Diego because he was fast becoming a star on the West Hollywood design scene and would be presenting a big show at a local gallery before opening his own showroom. I told my editor that I would need to think about it.

Apparently Diego was getting to be a local celebrity, but I had never heard of him. I did some background research and took a look at his Web site so I could see his designs. The rooms he put together and the houses he redecorated looked beautiful. He was into mid-century modern design. All clean lines, black-and-white palettes and earth tones, and high-quality, uncluttered materials.

This was going to be interesting. I started making a list of questions for him so I could learn more about his personal style, his design philosophy, and his story. When I clicked on the biography section of his site, I started to read his story and then took a look at the promotional photos of him.

That was when I realized . . . Diego was hot. Totally, objectively, inarguably hot. Of course, he knew he was hot since he was the one who had put up all those titillating photos on his own Web site, but I kind of admired that confidence.

Diego was Latino, with mocha-brown skin, wavy black hair that he periodically cut to follow the latest hairstyle trends, soulful brown eyes, a beautiful white smile, a muscular body from the hours he spent installing furniture and fixtures, and some sexy tattoos snaking sensually along the rippling muscles of his arms.

I called my editor back and agreed to the story. Then it was only a matter of talking to a friend at the PR agency, and suddenly I had a date . . . er, interview . . . to conduct.

After a little haggling, I arranged to meet Diego at his design studio—which was also his house—up in the Hollywood Hills. Just him and me. Alone at his house. Granted, as an objective journalist, I would have to behave and take copious notes, but it couldn't hurt to flirt a little, right?

The day of the interview arrived, and I spent the morning trying to pick out a hot outfit to wear. Though the sun was shining, as always, it was a crisp December day. The air was clear, and there was a light wind blowing. I was set to meet Diego at 11:00, so I spent the first part of the morning trying to pick out a hot outfit. I settled upon a new pair of tight dark blue jeans that I had just bought, a form-hugging black cashmere V-neck sweater, and some cute sneakers. On top of that, I layered an argyle scarf and a herringbone blazer that lent me a studious air. I took one last look in the mirror of myself in my completed ensemble and thought I'd gotten it just right.

I drove up to Diego's house along the winding roads through the hills, practicing greetings that would sound cool. When I got to the house, I checked my breath, then walked up the path to the front door and rang the bell. I waited several moments, but heard nothing, so I rang it again. Nothing. Uh-oh, had I made a mistake with the time? I started to check my e-mails on my BlackBerry to see if I could find the message with the appointment time, but just as I was scrolling through them, the door swung open, and there was Diego talking to someone on his cell phone and looking annoyed.

He was wearing a tight silk-screened T-shirt, black jeans, a black scarf, and shoes that looked like moon boots. He didn't look happy, but I smiled uncertainly as he sized me up. When he met my eyes, his expression changed, and he grinned while cutting his conversation short, saying, "Sorry, babe, I've gotta go. Yeah, I'll talk to you later."

With that, he hung up and turned his attention to me. "You must be Brad."

"Yes," I said, still a little flustered. "I hope this is still an okay time for our interview . . . ?"

"Definitely, come in, come in," he said quickly, ushering me inside and shutting the door behind me. Then he took my arm and led me quickly to the office he kept at the back of the house with a view over the city. He quickly opened the door to it, quickly arranged the papers on his desk, quickly checked his e-mail on the laptop, quickly held out a chair for me, and quickly got us both waters. Everything he did, he did quickly, as if there was not enough time in the day.

For my part, I paused at the window, taking a moment to absorb the glorious view. I breathed in deeply, feeling serene above the city. Diego shot me a quizzical look, then shuffled over and joined me. He stood right next to me so I could smell the faint fragrance of his cologne.

"Yeah," he said, responding to my unspoken statement. "It's beautiful, isn't it? Sometimes I forget to appreciate it, you know?"

Breaking the spell, I turned to him and said, "That's understandable. You've got a lot going on, haven't you?"

He let out a sigh and agreed.

"Tell me about it," I said, sitting down at the desk and opening up my laptop to start the interview.

Over the next hour or so, Diego told me about all the projects he was working on, shared his tips for finding hidden treasures at area furniture stores and antique dealers, how people can develop their personal taste, and little things everyone can do to add designer touches to their homes.

Every so often, he would throw in a little joke or crack a smile. That was when he was handsomest. Though he looked careworn and thoughtful when he was being serious, when he smiled his face completely transformed into that of an eager young man engaged by the world. Plus, he had these really cute dimples.

After an hour or so, I had all the material I needed for the interview portion of the article, so we just started chatting casually. Diego asked me about myself, trying to wrinkle out every detail of what I did for a living and what sort of things I was interested in writing about. He seemed just as interested in me as I was in him, and every time I mentioned an article I had written, he made a note of it as though he was going to look it up and read it when he had a free moment.

I was flattered by the attention, but I still needed to see his studio and the rest of the house so I could take some pictures of his designs.

"Could we take a look around the house now?" I asked, innocently enough.

"Sure, let's start with the kitchen," he said.

We walked through the house and Diego pointed out certain pieces and fixtures as he made points about the look he was going for. We went through the little house room by room, pausing every now and then to make a point or ask a question. When he got excited about something, Diego would put a hand on my shoulder or on my arm as he talked, as though to make his point clearer. It was all I could do to concentrate on what he was saying as he looked deep into my eyes with those penetrating brown irises of his. Maybe it was just me, but I thought he was touching me a lot more than he needed to, and pulling me back and forth across the room to see this and that. But I wasn't complaining.

Finally, there was only one room left to see: the bedroom. I was a little nervous because things were clearly building between us, but Diego seemed as cool as a cucumber. Until he fumbled with the doorknob. Then blushed. He was nervous, too! Suddenly, it seemed like anything could happen.

We walked into the room, and it was one of the most unabashedly sexy, masculine rooms I'd ever been in.

Everything was patterned in either black and white or silver and gold, like a hot retro mix between disco fabulous and mid-century chic. The bed had an oversized black leather headboard that was tufted with giant metal studs. The sheets were silver and black, with a sumptuous faux fur throw draped artfully across it. I could just picture Diego bringing his conquests back here and sprawling across it naked like a '70s porn star.

His two nightstands were littered with design and art books, though I spotted a biography of Frank Lloyd Wright and a few novels sprinkled into the mix. I also thought it was cute that he had a pair of reading glasses lying ready next to the lamp. Then the suave persona returned as I glanced around and spotted a mini wet bar in one corner with a beautiful antique cocktail set at the ready. From his bedroom, he had a view of the entire city, and the only thing that would have made it better would have been a private deck that he could take someone out on to share it with.

Diego nonchalantly reeled off a list of facts about the room—where he'd gotten certain pieces, the aesthetic he was working toward, where people could draw their own inspiration from when designing a space for themselves. Then he said he wanted to show me the bathroom.

We walked through the door to the en suite commode, and it was a beautiful combination of shiny black tiles and more muted white marble. The vanity had his and hers sinks—though only one of the sinks was used regularly, I noted—a separate water closet, and then the room opened up into a second, larger space that housed a huge, deep Japanese-style black granite soaking tub on one side. The other half was taken up by one of the largest showers I'd ever seen, fully enclosed by a wall of glass, with every kind of spigot imaginable. I counted them, and there were a dozen.

Diego explained that the shower was his one great luxury. It had a rain function, a steam function, jets positioned all over the place to hit you at various invigorating angles, and a two movable showerheads so you could really play around in there.

"Play around?" I asked him.

"Oh yeah, I spend a lot of time in there. It's a great place to think, to talk things out, and just to let your mind wander. You know, I also think that the bathroom, and the shower in particular, is the sexiest room in the house." He waggled his eyebrows suggestively at me as he intimated this.

Falling back upon old habits, my first thought was to defuse the situation, so I asked him a half-joking question that was still arguably on point. "You know, Valentine's Day is coming up, and a lot of couples are looking to put a little spice back in their relationship," I started, playfully. "Do you have any suggestions about what a couple can do to make their bathroom a sexy and romantic place?"

Diego looked at me uncertainly for a moment. I could see his mind whirring. Was this an opening, he was asking himself? I didn't really know myself whether I was inviting him to play, but I took a chance, and smiled at him invitingly.

He took the bait. "You know, there are lots of things you can do . . . with the right designer," he said, stepping closer to me.

"Such as?" I said, inching toward him.

"I work visually, so I think it's better if I show you."

With that, he pulled me all the way to him and started kissing me. His red lips were as luscious and pillowy as I'd imagined they would be while I'd been staring at him talking during the interview. They moved deftly over my own, creating the perfect combination of moisture and fusion as our faces joined together. I never wanted that kiss to end. As the moments passed and we started to embrace, his tongue slithered its way gently into my mouth and encircled my own, teasing me, prodding me, daring me. I tried to restrain myself as long as possible, but I was just so aroused that I started to mash my mouth against his and crushed his body against my own.

He gave as good as he got from me, and kissed me back with the same force and passion. I thought it was crazy that this was happening, but I couldn't stop, and I loved the fact that normally staid and stable me was about to fuck the shit out of this beautiful, artistic, confident man.

As I mentioned, I had decided to wear a new, tight pair of jeans that, in addition to showing off the juicy curves of my buns, was also strained tight by the size of my quickly swelling package. I pushed my hardening cock against Diego's crotch, and I could feel that he was getting just as aroused as I was. His meat was tenting out his black jeans, just asking to be unleashed.

I released Diego from my grip so that I could remove his shirt, quickly whipping it off over his head, then laying my hands on his hairy chest and stomach. Unlike most West Hollywood boys, Diego didn't wax his chest, instead letting the black hairs there grow naturally. He wasn't too hairy, but he still felt like a real man, and despite the Dolce and Gabbana cologne he was wearing, he smelled like a man, too—a mixture of clean soapiness with a touch of cigarette smoke, some shaving cream, and the faintest hint of sweat. It was a heady mixture.

My jacket and shirt came off next. I carelessly threw them in the bathtub, and by the time I'd turned back to face Diego, his head was level with my nipples. He began to lick at them, tracing their small circumferences with his tongue and squeezing the rounded muscles of my pectorals in his hands, really getting a good grip. I lost my breath when he bit down lightly on one of my nips, and he reacted by biting it even harder. It hurt, but it also felt so good that I didn't stop him. Instead, I grabbed his full head of wavy black hair and pressed his mouth even harder into my chest.

I felt his hands move down my tight stomach to my belt and start to unloop it. Then he was unbuttoning my pants and pulling them down, along with my briefs. He had a little trouble getting them over the ramrod-straight flagpole of my cock, which was at more than half-mast now, but he got them down, then kneeled in front of me.

Luckily, I'd groomed that morning, so my natural wilderness of my curls was tamed into a tidy little semicircle around the base of my dick. Diego began by licking at my low-hangers, making them curl up closer to my body. I'd shaved them this morning, too, so the skin was soft and smooth, the wrinkles like little marshmallowy dells. Diego seemed to appreciate the texture since he took one of my balls in his mouth and sucked at it until it was hanging low again, tender and slightly sore. Then he licked at the other one, greasing it with his saliva 'til it was as slick as an oil patch.

His tongue darted into the crevice between my ballsack and my thighs, getting a good, tangy taste of my skin, and

driving me wild with a ticklish feeling. By now, I was totally hard, and I wanted him to suck my cock, so I sat
down on the edge of the soaking tub, laid a hand on his
clean-shaven cheek, and guided his mouth to my rod.

He began by lapping at the head, covering every square
inch of its full roundness with his tongue several times
over. Then he opened his mouth wider and started to suck
farther and farther down my stem until it was totally
buried in his throat. He sputtered once but kept sucking
me, suppressing his gag reflex.

Next his hand got in on the action, following the me-
thodical motions of his head, up and down, up and down,
working my hilt into more and more of a lather. When his
hand got to my knob each time, he gave it a flamboyant
little twist, lighting up all the nerve endings and making
me shiver with arousal. I could feel the blood surging
through my cock and balls, and I thought that I would
come soon if I didn't stop him, so I pulled his head off of
me and brought his face up to level with my own so I
could kiss him.

As we made out some more, I could taste my own cock,
my precum, and his spit all mixed up in his mouth, and the
combination reeked of reckless sex, making me even hun-
grier to taste his cock. Staying seated on the tub, I made
Diego stand up, taking a second to run my hand along the
rigid outline his penis made against his jeans, then undo-
ing them slowly while looking up into his eyes lasciviously.
He was so patient, but I could see it in his eyes that he
wanted to get fucked. Badly.

Within another moment, I had his pants down around
his ankles and was staring at his brown hunk of chorizo. It

was an inch shorter than my own lengthy tool, and so much darker, disappearing into a mass of fine black hairs. It had a bulbous pink head that was much shinier and wider than the dark, rubbery skin of the shaft. I only had time to lick at the small line of precum dangling from the hole, though, before Diego cupped a hand under my chin and said, "Come with me."

I was in no position to argue, so we both kicked our shoes and pants off in a hurry, and he took me by the arm, leading me to his enormous shower. He turned on the steam function, and the room immediately fogged up with billowing, warm clouds of water. Then Diego turned on one of the sets of spigots along the wall, spraying us with hot jets. We kissed as the water ran down our bodies, and I didn't even notice as Diego unlatched one of the shower-heads from its holster on the wall and turned it on, spraying us both down with its gentle stream.

He whispered in my ear, just audible over the hiss of the water, "I want you to fuck me in here, but first I'm gonna warm up a little."

He moved me over to one side where there was a little ledge I could sit on, then seductively used the showerhead to spray himself down from head to foot, pausing at his crotch and getting his cock and balls as clean as could be. I could see how much he was getting turned on by the show, his brown cock extending to its full seven inches, and it was making me hard again just watching as he soaped himself up and got suds all over himself.

Then he turned around to show me the back view. The tattoos that ran along his arms continued up his shoulders and met in the middle of his back. It was a beautiful piece of art, and I was mesmerized watching it move as he moved. Finally, he bent over slightly so that the muscles of his back contracted and created a groove down the middle. His legs were positioned more than hip-width apart, so that when he leaned over, his ass was right there for the taking, his sausage just visible past the twin globes of his dark brown balls.

I didn't want to help him out just yet, though. He was doing a fine job all by himself. He brought the showerhead over his shoulder, letting the water run over his back and down the ravine of his butt. Then he shifted it to his other hand and brought it right up under his ass, shooting the water all over his undercarriage. He was so clearly keyed up by it, starting to squirm and shimmy with each gush of hot water.

Watching him got me hot and bothered, too, and I had tugged my cock back into a full woody. It was time to fuck him. I stood up and came behind him, taking the jet out of his hand and rubbing the length of my dick up in his furry ass cleft. I replaced the jet in its holster and continued to dry-hump Diego. For his part, he flexed his ass muscles around my dick and pushed up against me, raising the intensity. He reached for a bottle in the corner and squirted some lotiony stuff onto his hand. Reaching behind him, he slathered my cock with the stuff and gave it a few last tugs before guiding it into his rectum.

At first, Diego seemed a little tense, and I had to push intently against him in order to fully penetrate his anus, but once I'd gotten the globular crown of my cock past his sphincter, he eased up and I had a clear passage. I reached down and pried his cheeks apart, so I could look at my